ANCIENT KINGDOMS OF LJÓS

ANCIENT KINGDOMS OF LJÓS

BOOK 1 OF
LIGHT AND SHADOW OF THE FAE

DAVID HARRIS

Ancient Kingdoms of Ljós is a work of fiction. Names, characters, places, and incidents are largely the product of the author's imagination or are used fictitiously. The author has used some historical names, places and events to create an atmosphere that is realistic for the place and time of this work of fiction, but any such historical references are not meant to be historically accurate. Any resemblance to actual persons, living or dead, is entirely coincidental.

Published in the United States of America by
Harris Publishing LLC, New York

Hardcover ISBN 979-8-9940505-2-1
Paperback ISBN 979-8-9940505-1-4
eBook ISBN 979-8-9940505-0-7

www.davidharrisbooks.com

1st Printing

* * *

MAP OF LJÓS

LAND OF LIGHT, HOME OF THE ÁLFUR

NORTHERN REALM

NORTHERN OCEAN

LÁN
× LÉARGAS

× VESË

FJALL REALM

Sjärna River

Mánen River

VATNID REALM

ABHAILE

RÉLEGUR
×

LAKE SOLAS

× TEILATUA

Vindsáng River

SJÁVAR REALM

WHITE HEDGE

GARMONIYA
×

Silverström River

VILNIS
×

EKAITZA
×

× TISKINA

SKÓGUR REALM

SOUTHERN OCEAN

× TULIPESÄ

EYDIMÖRK REALM

MAP OF GWYNEDD, POWYS AND DYFED

KINGDOMS OF THE BRITONS

CONTENTS

CHAPTER ONE

Chieftain of Powys

Fifteen Weeks Before Winter Solstice

The day began with a deceptive calm.

The sound of children's laughter outside greeted Griffin as morning sunlight filtered into his family's home, but it was the smell of breakfast that drove him into the dining room.

"Morning, Ffion, what's for breakfast?" Griffin asked the matronly woman bustling about in the kitchen.

Ffion Lewis was the talkative housekeeper, clear of eye and sharp of tongue. Her quick wit was very familiar to the family, as was her penchant for drama and mystery delivered with a knowing look.

"Good morning yourself, Master Griffin," she said. "I've freshly made oatcakes and cold water from the spring. Your father wants to see you and Madoc at the skirmish field right after breakfast. He's already been out there for some time,"

Ffion raised both brows at this in emphasis. "You should probably go and wake your brothers. They'll need to go with you—and Dylan and Bedwyr are always hard to wake."

"All right, but oatcake first," he told the plump cook, snatching one of the piping hot flatbreads from a stack as he headed for the stairs.

Ffion had come to the family when the mother of the three older boys had died. And she had stayed on when Bedwyr's mother had mysteriously disappeared all those years ago. She'd looked after them like they were the family she'd never had.

"Oi, Madoc, get your lazy arse up! You too, Dylan, Bed'," Griffin said as he shook his head at the sight of his disheveled brothers trying to wake themselves from sleep.

"Geroff! Just cuz you're the eldest, don't badger us awake," grumbled Madoc.

"An' stop enjoying yerself so much," grunted Dylan from somewhere under the bedclothes.

Bedwyr just sat up and rubbed his eyes, his dark hair all tousled.

The four brothers had a stern father. Cynfor was the leading chieftain of the king of Powys, as well as the king's brother. He was a fierce warrior in his own right and a harsh taskmaster for his sons, all of whom had dark hair and eyes, and strong, broad-shouldered builds. All exuded strength and confidence.

Griffin was the oldest and a daunting warrior like his father but, unlike Cynfor, he had an easy-going demeanor and a good sense of humor. Combined, it gave him the bearing of a natural leader.

"Father wants us on the skirmish field early this morning, and you know what he'll be like if we're late," Griffin said. "I'll not bear the brunt of his foul mood for keeping him waiting!"

"Hurry up, Bedwyr!" shouted Madoc. "We've got our swords and shields already an' you're still donning your tunic."

Madoc was the second oldest and had much less of a sense of humor than Griffin. Dylan was the bull of the family, older than Bedwyr by a year. Heavily muscled, he could cleave an enemy's shield with one mighty swing of his two-handed battle-axe and drink everyone in town under the table. Bedwyr was the youngest and prone to daydreaming. Despite the occasionally harsh treatment he received from his older brothers, he idolized all three of them. Cynfor told him repeatedly that he was more like his mother's family; taller and leaner than Dylan, and a philosopher—unlike pragmatic Madoc and Griffin—he was also broad shouldered and rugged looking.

———— •✦• ————

"Ffion, as you can see, I have brought my hungry brothers to your breakfast table," Griffin announced. "Please feed them well so they've no excuses for the beating I will give them on the skirmish field this morning."

"Aye, I have a hearty breakfast here for all of you," Ffion replied, a twinkle in her eye.

The brothers sat at the table and wolfed down Ffion's oatcakes as young men are wont to do.

"What were you talking to Ladwys about just now?" asked Dylan, munching. "She scurried off with a very sour look on her face."

"Oh, she was asking me about some of the old tales of the Fae," Ffion said whilst dusting a bread board. "Tales that have been passed down from mother to daughter for many generations."

"Why was she asking you, Ffion?" Dylan asked suspiciously. "And why now?"

Ffion chuckled as she replied, "Well, the common folk hereabouts know my family and I've preserved the old tales better 'un anyone." Her red hands kneaded a knot of dough. "She's askin' now as rumors are spreading ... strange and unexplained things are afoot in our woodlands. As you well know."

"What old tales of the Fae?" Bedwyr asked around a mouthful of cake. "Tell us! Please!"

Ffion's busy hands rolled and shaped, flour escaping in puffs as she worked, and she smiled as she began, treating their attentions much like her careful working of bread.

"Well, many different creatures were part of the Fae world. The most important, though, were the High Elves of the Álfur and the *Darklings*, or Dark Fae," Ffion said as she worked. "The Leaders of the Álfur had a terrible beauty and majesty about them. They were not outright hostile to men but aloof and indifferent unless brought to anger by the foolishness of man. These were immortal beings, alive for thousands of years, cunning and strong, here for countless millennia before the arrival of humankind. The Álfur were tall and slender but very strong, their royalty and wizards wielded powerful magic, and they often walked away from men for hundreds of years, retreating to a mysterious realm, or disappearing into the deep forests and remote moors, surrounded by night's darkness or heavy mists in the gloaming." She paused to raise an eyebrow at Bedwyr who'd stopped chewing. "For more than a thousand years now, no man has seen the Álfur nor the Dark Fae, and their magic has ceased to touch the realm of humankind ... Or that is what was thought until recent events," Ffion concluded with an air of mystery.

"So, what've people been seeing after all these years?" Dylan asked.

Ffion wiped her hands on her apron and began bustling with the pots and pans.

"Dark things," she said, "with no easy explanation. Folk are troubled and talk of the old tales of the Fae is rising for the first time in many years."

Madoc rolled his eyes and snorted. "Drama!" he said, obviously unconvinced.

"You boys put these old tales out of mind and join your father on the skirmish field before he loses his patience!" Ffion concluded.

⋆◆⋆

"It's about time! The day unravels, and we've not yet had our first practice skirmish," Cynfor admonished. "Woe betide you all if it takes you this long to engage the enemy in battle."

The skirmish field was one of the only large, flat, grassy areas near Cynfor's keep, a secure location in eastern Powys surrounded by rocky hills with steep ravines. Treacherous ground for any would-be invaders.

"Rival Britons to the south and the damn Saxons everywhere to the east. Thank God we can depend upon Gwynedd to the northwest," he said gruffly. "We can't afford to be sallying out late when called upon. Not for battle nor for skirmish." He eyeballed each of his sons, his gaze lingering on Dylan. "The King of Powys is coming to visit us, and I want him to see us at our very best."

At this time, the major kingdoms of the Britons consisted of Powys, Gwynedd, and Dyfed in the west, with Dumnonia on a separate peninsula to the southwest. Strathclyde was in the north. There was also Armorica across the Channel and several smaller kingdoms, desperate to expand at the cost of their neighbors. It was a time when the Saxons grew ever stronger in the east, drawing strength from their heptarchy like a vicious dragon. The kingdoms of the Britons were under constant threat, their territories constantly changing, particularly in the center and the west, where Powys, Gwynedd, and Dyfed lay.

Griffin and Madoc circled each other with their practice swords held at the ready. They looked enough alike to be twins.

"Tis the day, older brother," said Madoc. "I've eaten enough dirt this week, thanks to you. Today, you shall have a taste."

"That'll take more than boastful words, minikin. You'll have to manage your feet as well as your sword arm if you want to keep your face clean," laughed Griffin.

Sure enough, Griffin tripped Madoc in the very next breath and then extended his hand to help his brother off the ground.

"Come, let's see how the younger ones do," said Griffin.

They watched as Dylan and Bedwyr faced off, looking far more mismatched. Dylan, with his stout, heavily muscled frame, and Bedwyr, sinewy and tall. Where Dylan had the advantage in strength, Bedwyr had the speed.

The pair circled each other warily. Dylan almost landed a mighty blow, but Bedwyr was no longer standing in the same spot. Bedwyr landed a glancing blow on Dylan's left arm as he glided into a new position and Dylan laughed as his backstroke prepared to do damage to Bedwyr's leg.

But Bedwyr simply said, "Look down, brother."

Dylan looked down and saw Bedwyr's sword, right in front of his neck. "I don't know how you wield that sword as fast as you do. I never even saw it! It's inhuman!" he gasped, pride in his eyes.

Hours later, battered and bruised, the brothers were all

in good humor as they left the skirmish field. Even Madoc. They had to get ready for the arrival of the King of Powys.

———— ✦ ————

Selyf ap Cynan himself was well-liked, but the sons of Cynfor were not at all fond of the king's two sons, although they were cousins. Arrogant and cruel were the most inspirational descriptions, and they were universally despised. In an army of straightforward men whose word was their bond, the sons of Selyf ap Cynan were not trusted. By anyone.

Griffin mused aloud as he buckled his best tunic, "I hear the king's daughter, Glynis, is everything her brothers are not. Tis a pity we've always seen less of her than of her brothers. Fair of feature, noble in bearing, and kind, I hear."

Dylan shook his head as he adjusted his leggings, they were too tight around his thighs.

"They say she has a calming influence on the king, which helps make up for the snakes he has for sons," Griffin continued, unabashed.

Bedwyr nodded as he finished dressing, Griffin always seemed to have the right of things. He tucked his medallion into his tunic, then paused and pulled it out again. It was held around his neck by a sturdy leather thong. The medallion itself was heavy silver, worn by many years of wearing and holding, but it had never tarnished. A large tree within a circle, the heavy roots were clear to see at the bottom, and the leaf-laden branches filled the top portion. Single leaves blew away from the branches. His mother had given it to him shortly before her mysterious disappearance years earlier. She'd told him that it had been in her family for many generations and that he should always treasure it.

Catching himself, Bedwyr finished tucking the medallion into his tunic and pulled on his boots. As always, he was the last of his brothers to be ready. He had to hurry to catch up and assemble in the courtyard to greet the King of Powys and his family.

The arrival of the king involved all of the expected greetings and tributes. Although Cynfor and the king were not close as brothers, they were enthusiastic allies. Cynfor was the leading chieftain within Selyf ap Cynan's kingdom, and he was a formidable supporter of the king during these troubled times. So, the king's arrival was accompanied by all the formalities their respective positions required, but the warmth of friendship was not a part of the occasion.

"Some of my men saw the strangest damn things on the way here," said Selyf. "Hardened soldiers refusing to go deeper into the woodlands we passed through. Something about shadows coming to life. One of our scouts disappeared without a trace!"

"Aye, we've heard some strange tales of late from our own who live in the deep woodlands," said Cynfor. "But let us cast aside these chill thoughts and welcome your arrival with food and drink!"

Everyone followed Cynfor and the king into the banquet hall where spirits would soon be lifted as people started eating and drinking.

"Maybe you'll get seated next to Glynis if you're lucky," Madoc joked with Griffin.

"An improvement from looking at your sour face while I eat," Griffin responded. "And Dylan's."

"None of us will be seated with Glynis; we'll be with her brothers, and she next to her father. Or in between her father and ours," said Bedwyr.

"Well, as long as there is plenty of food and drink, I'll be a happy man," said Dylan.

Bedwyr was right. None of the brothers were seated with Glynis. She was at the center of the high table, between her father, the king, and his brother and leading chieftain, Cynfor. Griffin and Madoc were at the right end of the table, with Afan between them, while Dylan and Bedwyr were at the other end, with Arawn.

Dylan was very happy, though, since the banquet involved the most impressive display of mouth-watering food that he could remember ever having seen. There was steaming hot wild boar, roasted goose, and countless baked trout, mounds of freshly baked bread and cooked vegetables, and of course, barrels of ale and hearty mugs. He wasted no time heaping portions on his plate.

Griffin was doing his best to engage in conversation with Afan while Madoc just glowered at him, his distaste and distrust clear on his face. Yet, the mood at the banquet was lifted higher by the arrival of Derwyn the bard of Powys whom everyone found very entertaining, whether he was singing songs or reciting ballads.

"What cheer do you bring us tonight, Bard!" exclaimed the king.

"Why, tales of brave Britons and cowardly Saxons, of course, Your Majesty!" Derwyn replied.

The men at the banquet banged their mugs on the table in appreciation of the bard's quick tongue and high spirits.

"I will tell you tales of us Britons and our island kingdom, stretching shore to shore, and the kings and heroes of long ago. And I will tell you stories of the coming of the Saxons, who push us out of *Lloegyr,* our lost lands," he sang as he strummed on his crwth. "Perilous tales of Britons pressed to the west, with Dumnonia to the south, across the Severn Sea, into the sea by the Saxons of Wessex! And lone Strathclyde in the north, beset in the west by invaders from Eire—to the north by the Picts—and to the east by the Saxons in Northumbria," he lamented. "Aye, lads," he continued, "Tales to fill your heart and boil your blood!"

After an hour or more of feasting and drinking and tales of brave Britons, Derwyn took a break.

"Pray, allow me to partake in merry revels and spirited toasts, Your Graces, ere I press onward in my quest."

"What recent tidings have you of our folk to the north and south?" asked Cynfor.

"Alas, Lord, I fear Armorica across the water is truly lost," Derwyn replied. "Rheged has succumbed in the north, and Strathclyde now finds itself in dire straits, beset on all fronts. A shadow doth loom o'er their fate," the bard continued.

"Aye, and of our cousins in Dumnonia, closer south of us?" the king asked.

"Sadly, my king, the Saxons in Wessex besiege them fierce. I fear it is a fleeting breath before they too, are lost to us Britons. Our kin may soon find refuge scarce, confined to these valorous lands that you and your fellow kings in Gwynedd and Dyfed guard, here at the heart of these western domains," the bard concluded. "Yet hark! Allow me to weave a tapestry of joy for the noble and gallant Britons gathered here in your hall this eve!" he roared as he sprang to his feet again

"In truth, ere the dawn of man's existence on this fair sphere, there echo tales of ages past, where civilizations thrived long before our kind did tread. Aye, 'tis hard to fathom, yet legends tell of a realm where knowledge, art, and marvels bloomed, gifting wisdom and grace to all mankind's race. Some worshipped the ancients as gods who turned brutish men into architects of great civilizations. Long ages past.

"Yet, alas, there were dark cousins of these ancients who brought dark thoughts and evil deeds to weak souls amongst all races of man. Darklings, some claimed, or fiends from the deep night, who sought to despoil all things pure and fair. With wicked glee, they tainted the innocent hearts of man, luring them unto shadow's embrace." Derwyn paused to further tempt his audience. "As the age-old tales do whisper, these spirits of yore, both virtuous and vile, were destroyed in a cataclysm of flood, while earthquakes and volcanoes shook the entire world like never before," he concluded with a flourish.

After a moment of silence, the banquet crowd erupted with loud approval and everyone's mugs were refilled. Derwyn was invited to sit at a special seat at the high table, where he was toasted by both Cynfor and the king.

A returning scout entered the banquet hall and hastened to Cynfor's side. The scout looked ragged and dirty, obviously just off the trail. He and Cynfor had a brief animated conversation before Cynfor surged to his feet, chair toppling backward.

"Saxons have been sighted crossing our border. Traveling in force. To arms!" he shouted.

The banquet hall erupted into a frenzy of activity. Fortunately, the feasting night was young and minds were clearer than they would otherwise have been. The fighting men of both Cynfor and Selyf ap Cynan poured out of the hall, pulling together their battle gear; swords, shields, spears, and helmets aclatter as the grooms brought out the horses for the leaders of this hastily assembled fighting force.

"We'll approach from two directions and catch the Saxons twixt our forces," said Selyf.

Cynfor would lead one force, supported by Griffin and Madoc with some of his men and those of the king, and the king's sons, Afan and Arawn.

"We will circle to the north of the Saxons and then run hard into their flank while you position your forces to the south of them," said Cynfor to his king. "We will be the hammer that drives them onto your anvil."

"Aye, Cynfor, we will smash these Saxons between us," said Selyf. "And we'll send the survivors scurrying back across their border. These incursions grow ever bolder and more frequent and we must halt their mischief and take our stand."

The scouts led the two forces of Britons through the hills of eastern Powys. One group to the north, and one to the south.

◆

Griffin's heart was pounding as he rode next to Madoc, just behind their father. Afan and Arawn rode behind them, with the combined forces they led, in trail. They had traveled fast and far into the dark of the night and were now approaching the Saxon forces to their south.

"Methinks we're blessed with just enough moonlight tonight," whispered Madoc. "Enough to guide us and not betray our movements to the Saxons."

"Aye, and we're further blessed with clear and dry weather," Griffin whispered back. "This would not have gone as quickly or quietly slogging through mud in the pouring rain."

Cynfor pulled up, and the leaders of their force gathered around him, along with the scout he was talking to.

"The Saxons are camped just over the next rise. It appears to be a larger force than we expected, but they are foolish enough to be sleeping. And with campfires burning," Cynfor said. "The scouts also tell us that the king's forces are in position to the south as we thought."

"We shall drive these Saxons into the king's forces just as we planned," said Griffin. "Lead us to victory, Father!"

Bedwyr and Dylan crept up to the top of the rise and looked north, down to the Saxon camp. The flatland where the Saxons were sleeping was within arrow shot from where the brothers lay silently. Bedwyr could see the rise beyond their own, where the advance force led by his father and brothers would charge into the sleeping Saxons and push them into the king's forces to the south.

"They should be riding down into that Saxon camp any moment now," Dylan whispered beside him. "'Tis going to be a challenge for us to remain rooted here but we must do as our king orders."

"We should have our own opportunity to wreak havoc on the Saxons if this battle goes as planned," Bedwyr whispered back.

Just as they finished whispering, Bedwyr and Dylan saw their father on his white steed charging down the opposite slope, with Griffin and Madoc right behind him. In the space of a heartbeat, they were in the center of the camp and charging towards the planted standard of the Saxon ealdorman.

Suddenly, a shield wall of Saxons sprang up in front of them. They had not been sleeping after all—and now formed a solid line of well-prepared soldiers. Fortunately, the rest of Cynfor's force, led by Afan and Arawn, was advancing down the slope from the north.

Another two lines of Saxons rose up on either side of Cynfor and his sons. They were now virtually surrounded by rank upon rank of sturdy Saxons.

Just as the reality of this new tactical challenge was sinking in, a line of Saxon cavalry emerged from hiding to form a line to the south of the encampment, between the king's southern forces and the encampment. There were now too many mounted soldiers for his southern band to advance upon. The Britons were outnumbered and outflanked. Both north and south.

As Bedwyr watched, horrified, Afan and Arawn held back the support forces from the north. They would not be leading that force to support the rescue of Cynfor and his sons. Six Saxons rushed at Cynfor, two each from the north, south, and west, and gutted his horse in the blink of an eye. Cynfor tumbled to the ground in the midst of his foes.

Bedwyr watched his father as he quickly sprang to his feet, yelling something inaudible as Griffin and Madoc dismounted in two single fluid motions, moving to stand back-to-back.

"Give those Saxon scum a ring of steel to chew on!" he hissed, motionless, eyes frozen as Cynfor, Griffin, and Madoc stood in the center of the Saxon camp, their swords bristling.

Promises of death whispered from that circle of bright steel and the Saxons paused.

"Ride down now, Afan and Arawn! Help them, you worthless curs! Now is the time," shouted Dylan next to Bedwyr from the safety of their southern rise

But the sons of Selyf ap Cynan stood their ground, holding back their forces from saving Cynfor and his sons. Bedwyr saw their treachery, and a cold chill ran down his spine. As he watched, the pause that had been holding back the Saxons ended. Ranks of heavily armed men began their advance on Cynfor and his sons.

Their bright ring of steel held back the first assault with bodies falling all around them. And the second, and the third. Now, the fallen Saxon comrades were forming a barrier to help defend the beleaguered Britons.

Suddenly, from behind the front ranks of the Saxons, a spear whistled out of the darkness, slipping between the brothers and striking home in Cynfor's lower back.

Cynfor fell to the ground and the Saxon ealdorman raised his sword and brought it down in a killing arc toward his neck. There was a loud clang as Griffin's blade stopped the ealdorman's as he stepped up to meet it.

Bedwyr heard Griffin yell but the Saxons surged again. The circle of bright steel had been broken.

"I cannot stay here and just watch this!" Dylan shouted at Bedwyr.

"We cannot do anything else! As much as it pains us, we *must* follow the orders of our king. And we must survive ourselves to take vengeance on these foul Saxons," said Bedwyr, tormented.

Helplessly, the brothers watched as surging Saxons over-whelmed Cynfor and his sons. Cynfor never regained his feet after the spear took him in the back, and Dylan and Bedwyr watched in disbelief as Madoc fell under the Saxon's rush. The last thing Bedwyr saw was Griffin standing astride his father, defending him to his last.

Then, they were lost in a wave of Saxons.

"Away! Away now! We must retreat, or we are all lost," shouted Selyf, his voice piercing the night.

"He's right," Bedwyr hissed, his visage dark with grief and anger, "our revenge must wait for another day!"

"Aye," Dylan muttered in reply, "but revenge we will surely have!"

Bedwyr followed Dylan and the king's forces south. Away from the Saxons. Away from his lost father and brothers. Away from the treacherous sons of the king. A dark hatred smoldered in his breast and he swore that he would have vengeance on them all.

CHAPTER TWO

Ambition and Treachery

Fourteen Weeks Before Winter Solstice

Bedwyr and his brother Dylan followed their king as he led his remaining warriors away from the Saxons and back to Powys. It was a mad scramble. First, they went south, and then they turned to the northwest and went back to Cynfor's keep. The mounted warriors were constantly shifting between riding ahead of their infantry to make sure the way ahead was clear and circling back to make sure that they were well and truly clear of the Saxons.

On any other day, Bedwyr would have gloried in the bright sunshine as they re-entered his family's territory within Powys. But not today. The rugged hills were a welcome sight as they lay within an hour's ride from Cynfor's keep but Bedwyr's mood was black. He mourned the loss of his father and brothers and he was filled with rage but had no ready target where he could unleash that rage.

"We must have vengeance," he said to his brother. "Somehow, someday, we will have vengeance on those cursed Saxons."

"Aye, brother," replied Dylan. "And we will have to talk to our men that went with Arawn and Afan. It looked like they held back warriors who could have saved our father and our brothers. I would know more of this apparent treachery."

"Arawn and Afan Selyf ap Cynan have never been liked in Powys," Bedwyr replied. "But outright treachery is unexpected, even for them."

"We are close to home now," said Dylan. "Once we get settled in our keep, I am sure the king will call a war council. We need to muster warriors from all corners of Powys to defend against these Saxon incursions."

There was a long, steady rise in the terrain leading home. Jagged rocky breaks disrupted the rolling green hills, and patches of small, wooded areas were scattered here and there.

The long, wide green hillside now in front of them was one of the largest open areas remaining on the trail up to the keep.

A large number of warriors were arrayed at the top of the hill, with yet more numbers visible on both the right flank and the left. These were fellow Britons, but they were not men of Powys. The positioning of their forces indicated hostile intent and they would have known from the approaching banners that it was the King of Powys who approached. They certainly knew that the land upon which they stood was Powys territory and not their own.

Selyf brought his own warriors to a halt and examined the terrain in front of them. His adversary had chosen his position well, holding the higher ground before the king's forces. He also had a larger number of foot soldiers, whereas Selyf seemed to have only one significant advantage: a larger number of mounted men.

"Dylan and Bedwyr," Selyf said. "Come forward with me and see this rogue who vexes his fellow Britons in these troubled times. These are your own family's ancestral lands within Powys, after all."

Three men from the intruding army came forward to meet them halfway between their forces. Their leader was a huge bear of a man with a large gold torque around his neck. He carried a heavy, two-bladed battle axe with a long handle.

"Eluad ap Glast!" Selyf exclaimed. "The renegade king of Dogfeiling. I should have guessed it were you, the uninvited shade, who darkens our doorstep."

"Aye, it is me," replied Eluad. "And lo! I should have seen with a glance, 'twas the base King of Powys limping home from Saxon clutches with his tail between his legs."

"What foul intent has brought you to my kingdom with a small army?" asked Selyf. "I declare this bodes ill for those noble Britons who would raise their swords 'gainst Saxons rather than stand as foe 'gainst Briton kin."

"Aye," replied Eluad ap Glast. "This day does bode ill for you and yours. More dire than you can divine." He watched Selyf gravely before erupting, "Bring them out here!" Eluad yelled to a small group to their right, "Let this erstwhile king see his hapless seed."

Two men were led forth, bound hand and foot. They stumbled forward, appearing to have difficulty staying on their feet and had obviously been harshly treated by their captors. One could easily see by the swelling of their faces and their bloody, matted hair.

"It's Afan and Arawn," said Bedwyr. "How have they come to be in the clutches of this foul man?"

"I'm not sure they're any worse off with him than they would be with me," Dylan replied. "At least by his hand, they still breathe."

"What say you, King of Powys?" yelled Eluad ap Glast. "Do you discern this refuse fleeing from the Saxons yonder? What woeful progeny you have sired. I would be doing you a favor should my axe take their heads right here, right now." He turned to his audience, arms outstretched. "I will make you a generous offer," continued Eluad. "I bid you to a fair contest, a man-to-man fight. If you best me, my army will leave in peace this day. If I win, I will spare your sons—but I will have terms! First, they must go into exile across the water to Armorica. Second, your warriors shall swear fealty to my throne, as Powys' new king as well as Dogfeiling."

All eyes fell on Selyf.

"Do you accept my terms?" yelled Eluad ap Glast.

"Aye, you mangy cur!" Selyf yelled back. "Let us hasten the task. I'll have your head on a pike outside poor Cynfor's keep before this day is done!"

While the two kings prepared themselves, their people prepared the ground where they would battle. Level ground with the boundaries clearly marked off.

Eluad ap Glast was heavily muscled and wielded his heavy two-bladed axe as lightly as other men wielded a sword. He wore a helm with a nose guard and carried a small round shield with a rampant bear emblazoned upon it.

Selyf ap Cynan was not as thickly muscled, but he was long of limb and bore a longsword that further extended his reach. He also wore a helm with a nose guard and carried a small, round shield. Yet his was adorned with a two-headed eagle.

The two kings circled each other guardedly, careful to stay within the designated boundaries. Eluad ap Glast whirled his two-headed battle axe more quickly than Selyf expected, but the blow only glanced off his shield. Another flurry of blows from the whirling axe was also ineffective and on one of them, Selyf's long arm and sword darted out.

"Hah, so you draw first blood!" Eluad said. "That will not matter when the shadows part this day." And he lunged forward and struck a mighty overhead blow on Selyf's shield with his axe.

Selyf fended off the attack, but he staggered back from the strength of the blow.

Sensing an advantage, Eluad pressed forward again, but Selyf was ready with his sword, biting deeply into Eluad's left arm. Now, the erstwhile usurper could not raise his shield to protect himself.

Before Selyf could take advantage, though, Eluad brought down his battle axe in another fierce overhead swing with his right arm.

This time, the axe caught in Selyf's shield.

Eluad was in a bad position. The huge beast of a man had no use of his left arm and no shield, and now his axe was stuck in Selyf's shield. With only one arm, he was unable to free it.

Selyf ap Cynan raised his sword and drew himself in closer to Eluad ap Glast for the killing blow.

"The last thing you will see in this life is my blade cleaving your throat," he gloated.

"You talk too much," replied Eluad. "It shall be your doom."

Eluad ap Glast twisted the handle of his axe stuck in the other king's shield. The handle came free, revealing a long, thin blade that glinted wickedly. He took advantage of how close Selyf had drawn himself in, and with a simple fluid motion, drove the knife through Selyf's eye and into his brain.

Selyf ap Cynan, King of Powys, staggered back with a look of surprise on his face, Eluad's unexpected blade protruding from his eye socket.

His lifeless body collapsed to the ground.

Eluad roared in triumph. He turned to his men, who were holding Selyf's sons captive, and yelled, "Kill them! Kill them all! I don't care what promises I made; I want them all dead!"

——————— ✦ ———————

Bedwyr and Dylan had been edging slowly away from the other men as the kings were embroiled in battle.

"All right, brother," Dylan said. "Now, we do as we planned."

"Aye," replied Bedwyr. "You ride northwest to Gwynedd, to our good allies. They shall be sorely grieved to hear these tales of treachery and strife."

"And you southwest to Dumnonia," said Dylan. "Follow Offa's Dike and you'll avoid most of Saxon Mercia, but you must cross Saxon Wessex to reach our allies in Dumnonia."

"Chaos and loss grip us," said Bedwyr. "But Father raised us strong and resourceful. We will avenge our father and brothers."

"And pull down this vile hex on our land, Eluad ap Glast," said Dylan. "Ride hard, brother, we shall meet again."

CHAPTER THREE

Clun Forest

Fifteen Weeks Before Winter Solstice

Dappled sunlight filtered through the tall trees and shimmered on the water's surface. Dragonflies flitted through the glade, and songbirds made cheerful noises in the surrounding trees. Alantir felt a light breeze lift her hair with a faint scent of wildflowers. She positioned herself so that she could feel the warm sunlight on her face, her thoughts trailing.

A splash of water startled her and interrupted her reverie. "Meriel!" she spluttered. "I should have known better than to try to relax with you around! Can't you sit still for longer than two minutes? We're not teenagers any longer."

Meriel just laughed and dove back into the water. "Come in and enjoy the water. You've a big competition just a few hours from now," Meriel said. "Stretch out with a few laps."

"Ok, ok," Alantir said as she jumped into the water with Meriel. "Just a few minutes, then we'll need to dry off and go home."

… Which was how they found themselves a short time later.

They looked so different. Alantir was tall, dark, and slim, whereas Meriel was shorter, with long, wavy blond hair and abundant curves. Alantir lightly and lovingly touched the bark of one of the trees as they walked along the path. She loved every tree in their forest.

All these magnificent specimens with trunks so wide that it would take a dozen or more of her people with outstretched arms to encircle one of them. *They must be thousands of years old*, she thought.

After a lifetime in this forest, all the known and hidden pathways were as familiar to her as her own home in Beechwood. The two friends trod softly on the forest floor, the afternoon sun filtering through the canopy far above as the scents of fallen leaves and rich soil filled the air.

Alantir was also familiar with all of the mysterious ancient stone works that served as demarcations of her own people's territory. Deep within Clun Forest, hidden behind sections of the wider forest, the tribes living beyond found it dark and forbidding. Alantir thought that their own hidden realm deep within the center was friendly and inviting. Still, outsiders never made it far enough to get beyond those dark center sections.

"What's for dinner, d'you think?" Meriel asked. "Maybe I should eat with your family tonight."

Alantir laughed. "Why should tonight be any different than almost every other night?"

The homes of Beechwood were just ahead on the path. An untrained eye would not see anything but more forest, but the two friends could well see all of the homes in their community built into the upper reaches of the majestic trees. To their eyes, the pattern of solid branches spiraling upward looked just like what it was: a spiral staircase.

Alantir and Meriel sprang up them to Alantir's family home. Her younger sister, Cerwen, was giving study lessons to her younger brother, Caradoc, on the history of their people, the woodland elves of Beechwood.

"Don't mind us!" Alantir said as they pilfered apples from a bowl in the kitchen past the study area and piled noisily into an overstuffed armchair to listen.

The sound of rustling leaves formed the acoustics in the open home, and softly filtered sunlight filled her vision in every direction. It was as if the forest embraced them.

"Long, long ago, in the time before the Great Sundering, our world of Terra had not yet been separated from the lands of Light and Shadow, Ljós and Myrkur. Magic existed in Terra then, and our people were kin to the …?" Cerwen gestured at Caradoc to supply the answer, her eyebrows raised.

"Uh, the high elves of Ljós?" he said, blushing.

"Mm," said Cerwen, continuing, "Others of the Álfur used magic, and often great good came from the use of magic with the Light. However, magic was also used with the Shadow for evil purposes. Our ancestors, the woodland elves, never had much use for magic. Our people's love was for the trees and other living things in our forest home. The war between Light and Shadow eventually led to the High-Elves' plan for …?" Her fingers began to tap.

Caradoc blew his cheeks out, floundering. His attention was, deplorably, only on Meriel and not his lesson. Cerwen exhaled loudly, exasperated.

"The *Great Sundering*. This would isolate Terra from the dark forces of Myrkur, but it would also isolate Terra from the Light of Ljós. Our ancestors had to make a terrible decision: stay with their beloved woodlands in Terra, forsaking their Álfur relatives, or move to Ljós with all the other elves and leave their beloved forest behind forever. If they chose Terra, then what—?" she broke off abruptly, as Caradoc slid his eyes downward guiltily, his fingers knotting.

He muttered something to the floor, inaudible and incoherent.

"Do pay attention Car'—or perhaps you'd like Meriel to give your lesson?" she quipped.

Caradoc went a violent shade of red at this and perked up long enough to deliver an answer. "They'd ah, they would also be choosing mortal life for themselves and their descendants. In the end, our ancestors chose to remain," he said.

Mollified, Cerwen continued, "They said farewell to their elven kin who moved to Ljós and have lived in these woodlands for eons, without the use of magic and living mortal lives."

"Difficult decision," Caradoc said dreamily. "That must have been very hard for our ancestors. I would not want to have to make a decision like that."

Cerwen's eyes narrowed suspiciously. "But we have deeply enjoyed our forest home ever since, so we are grateful that our ancestors decided as they did," she said.

"We have to get you ready for the tournament," Meriel said, laughing good-naturedly. She winked at Caradoc before turning to Alantir. "You'll miss the start if we don't hurry."

Alantir was considered the best young archer in their community, but she had several rivals. Beryl was a particularly close rival. The annual tournament was their opportunity to displace Alantir and win possession of the Ash Arrow. The Ash Arrow was a special brooch that was awarded to each year's winner to wear proudly until there was a new winner. Alantir had worn the Ash Arrow for three years running now, and Beryl was more determined than ever to win this year.

The competition took place in a large clearing some distance from Beechwood. Close to one of the ancient stone markers that had traditionally defined the border of their own realm, and deep within the forest. Lingering magic from the time of the Great Sundering was embedded in these stone markers and helped keep the humans from wandering into their realm.

Each archer had three opportunities to split one of the narrow willow wands that were embedded in the ground before several different mounds of forest debris. The willow wands wavered in the light breeze. The afternoon sun that filtered through the forest canopy had more shadows than they would have seen at midday. The archers kept taking turns as long as they split a willow wand with at least one of their three shots. After several turns, however, it was down to just four archers, including Alantir and Beryl.

"Beryl is presenting a real challenge this year," whispered Meriel to another bystander. "She looks more determined than ever to win the Ash Arrow this year."

The rules changed slightly once the competition was down to just two finalists, Alantir and Beryl. For this final round of competition, a single miss caused a loss. As last year's champion, Alantir had the right to go second.

Beryl went first. She split all three willow wands, although the third one was close.

Alantir went second. She split the first two willow wands quickly, but a stronger breeze was rising. She pulled her fingers back to her right ear with her third arrow and watched the target willow waving in the strong breeze. She did not sight her arrow but instead, tried to visualize where she wanted her shot to end.

Sure enough, she split the third willow wand.

Beryl went again. She split the first willow wand but missed the second shot. The strong breeze was just too much of a problem.

"Alantir!" whooped Meriel. "You won again!"

"Nobody has ever before earned the right to wear the Ash Arrow for four years in a row," said Meriel. "Your family will be so proud!"

Alantir lined up with Beryl and a stern-faced boy who'd reached third place to receive their awards in front of an excited crowd. Before the ceremony could be completed; however, a runner burst into the clearing.

"Humans have been spotted inside our borders!" the runner shouted. "This has never happened before!"

"Where have they been seen?" asked one of the judges, twisting in his seat.

"Heading right towards Beechwood," answered the runner. "Hurry! We need more defenders as soon as possible."

Alantir grasped the medallion that she always wore around her neck. She tended to reach for it whenever she was anxious, her mother had given it to her. She took a deep breath and looked at Beryl who returned her intense gaze with a look of firm resolve. They nodded at each other and sprang into action.

"Archers," shouted Beryl. "Line up behind me and Alantir. We will each lead a band along two different paths back to Beechwood."

Alantir and her group of archers jogged down their chosen path back to Beechwood. Her group would be approaching Beechwood from the north, and Beryl's from the east.

Just before they reached Beechwood, Alantir smelled a sharp tang that was not part of the forest. And now she could hear sounds that did not belong either. Rustling leathers and softly jangling bits of metal. Humans!

How could this be? Alantir thought to herself. *The magic in the ancient stone works at our borders must have failed for some reason. What could possibly have disrupted the spells that have concealed and protected our forest realm for eons?*

There was no more time to wonder. Humans were just outside the boundaries of Beechwood, and they needed to be stopped. Now. There was no time to wait for further assistance.

"I want half of you lined up just ahead on the far side of their path," whispered Alantir. "And the other half just ahead on this side."

Once she had her archers set up where she wanted them, Alantir stopped to watch the humans approach, her dark brown eyes watchful and pointed ears alert. Her dark green tunic and deep brown leggings helped her remain concealed in the forest just a step off the path. Her brown hair was bound in a long braid that hung to the middle of her back and she wore a belt knife on her waist. She wiggled her toes inside her soft leather moccasins as the humans drew closer, as she often did when she was nervous. *These humans look bigger than I ever imagined*, she thought. *We would never have a chance against them in a test of strength. In any fight we must be swift and silent, decisive as well as cunning.*

Alantir stepped out of the forest and onto the path in front of the small group of humans.

"Halt," she declared firmly. "Why are you trespassing in our woodland realm?"

The humans were startled. They had not seen where she had come from. She had just seemed to materialize in front of them.

"Who are you to tell us where we can and cannot go?" a man who appeared to be their leader snorted. "You're just a slip of a girl, standing alone in this forest in front of my armed and dangerous men."

"Things are not always the way they seem to be," cautioned Alantir. "Turn around now and never tread this path again. Nothing but woe and ill tidings will your womenfolk know of you if you do not heed my warning."

The man slung his shield forward, widened his stance, and lifted his sword slightly above his waist. "Nay," he stated. "It will take more than a mouthy young girl with a slender bow to tell me and my men what to do and where to go."

He lunged forward and raised his sword above his head, poised to deliver a mighty blow.

Alantir drew and loosed her first arrow and had another nocked in the space of a single heartbeat, her first piercing the wrist of the human's sword arm.

As he howled, she said, "The next arrow goes through your eye. Heed my final warning, human. Leave now and never return, and your company will keep their lives. Or ..." she cocked her head. "this 'slip of a girl' will be your doom if you wish."

The two groups of archers stepped out of the forest, flanking the humans, their bows fully drawn and ready. Human and elf stared at each other, both breathing heavily. The humans blinked.

"Aye," their leader spat. "You can keep your stinkin' woodlands. Ain't nuthin' here worth spit anyways."

Alantir and her archers followed the small band of humans as they left, stopping at the stone markers. They watched the humans disappear into the gloom of the dark forest that surrounded their own hidden realm.

Later that evening, the woodland elves relaxed around a blazing bonfire. Alantir toyed with her medallion. It was heavy silver with a large tree within a circle.

"Why were the humans able to enter our realm?" she asked her mother. "Why didn't the magic wards conceal our hidden paths and misdirect them as they have always done?"

"Something has changed," Gwendlyn said, her long hair falling alongside her narrow face. "More changes are coming. I have a foreboding that grim tidings are ahead," she said. "I feel that magic is returning to Terra. And the Light and Shadow of the Fae are returning with it. Fell creatures of the Shadow are stirring, as are bright champions of the Light." As the spiritual leader of their community, Gwendlyn was more sensitive to hidden currents than anyone else. In her dreams, she had seen visions of what the future might hold. Leaders of men and elves corrupted and turned to evil deeds. Foul creatures of the Shadow running amok, killing innocents and enslaving others. Good people overwhelmed by dark magic everywhere in the world. This was only one possible future, and it might not come true, but the visions chilled Gwendlyn to her core.

Alantir gazed into the flickering flames of the fire and wondered what her mother's insights would mean for their future. For her people. And for herself.

CHAPTER FOUR

Shadows in Terra

Fifteen Weeks Before Winter Solstice

◆━━━━━━━◆

"I wonder if there is something wrong with the stone border marker in the area where the humans crossed our border?" Meriel said. "You know, maybe something is broken inside the rock."

"Hmm," Alantir replied. "Maybe we could investigate the stone marker in that area and then go examine the next one along the border. See if we can find any obvious differences.

"That's a great suggestion," Meriel said. "If we think we have found something, we can return to Beechwood and tell your father. He would know what to do next."

Alantir's father was Tarandyl, chief architect of the woodland elves, and a member of their ruling council.

"There is actually another stone marker that we can investigate on the way to the marker, the one where the humans crossed our border," Alantir pointed out. "That closer one is just past the waterfall."

Alantir made sure that her quiver was full of arrows and gathered up her good cloak and two skins of fresh water. Meriel was going to bring food.

"Tell Mother and Father that I'm going on a long hike with Meriel," Alantir told Cerwen. "We should be back before dinner."

The path to the waterfall was often shared with abundant wildlife. Foxes and deer, along with squirrels and hares, were seen moving through the brush just off the path. Birdsong was a constant accompaniment on their walks. It was a beautiful sunny afternoon as Alantir and Meriel set off for the waterfall.

"I noticed that Gareth was admiring your performance at the tournament yesterday," Meriel teased her friend. "He may be your greatest supporter."

"Gareth is only interested in my archery skills," replied Alantir. "On the other hand, his eyes cannot seem to stop admiring your curves whenever the two of you are together. Don't you notice?"

"Of course, I notice," giggled Meriel. "And I love the fact that he is attracted to me--clearly he would fancy a cuddle. But it's you who fascinates him—he wants to go for a long walk in the woods with you."

"Well, he's not here right now, so he's not getting a walk or a cuddle," laughed Alantir. "Let's enjoy our own time together."

"Look at the vixen stalking the goldfinch," whispered Meriel. "She must be hoping to bring something back to her kits. "

"If her kits are hungry, perhaps she should try for easier prey than that goldfinch," said Alantir.

The path narrowed as they approached the waterfall, the branches from the trees interlocking above their heads. It created the feeling of a natural corridor through the forest, softly carpeted with fallen leaves. In the near distance, the two friends could hear the sound of falling water and after a second's hesitation, hurried their pace.

Meriel rushed to the edge of the water, stripped to her undergarments, and dove right in.

"Hurry, hurry!" she exclaimed. "The water's delightful after our long walk."

"I'm not as quick as you to pull off all my clothes," Alantir drily observed. "Make room, or I shall be right on top of you."

"Remember how we used to hide behind the waterfall when we were younger," reminisced Meriel. "We loved that the falling water made us invisible in that little cave back there. People couldn't see us even when they were looking straight through, standing in the pool in front of it."

The warm sun felt good on her face as Alantir dried off on the grassy bank. Combined with the sound of the waterfall and the smell of the grass, it made for a very relaxing break in their hike.

The walk to the first stone marker from the waterfall was short. As they approached it, they noticed nothing that seemed amiss. There was a small clearing set back from the path and in the center was a circle of twelve smaller stones, all roughly hewn gray granite, buried deep in the ground. Only a short rectangular top of each stone was visible.

In the center of that circle of stones was a large, round stone. This was also gray granite, but the section above the ground was much higher than the surrounding stones, up to the height of Alantir's waist. The center stone was smooth and polished, and the top was cut at an angle with deep engravings. The image was of an intricately carved and interwoven four-cornered knot. A quaternary knot.

At each corner of this engraved sigil were symbols. Just outside of one corner was a symbol of Fire. At the opposite corner, there was a symbol carved for Water. In the third, one for Earth, and in the fourth, Air. There was also a line of runes engraved above the quaternary knot and another line of runes carved below. The meaning of the runes had been lost to her people long ago, but she had often come to the stone monuments. Alantir enjoyed running her fingers over the engravings. She could feel a faint tingling sensation, probably her imagination. These clearings always had a hushed silence and a sense of latent power.

"I don't see anything amiss here," said Meriel. "Do you?"

Alantir squinted. The clearing itself looked as it should, the stone undisturbed. She walked slowly around the clearing, looking at things from every angle. "No", replied Alantir. "I don't see anything wrong here either."

"So much for my crazy ideas about 'broken stones,'" laughed Meriel. "Now that I think about it, how could stones even be broken?"

"Don't be so quick to doubt yourself," replied Alantir. "We still have a second stone marker to inspect. And this next one is in the area where the humans found their way across our hidden border."

"All right," said Meriel. "Then let's get started. It is already mid-afternoon."

The path to the second stone border marker meandered through the forest and took them to the top of a large hill. From the top, Alantir and Meriel had a good view of the landscape, all the way to the next stone border marker.

"Meriel," Alantir said. "Do you see anything unusual down there?"

Meriel shaded her eyes from the afternoon sun. "Yes," she replied. "That area of the forest looks sort of dark compared to the sunny area around it."

"Almost like there was a clump of clouds casting shadows

on the ground in that area," said Alantir. "But not a single cloud in the sky."

"You're right," replied Meriel. "How strange."

"Let's go take a closer look," Alantir said.

As they got closer to the location of the second stone monument, less sunlight filtered through the forest canopy and fewer animal noises sounded from the trees around them.

Then, there were no animal sounds at all. None. And no sunlight.

"Alantir," Meriel gasped. "I don't like this. This clearing frightens me, and I don't know why."

"Something is wrong here," answered Alantir. "Let's be very careful."

They entered the clearing slowly. The twelve smaller stones encircling the larger center stone all looked as they should.

"Oh, by all the stars in the sky!" exclaimed Meriel. "Look at the center stone!"

"It looks like it was struck by lightning," replied Alantir. "There's a large section missing from the top, a crack from there to the bottom, and a blackened area around it."

"And look! Behind the stone!" exclaimed Meriel. "Look at the trees, on the outside of our border. Some of them are all black and charred. Like a fire swept through them."

"Yes, but just in a narrow swathe," replied Alantir. "Right up to our stone border marker. I can't imagine what could have caused this, but this is bad. Much worse than we thought. We need to leave this place right now."

The two friends turned and ran out of the clearing. Back down the path they had come. The forest around them was even darker than it had been; the shadows between the trees seeming to flicker, like a dark version of a candle's guttering flame.

The shadows between two trees suddenly flickered towards Meriel and she was suddenly snatched and whisked from sight, into the deeper dark of the forest behind the path. Alantir was stunned. It had happened in the blink of an eye.

Belatedly, she stirred into motion and lunged into the forest to save her friend. "Meriel!" she cried out. "Where are you? Merry! Yell so I know where you are! I can't see anything here; it's so dark!"

Alantir edged her way further into the darkened forest. She grew increasingly anxious as more time passed without any sign of Meriel. It had all happened so quickly. One minute, they were moving quickly down the path back to the waterfall, and a heartbeat later, the shadows had come to life and Meriel was gone.

Alantir heard a noise to her right and stumbled forward in that direction. "Meriel? Is that you?" she exclaimed, fighting her way through dense foliage.

There, on the forest floor, lay Meriel, small and still.

Alantir dove forward, relief flooding her senses as she neared her friend. "Meriel!" she almost sobbed.

The lack of response caused Alantir to falter. *Please don't let it be bad.* Her eyes darted to the shadows on either side where nothing moved and she advanced warily, until she reached Meriel. Alantir touched her friend gently, stroking her arms, her disheveled blonde hair, her face.

Why won't you answer me?" Alantir asked as she knelt, cradling Meriel in her arms.

Finally, Meriel's eyes fluttered, and she drew small gasps of air. "Don't—" she stammered. "Don't let them … Don't let them get you!"

"Who, Merry?" Alantir asked softly, not wanting to cause more distress.

"I am so cold," Meriel managed. "It's so dark. Help me!"

As Alantir hunched over her friend, she could see that where her skin had been blotchy a minute ago, it was now turning ashen gray. Her skin was icy cold to the touch.

Between herself and her cold friend, Alantir could feel something warm, but her focus was on reviving her friend. She hugged Meriel, rubbing the other girl's arms, but the stricken girl began to shake violently. Her whole body convulsed, her limbs extending straight out. Her eyes rolled back in her sockets, and her skin flushed a dark gray. Meriel stopped moving, and then she stopped breathing.

"No!" cried Alantir. "No, Meriel! Not like this."

Alantir rocked back and forth, holding her friend's body in her arms as her wails tapered to shaky moans. They were alone, no help would come. She smoothed Meriel's hair away from her face, although looking at that dark gray face was hard. Lifeless now.

Meriel's eyes suddenly snapped open and Alantir clutched her friend in shock. But the red eyes framed by the dark gray face did not resemble Meriel's. A low animal growl emitted, and a small wisp of what looked like black smoke escaped from her mouth. Hands that looked like claws reached for her.

Alarmed, Alantir pulled back, jumping to her feet. As she did, her medallion swung out from inside her tunic. It was glowing! A soft green light pulsed from it and she instinctively clutched it and felt that it was warm to the touch.

"Help me, please help me," she exhorted. "Whatever power is in this charm, please help me save my friend or ease her passing."

Her medallion grew even warmer, and the green glow brighter. A shaft of light escaped between her fingers and shone on Meriel as if seeking her. As it touched Meriel's body, it burst into a bright green glowing sphere. Warmth and illumination cascaded from its green glow.

Meriel's body once again convulsed, violent shaking lending her the appearance of a rag doll as the awful gray fled her features. Then she relaxed, her limbs still once more, and her features softened. The bright green glow faded to a soft flicker and then faded completely.

Alantir reached down to close her friend's eyelids, her wide eyes blue again. "Light and warmth," said Alantir quietly, tears streaming down her face. "Light and warmth eased your passing."

Suddenly, Alantir heard rustling behind her and saw movement in the shadows. Terrified, she prepared to flee and a realization clarified their—*my*, she self-corrected—situation. There was danger here, something had gotten to Meriel and killed her. She had to leave. She was strong, but not strong enough to carry Meriel all the way home. Agonized, Alantir cast about for a solution. She hated to leave her friend's body behind, and there was nothing here with which to mark the area. What to do?

Alantir's dismantled thoughts harried. And then she thought of the waterfall.

Don't hate me, Merry, she thought as she tore off strips of Meriel's hunting cloak, wide enough to use as bands, and began to fasten them around Meriel's dead ankles.

By the time Alantir was halfway back to the waterfall, the forest around her looked and sounded normal again. There was no sign of that unusual darkness or the unnaturally long, creeping shadows. She sat briefly on a fallen log to rest. Meriel was heavy but they were almost there.

She picked up Meriel's heels once more, the bound cloth about her feet forming a useful grip to help her pull and slowly continued down the path. Meriel's long blonde hair caught the leaves and twigs as she was dragged, but the grief was Alantir's alone to bear. Meriel no longer cared. When they reached the waterfall, Alantir waded through the water and stepped behind it. There, in that small hidden space, she arranged her friend's body.

She kissed Meriel's forehead, her tears invisible in this place. *I will come back for you, Merry,* she promised.

Then Alantir left her dead best friend for Beechwood. She had to warn her people—now!

CHAPTER FIVE
Alantir's Flight

Fourteen Weeks Before Winter Solstice

Alantir paced back and forth. She had just recounted her experiences to the citizens council. The senior members of which were now discussing what they should do to address this overwhelming new threat. An hour had passed. And then another hour. After several hours, Alantir's Tarandyl emerged with most of the other senior council members.

"Well, we do have a plan," he said. "None of us likes what we must do, but it seems there were no viable alternatives." His face hardened, with a wry twist of his mouth, and his eyes rested gravely on Alantir.

"First, we will send out a team of rangers to the ring of stones by the waterfall. They will be able to determine the extent of the problem and how quickly it is spreading," he continued. "They must also conduct some experiments to confirm your observations of light and heat halting the spread of these shadow creatures."

"How long, Father?" asked Alantir.

"Two days," he replied. His tone was kind as he spoke to his daughter, compassion for the passing of her friend. "If they confirm the threat and the impact of light and heat, we must ... with heavy hearts ... cut down some of our beloved trees in various forest areas."

There was an audible gasp and murmuring suffused the room in a low and angry hum. Trees were sacred for every elf in Beechwood.

"We must create a wide strip of bare land that encircles the central portion of our hidden realm and ensure that the affected areas of forest are too far apart from our dwelling for the shadows to cross the gap," Tarandyl explained. "During the day, sunlight will flood the gaps we create, keeping the shadows at bay from the newly isolated center of our realm. And during the night, teams of rangers will keep large bonfires lit all along these gaps. As the area of contamination is to the northeast of Beechwood, we will start by creating boundary areas in the north and the east."

"It's too bad that our people gave up magic at the time of the Great Sundering," Alantir said. "Magic-wielders could probably fight these shadows without sacrificing our trees."

"Agreed," Tarandyl sighed. "Yet we do not have those capabilities anymore, so we must do what we can."

Several days later, Alantir and Gareth were working with a team to the north of Beechwood. It was a grim task and as each tree was felled, many cries could be heard. Still, they had made good progress in clearing their area in the north. Alantir's parents were working with a separate team to the east of Beechwood. Fear drove them forward, that these strange shadow creatures would reach them before they could complete their preparations.

"How are your parents, Alantir?" Gareth asked. "It must be difficult for them to leave your younger brother and sister behind while they do this work on the eastern boundary."

"They are doing as well as anyone. Thank you for asking," replied Alantir. "They are glad to contribute to our defenses even though they have to leave my brother and sister behind for a while. You also have younger siblings behind in Beechwood, don't you, Gareth?"

"Yes, I have two younger brothers back there," said Gareth. "My parents did not want to leave them alone, so my aunt is with them now."

By now, Alantir's group had cleared a large number of trees from the space between the protected central section of the forest and the shadow-infested outer regions. One part of their group was now working on the trenches in the middle of the cleared space, while another prepared stacks and stacks of split wood to be used to fuel the bonfires that would burn in the trenches. As Alantir looked back to the west where they had begun, she noticed a commotion. A growing number of people appeared to be yelling and waving their arms out toward the western edge of their cleared area.

"I wonder what all the fuss is about,' said Gareth. "Look! They're dropping their tools and running off."

"Let's go see," replied Alantir. "It must be something important."

Gareth and Alantir edged their way into a group having an animated discussion.

"These damned shadow creatures are moving in quickly from the west," one man said. "We were supposed to be safe in that direction, so we don't have any defenses prepared."

"The shadows are heading straight toward Beechwood," somebody else said.

"Gareth," Alantir said. "We have to warn our families in Beechwood and out on the eastern boundary."

"We will have to split up then," replied Gareth. "I'll go to Beechwood and you take the eastern boundary."

"Where should we meet?" yelled Alantir as she gathered her gear.

"South," replied Gareth as he started to run. "Just get everyone to head south. That seems to be the only safe direction."

Alantir slipped the strap for her full quiver of arrows across one shoulder and her bow across the other. She didn't know what good they'd do against these shadow creatures but she wasn't going out into all the chaos around them without any weapons. Alantir broke into a run, eager to reach the eastern boundary area as soon as possible.

Alantir cut through the protected central section of their forest realm. As she approached the eastern boundary, she saw that the felling was even further along than theirs on the northern boundary. Here in the east, the area was fully cleared, the trenches completed, and huge piles of split wood were already stacked and waiting along the interior edge of the cleared area. The remaining stumps were a grisly sight, like gigantic broken toothpicks. Although they'd been shorn short, they stood as a sad testament to what had once been.

She shivered. There were no woodland elves in sight. Where could they have gone?

Alantir wondered if they might have heard the news and returned to Beechwood. But if that were the case, she was certain that they would have left someone behind to say so. Movement on the far side of the cleared area caught her eye, and she headed off in that direction.

A large number of elves were going in and out of the forest on the far side of the cleared area. Some of them seemed to be dragging bodies into the sunlight. Alantir rushed up to one of the men coming out of the woods. He was dragging a woman's body with the same ashen gray skin Meriel had had, after she was attacked by the shadows. Once the body was in the sunlight, the woman's appearance was transformed, just like Meriel's.

Alantir looked at the man's tear-streaked face. She did not want to intrude on his grief, but she needed to know what was going on.

"I am so sorry but where is everybody?" she asked him.

"It started with just a few elves," the man said. "Yelling for help, and more elves went in to save them. It all happened so fast. More and more elves were going in. I resisted the urge to help until I heard my own poor wife screaming for me. And now she is lost forever."

"I'm so sorry for your loss," Alantir said, touching the man's shoulder as she saw somebody she recognized dragging another body out of the woods. It was Gareth's father, Bryn.

"Gareth is OK," she told him. "We received word that these shadow creatures were somehow coming in unexpectedly from the west. Heading toward Beechwood. Gareth went there, and I came here for the parents."

"Thank goodness he's alright," Bryn replied. "These living shadows are coming at us from all directions. I pray he stays safe."

"Everywhere except south," Alantir said. "Have you seen my parents?" she blurted.

"Yes, sorry, they're working with my wife to save more

elves," he replied. "I'll take you to them. But be on your guard in there. The shadows seem to appear out of nowhere."

"We found out early in the attack that we can help ease the passing of those afflicted by dragging them into the sunlight," he continued. "Even if their lives can't be saved, at least we can ease their passing from whatever horrors they would otherwise face."

"Please take me to where you last saw my parents," Alantir asked.

She followed Bryn into the forest. There were terrible screams all around them, and people were crying as they hugged afflicted loved ones or dragged their thrashing bodies into the light.

Alantir kept a careful eye on the dark spaces between the trees.

"This is the area where they were helping the last group," said Bryn. "Blazing stars! I see your parents, but it does not look good!"

"Please help me," Alantir cried. "Maybe it's not too late."

But it was.

When they reached her fallen parents, Alantir was horrified to find them both on the ground. Shaking and convulsing, with dark gray skin. Alantir choked back her tears and took hold of her mother's body. Bryn grasped her father.

Once they had dragged both of her parents' bodies out into the sunlight, that dreaded gray skin color receded. Alantir sobbed over the sudden loss of her parents.

"I have to find my wife," said Bryn. "Will you please help me? I am sorry to take you away from your grieving, but I really need your help."

"Yes," sobbed Alantir as she slowly rose to her feet.

They returned to where they had found Alantir's parents and then went further into the forest. Gareth's father called his wife's name out over and over. But there was no response.

"I think that I see something over there," he said.

Alantir felt a tingling sensation on the back of her neck. She carefully examined the forest around them and saw movement to the left and then also to the right. "Bryn!" she shouted. "Something is not right here. There is movement on either side of us." A sobering realization came to Alantir then. The living shadows were now positioned between them and the cleared area in the sunlight. "They've cut us off!" yelled Alantir.

"Run! Run south!" Bryn shouted back. "Save yourself! You have done everything that you can. Now save yourself, Alantir!"

Blinking away her tears, Alantir ran desperately. She could hear rustling all around her and saw flickering shadows in her periphery. *They don't want anyone to escape*, she thought.

Alantir clutched her medallion, feeling its warmth in her hand but did not break her stride to see if there was light again.

"Please help me," she said out loud. "I don't know how any of this works, but I know that I need help to escape these evil shadows."

Heat pulsed from the medallion, and a shaft of green light shot forward from her hand, cutting through the dark and gloom around her, and illuminating a clear path forward off to her right. Alantir followed this illuminated path to safety.

She ran and ran, no longer aware of her surroundings, until she entered a large clearing lit by bright sunshine. Alantir collapsed on the green grass, covered from head to toe in golden rays.

CHAPTER SIX

White Henge of Ljós

Fifteen Weeks Before Winter Solstice

Taorlyn entered the stone circle from the east. The full moon illuminated the towering white pieces. The roughly hewn rocks seemed to have a faint glow about them as though illuminated from deep within. The moonlight added to the effect. This ring of twelve towering white stones also emanated a palpable aura of latent power. The White Henge of Ljós had been here at the center of the realm of the silver elves from the earliest days of their people. The surrounding land was flat for miles and miles around them, although there were snow-capped mountains beyond those flat plains.

It had been a long time now since he had served as Warden of the North. Those had been the days before the Great Sundering. Now, he was Warden of the West. Time passes and things change. Taorlyn of the Álfur proceeded around the large, round stone at the center of the White Henge. He watched the Warden of the South, Neldorin, take her assigned post, followed by Vaelwyn, the newly appointed Warden of the North. Vaelwyn was the youngest of her people ever given the honor and responsibility of a Warden. Aldorthyn, the Warden of the East took his position, and Caedwyn, the Warden of Midgard, senior of their order, took his position at the center of the round white stone dais. Finally, Aneirin, the king of the silver elves took his position at the southeast point within the stone circle. His hair was swept back from his head in a silver clasp and his garb was cut for movement.

Taorlyn thought back over the past month. There had been a growing sense of foreboding amongst all twelve of the Prime Adepti, especially the five Wardens. They could all feel that something was *wrong* across all of the realms. They had agreed that a special conjuring was required where they would invoke the power of the White Henge to help them visualize what was causing such disturbance. Once they could visualize the problem, they planned to use the power of the White Henge to assist in devising a solution.

Aldorthyn, Warden of the East raised his long white rune staff with both hands. The polished surface was engraved with silver runes of arcane power. The rune staffs of the Adepti held much of the power of their people; they harnessed and focused this to amplify the native power of each individual to whom they were attuned.

As he raised his rune staff with both hands, he intoned, "Ceiliúradh a dhéanamh, Solas!" *Celebrate light!* and then inserted his rune staff into the prepared slot at the eastern edge of the central dais.

The east section of the round white stone glowed softly, illuminating the Warden of the East.

Taorlyn, Warden of the West, felt a warm breeze rustle his long silver hair. He raised his own staff in both hands and uttered another phrase, "Solas, an iarthair! Cuir isteach, an chloch!" *Light of the West! Enter the Stone!* and placed his rune staff in the slot prepared for the West.

The western section of the white stone dais now also glowed from within.

Neldorin, the Warden of the South paused for just a moment. All the Prime Adepti were assembled here, including the king of the silver elves, and the light of the full moon highlighted their faces as well as the imposing ring of stones that encircled them. She raised her rune staff and repeated the ritual of the others. With her staff inserted in the round white stone, the southern section now glowed too.

Vaelwyn, Warden of the North, followed suit and a complete glowing ring now formed around the central section of the dais, activating the east, west, south, and north.

Caedwyn, Warden of Midgard raised his rune staff in both hands, intoning "Solas, an t-ionad! Cuir isteach, an chloch!" *Light of the Center! Enter the Stone!* His staff crackled with energy.

The entire round white platform was now glowing, pulsating with power.

Finally, the king of the silver elves raised his rune staff and tapped twice on the towering white stone at the southeast point of the White Henge. It had a glow, brighter than the rest, appearing illuminated more strongly from within. Aneirin moved to the southwest point of the White Henge and repeated the process. Then the northwest and the northeast. Four points of the White Henge itself were now brightly illuminated and pulsing with power.

In unison, all twelve of the Prime Adepti of the silver elves chanted the words required for the special conjuring. They all raised their arms to waist level with their palms open and facing upwards. The air above their heads began to shimmer, and a visualization slowly took shape above the center of the platform.

———————◆———————

"This will be a monumental task," said Caedwyn after they had taken in the visualization in the White Henge.

"There is no denying that fact," replied Aneirin. "We will need to appoint an Elven leader and we will also need a Guardian from the Breacadh an Lae; a Caomhnoir who represents the best of their people."

The Caomhnoir were the guardians or warrior princes of the Dawn Kin, the Breacadh an Lae. The Breacadh an Lae were an early race of beings predating mortal men. Although they were not Fae themselves, they had always been closely aligned with the Álfur folk since the earliest times and as such, were referred to as the Dawn Kin. They had extremely long lifespans but were not immortal like the Álfur. Physically robust, they made terrifying warriors. They had always been few, and their numbers had shrunk dramatically in recent centuries. They had always considered themselves cousins of the younger race of humans who came along long after the Álfur and Breacadh an Lae. Some wondered if their decision to join the Álfur in Ljós at the time of the Great Sundering was bad for their people, separated as they were now from their human cousins.

"I recommend Vaelwyn as our own appointed leader," said Caedwyn. "Although she is young, she is also the most powerful Prime Adeptus that we have seen since the days before the Great Sundering."

"But can she muster the Breacadh an Lae?" replied Aneirin. "Along with the fractious Álfur and all the warring tribes of the humans?"

"She can, and she must," said Caedwyn. "Let's meet with her now."

"If she agrees, we must hasten to get her started," Aneirin replied.

Vaelwyn was unique among the Prime Adepti. She was incredibly young by elven standards, having been made a Prime Adeptus when she was only a few hundred years old. Vaelwyn was the most powerful silver elf seen in thousands of years. She had been left behind while still a child when her parents' ennui compelled them to trek through the Eydimörk mountains to undertake the Sojourn; a choice made by only a few hapless elves each year.

Vaelwyn made a striking appearance with her tall, athletic build. She was tall even among the elves, with an ample chest, and she wore her silver hair in a long braid. Vaelwyn had deep green eyes, set in a face that was beautiful but strong, with a penetrating gaze that often made others feel uncomfortable. She spoke with a commanding voice, often described by others as 'steely'. Vaelwyn carried a white rune staff, shoulder-height, engraved with silver runes—as did the other Prime Adepti. She wore a white tunic, intricately embroidered with small white pearls, and a black cloak with a large hood and a brown fur collar. Vaelwyn's cloak was clasped with a heavy gold brooch at her left shoulder, and the same heavy gold pattern served as the buckle on her right hip for a sword belt. She also wore a gold ring on her right hand, set with a large red ruby. And a gold necklace with a broken bottom half of a mandala, with a deep green emerald set in the center. Her friends noted that she exuded a unique combination of strength, beauty, intelligence, and authority. Her detractors noted that she was an arrogant and insensitive bitch. All agreed that she was always calm, confident, and unflustered—even under the most difficult of circumstances.

"In principle, I understand what must be done to fully restore and maintain the separation of the realms put in place by the Great Sundering," said Vaelwyn after she had listened to Caedwyn and Aneirin. "But I do not fully understand why the mortal folk from Terra must be involved. They are so fragile and so difficult to reason with. And I also do not understand why the Breacadh an Lae must play a part in all of this."

"You saw the conjuring at the White Henge, just as the rest of us," answered Caedwyn.

"Yes, but as we all know," Vaelwyn answered with strength and clarity in her voice, "some things are clear in such a conjuring, some hazy, and some things are simply hinted at. There is ample room for very different interpretations."

"It is clear that a Caomhnoir of the Breacadh an Lae will be needed, although not why," replied Aneirin. "It is unclear what wider role may be played by the Breacadh an Lae. It is also clear that mortal folk from Terra will be important, but the full depth of their involvement remains unclear."

"What is clear," Aneirin continued, "is the return of The Six to the mortal realm."

"Yes, I saw the disturbing images of the gölge yürüteç, the Shadow Walkers, in our conjuring," replied Vaelwyn. "These fell creatures are powerful and the Shadow has always worked his most wretched evil with their eager assistance."

"You are too young to remember the horror that all Álfur felt when those six of our most talented and powerful left the Light—seduced by Shadow."

"Now, you and Caedwyn must travel to the Breacadh an Lae and convince them to appoint a Caomhnoir for the first time in long ages," continued Aneirin. "He must be dispatched to Terra on one of the hidden pathways. Once there, they must locate the two mortals who bear the amulets of Earth and Air, and escort them safely back to Ljós."

"I will meet the Caomhnoir and the mortals when they are brought back to Ljós and escort them all to the White Henge," said Vaelwyn thoughtfully. "Once there, we all hope that the next ritual will provide clarity for the tasks ahead." She lifted her head, looking intently at Caedwyn. "By then we must know what, exactly, will be the critical role the mortal folk must play."

CHAPTER SEVEN

Breacadh an Lae

Fourteen Weeks Before Winter Solstice

———◆▬▬▬———

"I will travel with you to the Breacadh an Lae's city of Abhaile," said Caedwyn. "There, I will introduce you and your mission to the king's council. They have had many dealings with me over the long years."

"Yes, that king's council is known to me," replied Vaelwyn. "And given their difficult reputation, your assistance will be greatly appreciated."

"We will be asking them to take action they will not be glad to undertake," said Caedwyn. "They have not made a formal appointment of Caomhnoir for many centuries now and will more than likely have some strong ideas about who should or should not receive this honor."

"As I think you perceive," replied Vaelwyn in a low voice

full of resolve. "I have a strong idea of who should be appointed as Caomhnoir for the task that I must complete."

"It is well that along our way to Abhaile we plan to visit Alderon, King of Lán Léargas in the Fjall realm," Caedwyn said. "Given his city's proximity to Abhaile, he knows more about the prevailing sentiments of the Breacadh an Lae than anyone else in Ljós."

An hour later, the two Prime Adepti of the silver elves met and set off for Fjall. They would follow a course that took them through the heathlands and moors that lay between the forests of Skógur to the west and south of their intended path, and the mountains of Fjall, to the northeast.

After several days of uneventful travel, Caedwyn and Vaelwyn approached the mighty Månen River that ran to the west of the mountain range containing the beautiful city of white stone that was Lán Léargas. The city gave its name to the kingdom of Lán Léargas, which was the northern half of the mountain realm of Fjall. The weather had been good for most of their journey, but a wind from the west was starting to rise. Their crossing toward the western end of the river took them close to the Fjall Bay and there was a smell of salt in the air, typical with the proximity of the sea. They continued to follow the well-worn path along the northern bank back to the east, up to the mountains.

As their path took them deeper into the mountains, the air grew colder, and the wind blew stronger. They eventually had to cross the Stjärna River and the path they followed after that crossing had sharp twists and turns. Some of the sharpest switchbacks were located where there was a fortified outpost on the craggy heights above them. The sky was a bright blue, contrasting with the browns and greens of the lower peaks. As they rose higher into the mountain range, the stark white of the snow-capped peaks more often contrasted with the piercing sky.

When they were deep into the northern range, they could see a wide valley stretching out before them, surrounded by mountains. There was a spectacular waterfall on the western edge of the valley that fed a river with clear sparkling water. Lán Léargas lay to the east. The city was built into the mountains behind it but also spilled out into the valley. There were wide avenues and broad stairways leading around it and rising ever higher like an abstract labyrinth. The elven builders had created structures that combined light and elegant features with an overall sense of solidity and strength. Bridges with beautifully carved balustrades and archways stretched over bustling footpaths and waterways, stairways with dramatically wide, low steps that created a feeling of majesty, and every detail seemingly dovetailing with the emerald greens of trees in their thousands.

The white stone city felt in harmony with the blue sky above, the white snow-capped peaks around them, and the greenery of the abundant plantings in the city and along the riverbanks.

The gates leading up to the inner levels of the city were emblazoned with King Alderon's arms of a white horse galloping across a light blue background. These northern elves were accomplished horsemen who loved the wide-open plains that spread out to the north and east of their mountain kingdom. The king ruled Lan Léargas from the Chariot Throne, appropriate for these elves who sometimes still rode their horse-drawn chariots into battle.

"Welcome back to Lán Léargas, Caedwyn", said the leader of a group of Fjall elves who met them at those gates to the higher levels of the city.

"It is a great pleasure to see you again, Prince Danderion," replied Caedwyn. "And you remember my companion, Vaelwyn."

Prince Danderion looked at their visitors. He had known Caedwyn since he was a small boy, and the Prime Adeptus appeared unchanged to him; vigorous, an air of unquenchable vitality, his fiery blue eyes sparkling with unshared mirth, although it did look like he leaned on his rune staff a bit more heavily than before ... perhaps. Prince Danderion had met Vaelwyn before but was not as familiar with her. She was taller than most elven women and seemed strong and robust for one of the Prime Adepti of the Silver elves. An attractive woman with bright green eyes and strong facial features framed by her long silver hair. There was no doubt that those bright green eyes did not miss anything that went on around her.

"Come with me," the prince said. "My father is looking forward to welcoming you. You must be tired after your travels, so we will let you settle in your guest rooms and freshen up first. We will welcome you in the king's private dining hall in an hour."

An hour later, King Alderon welcomed the two visitors. Alderon was one of only ten elven Lords of Ljós, a number that excluded the king of the Breacadh an Lae, since he was not one of the Álfur. Alderon was a gracious host and welcomed them warmly.

"I understand you are bound for Abhaile to meet with the king's council for the Breacadh an Lae," said King Alderon. "And that you seek my input on the best way to approach the current members of that council."

"Yes, Alderon," replied Caedwyn respectfully. "Any insights you have would be most appreciated."

"Well, of course, the Breacadh an Lae have always led a somewhat insular existence here in Ljós," said Alderon, scratching his chin. "Although the Dawn Kin are friends and allies of the Álfur, they keep to themselves on their island home much more since the time of the Great Sundering."

"Yes," replied Vaelwyn. "I have always felt that their people mourn the loss of contact with the humans of Terra far more than we Álfur do."

"Indeed," continued Alderon, nodding. "In recent times, some of the newest members of the king's council in Abhaile have developed extremely blinkered views. I fear they will seek to influence the other members away from any decision to help a mission that comes from the Álfur."

Vaelwyn's stoic expression shifted, her eyes flicking to Caedwyn. Her clenched teeth gave a stern set to her jaw.

"You need to be prepared to present them with something that is truly compelling," concluded Alderon.

After they had finished dinner, Alderon invited them up to his solarium. It was located at the top of their highest peak and offered a breathtaking 360-degree view. Lán Léargas was situated at the northwest corner of Ljós, almost as far west as Garmoniya in the Skógur realm, and almost as far north as Vesë in the Vatnid realm. From this location, they could see the shores of the great lake that contained the island home of the Breacadh an Lae. Located within Ljós yet set apart. Like many other aspects of the Dawn Kin.

Sometime prior to their visit, King Alderon had been traveling to several villages in his kingdom. As he was wont to do, he traveled incognito. He wore plain, well-worn clothing and boots, carried an old, plainly wrought sword and scabbard, and wore a cloak with a large hood, which he kept pulled up to conceal his face.

In the first village he visited, he stood quietly in the back of one of the school classrooms. He enjoyed listening to the teacher's lesson and the questions and answers from the young elves. When the students ran outside for recess, the cloaked king went to speak with the teacher. He complimented her and kindly inquired whether there was any student whose family required assistance. The teacher was able to identify one who had suffered the loss of their business due to a recent casualty and were still struggling to recover. The king left a small leather bag and asked her to use it to help the family.

Understandably baffled, the teacher watched the cloaked stranger walk out of the door. As he mounted his horse outside, she opened the small leather bag that he had left in her hands. She was surprised to see the gleam of gold coins inside.

In the second village visited by incognito Alderon, he went to a local healer and waited while several patients who had arrived before him were treated. While he did so, he listened to the villagers talk about their ailments and how much the healer had helped them in the past. He was particularly interested in a poor widow with six children. All present were concerned that, despite the healer's best efforts, the widow might not recover without expensive healing potions that could only be purchased in Lán Léargas. The healer was willing to make the trip, but there was no money to pay for the potions.

When it was time for the cloaked stranger to be seen, he handed the healer a small leather bag and instructed him to see to the needs of the widow.

As Alderon trotted his horse into the third village, it was approaching evening, and daylight was fading. He sat in a shadowed corner of the local pub and listened to the villagers. They talked about the weather and gossiped about the other villagers. Then the talk in the pub shifted to discussion of their king. One of the villagers asserted that the king could be doing a lot more to help his villagers but was immediately shouted down by a chorus of voices defending him. Various stories were told about King Alderon's brave deeds and generous acts. The villager who had initially spoken out looked abashed. Alderon smiled to himself, somewhat relieved.

As he stopped at the bar on his way to the door, he left a small leather bag and muttered to the innkeeper. There was enough to buy several rounds for all the punters.

King Alderon rode home in the dark; he was pleased that he had spent the day learning more about his villagers and helping a bit here and there. Yet he spent much of it thinking about what more he might do the next time he rode out for a visit.

Vaelwyn waited outside the stable where their horses were being tacked up. She was enjoying the morning sunshine and birdsong while she waited for Prince Danderion and was surprised that he had invited her to go riding with him during dinner the night before. Either way, she looked forward to the fresh air and exercise. Truth be told, she was also looking forward to spending some time with the prince. Vaelwyn knew his father, King Alderon, from his occasional visits to confer with the Adepti, but she was less familiar with the prince.

"An early riser?" the prince greeted her. "You look much more wide-awake than I feel."

"I have always been a morning elf," Vaelwyn replied, smiling. "I welcome the early quiet before everyone else is up and starting their daily activities. Where do you plan to ride this morning?" she asked.

"I was thinking north?" Danderion replied. "Across that large open plain toward the wildwood in the far north."

"Across the open plain should give our horses some good exercise," she said. "Although don't you think that all the way to the wildwood itself might be too far for a simple morning ride?"

The grooms brought out their horses, and they mounted up, trotting the animals out of the valley of Lán Léargas. The horses seemed eager to reach open ground where they could break into a gallop. As they worked their way down through the winding mountain passes, Vaelwyn could see the open plains in the distance.

"Last night, your father expressed concerns about a recent increase in reported sightings of goblins. Do you share his concerns?" she asked Danderion.

"Yes, it is a concern," he replied. "But I am not sure how genuine all these supposed sightings are. Our village elves can be … somewhat ignorant," the prince continued carefully, as if choosing each word. "Gossip and rumor have a stronger place in their lives than fact and reason."

"That is a fairly harsh view of the village elves," Vaelwyn said. "In my own experience, they are just as smart as city dwellers and may be even harder working. And I have found villagers to be very alert to changes in their territories."

"Hard working, perhaps," laughed Danderion. "But you cannot deny their love of rumor and gossip. Especially in the pub every evening with a mug of ale to loosen their lips." Conversely sobering at his own words, he continued, "I just think that the reports are likely to be exaggerated. There may be a kernel of truth in there somewhere, but it will be for my father's riders to validate how genuine the threat really is."

As they emerged from the last of the northern foothills, they cantered onto the wide-open plains. There were open grasslands as far as they could see, stretching out in front of them.

"And now," said Vaelwyn. "We have open ground ahead of us. We can let our mounts lengthen their strides for a while."

Further north from where they'd emerged, they could see a band of figures moving across the plains toward the northern foothills of Fjall's mountains. It was too far to make them out clearly, but they were on foot and heading toward the hills in a line that could be traced back to the northern wildwood.

"Do you see that band of stragglers up there?" Danderion asked, pointing.

"Yes," Vaelwyn replied, her voice rising slightly. "I see something. But they are too far to make out clearly."

"Let's ride!" exclaimed Danderion.

As they thundered north toward the interlopers, they could see the first of them scrambling into the foothills. It looked like the whole band might get safely away before they could reach them.

"They are not Álfur!" Vaelwyn cried out. "They are too short and misshapen."

"It's a warband of goblins," Danderion replied. "Finishing a nighttime run from the northern wildwood to the northernmost mountains in my father's realm."

"Well," said Vaelwyn, flashing her teeth. "Perhaps the village rumors are indeed true!"

"And they picked a rugged section of our mountains to disappear into. We'll never be able to get our horses to follow them in there."

"Let's get close enough to the last of them to be able to confirm our sighting before they disappear into the rocks completely," Vaelwyn said.

"Goblins!" seethed the prince, "Once we've confirmed, we'll have to ride hard for Lán Léargas to report this to my father. He must know right away."

Kernel of truth, indeed! Vaelwyn thought to herself.

———— ✦ ————

Later that day, Caedwyn and Vaelwyn were waiting at the waterfront of the great lake where they would board a ship for Abhaile. It had been a week now since they'd left the White Henge. Their ship approached the city on the island of the same name, and they were once again impressed by its scale and grandeur.

The entry to the harbor of Abhaile was flanked by two gigantic statues of Breacadh an Lae warriors. These people could be savage and war-like and they celebrated their martial culture. Young men were separated from their families at an early age to be trained and conditioned as warriors. The two enormous statues flanking the harbor entrance reflected their ideal, with fierce expressions on their bearded faces, fully armored with helms and byrnie. Their inner arms formed an arch over the harbor entry and had upraised palms facing outwards. The message conveyed was 'Halt' rather than 'Welcome.' The outer arm of the left statue held an upraised battle axe, and the outer arm of the right statue an upraised sword.

"Welcome to Abhaile, Vaelwyn," said Caedwyn. "As you know, we Álfur must always be careful regarding contact with iron here. The Breacadh an Lae, like the mortal humans of Terra, freely use arms and armor of iron and steel. Contact would be fatal to our own Fae people."

The harbor front of Abhaile led directly to the center of the capital city whose hulking scale matched the large size of its people. The smallest of the Dawn Kin were seven feet tall, with the largest over eight, and they were all of a robust, muscular build, not slender like most of the elves. Before the Great Sundering, some of the humans of Terra described the Breacadh an Lae as giants, and some of the humans described them as gods.

The central square of their capital was wondrous to behold. Framed by three colonnaded buildings, all with massive columns and a long run of rising stairs. The Hall of Treasury was to the left, the Hall of Justice to the right, and in the place of honor, at the head of the square, was the Hall of the Warrior, behind which was located the king's palace. One entered the Hall of the Warrior if one visited the king.

The stairs to the Hall of the Warrior entrance were flanked by torches that were kept always burning. The torches themselves were more than fifteen feet high, and the rise of each step almost two. The double doors of the entry to this Hall were both open, made of oak four feet thick and banded with heavy iron bands that were dotted with fierce iron studs. Each of the two doors was thirty feet high and ten feet wide. Everything was on a grand scale—and imposing.

As they entered the hall, the ceiling rose high above their heads, and their steps on the marble floor sounded muffled by the oppressive space around them. More columns and torches lined the center corridor of this great entry hall. Shields emblazoned with colorful coats of arms were hung on the columns on each side, too numerous to count. Behind the columns were weapons displays, some in places of particular honor in special displays.

"I am always newly impressed by this city's grandeur," Caedwyn said. "The scale of it, the history behind it, and the pride of our friends, the Breacadh an Lae."

"Yes, you've spoken truly," Vaelwyn replied. "Their vanquished foes must tremble and quail when brought before them here in chains. I am glad that this tribe of giant warriors is our ally."

"King Delbaeth is large and hearty, even by their standards. And he likes to play the jovial host," said Caedwyn. "But don't be fooled by his easy demeanor, he is one of the sharpest and shrewdest kings in Ljós."

"Why does he bother with this council that he has assembled?" Vaelwyn asked. "After all, he is the king here."

"Good question. I think that he likes to engage the most powerful leaders in his realm by inviting their participation through this council. They feel important ... and the king keeps them under his watchful eye."

Farther down was the king's formal reception area. Although the throne sat on a raised dais, it was only slightly elevated from the benches that flanked both sides of a large rectangular central hearth. Bright fires burned within— warming benches filled with King Delbaeth's favored. This warm central portion of the grand hall was reminiscent of a Norseman's longhouse from the mortal realm.

"Hallo, Caedwyn," boomed the king's voice. "I bid you a warm welcome on your return to Abhaile. It has been too long since your last visit."

The travelers stopped respectfully, bowing low.

"Your Majesty," spoke Caedwyn. "As always, your kingdom is truly a sight to behold. King Alderon was generous enough to host us in Lán Léargas last night," he continued. "He bid me convey his kind regards."

"And I am sure he advised gladly on how best to 'handle us,' myself and my council," replied King Delbaeth, a throaty chuckle seizing his appreciable girth.

"Ah," began Caedwyn, momentarily surprised out of a better retort.

"Fear not, good Caedwyn, I take no umbrage. I am too long in the tooth for such and my relations with Alderon are healthier than my teeth, at least!"

"Good king," Vaelwyn said, "Thank you for your warm welcome. King Alderon spoke quite highly of you, and at great length. My name is Vaelwyn and I have been chosen by my own king to lead a special group to oppose the latest plans of the Dark Fae. I will look forward to explaining more at our meeting later."

"Well met, Vaelwyn of the Prime Adepti," replied the king. "I am eager to learn more of this task that you have been assigned. We have no love of the Dark Fae here. We will convene our council again after you both have rested here for a while and refreshed yourselves a bit.

The warm fires in the hearth felt good as Caedwyn and Vaelwyn relaxed and enjoyed some casual banter with the king's companions.

———— ◆ ————

Four of the six appointed members of the king's council had attended a meeting held earlier that day. Talendorf, the pompous fool who sought every opportunity to curry favor with the king was there early. And Eltaneth was also there early, turning his suspicious gaze on one council member after another. Vonteil sat there quietly and pushed her hair behind her ear, hoping that she would not have to listen to these fools for too long. Oxmyr came in with a brisk stride shortly before the king himself, and sharpened his dagger while they waited for the king.

Once he arrived the king did not waste any time getting started.

"Thank you for coming to this impromptu meeting," he said. "I will keep this short and to the point. We will be having a full meeting later today with two of the Prime Adepti of the Álfur. I want that meeting to go smoothly, with no dissension or disruptions. So this meeting, here and now, is where I want to get any reservations voiced about helping the Álfur."

"Once again…" said Eltaneth.

"Yes, once again," replied the king. "And for good reason – as always."

"My king," Eltaneth began in his unctuous voice, "We all want to help the Álfur whenever it is reasonable, and of course, rewarding, for our own people. But how much do we really know about this most recent folly of theirs?"

"You make mockery of our friends, Eltaneth," the king said. "For what reason? How many times over the long eons have we Breacadh an Lae stood shoulder to shoulder with the Álfur? With good results for all …"

"Yes, but …" Eltaneth interrupted.

"You must take our friends seriously today, Eltaneth," said the king. "And you must not seek advantage for yourself from this situation. Am I clear?"

"Well said, my king, well said," Talendorf interjected. "And if I may say so, we should make every effort to aid our friends the Álfur in any way that we can."

"As long as I can wield my sword and bear my shield, I am ready to battle the Dark Fae," Vonteil spat out. "And all of my battle-hardened warriors fight with me."

"Aye, she has the right of it," said Oxmyr. "I am ready to slay Darklings anytime and anywhere. Let's just get to it!"

"All right," said the king. "You have all made your positions clear. Let's see how we can help our friends when we meet with them later today."

———— ✦ ————

After a short time spent warming themselves by the hearth in the king's reception hall, Caedwyn and Vaelwyn were escorted to the council chamber. Six members appointed by the king were already seated and waiting there, along with the king. The atmosphere was somber, a change from the jovial reception. One of the members, a spry and spindly man called Talendorf, rose to begin the meeting.

"We should not waste too much time on preliminaries here," he said. "Please tell us why you have requested an urgent meeting with this council."

"Of course," replied Caedwyn. "You are familiar with my presence as we have had many dealings over the years, and you all know I would not waste your time with trivial matters."

Seven pairs of eyes watched him carefully, the king laced his fingers, waiting.

"We live in momentous times," continued Caedwyn. "The silver elves' Council of Prime Adepti has conjured a vision, and we now believe we know what is behind the disturbances in the spiritual realm. Evil is stirring. Light and shadow are becoming unbalanced, and balance must be restored. Vael-wyn—" he gestured to her, on his left. "has been appointed to lead a mission to address these dark developments," Caedwyn continued. "But she will need the assistance of your people."

"Don't take the long way to the point, old friend," spat Eltaneth. "Just tell us exactly what the problem is and what you are seeking to extract from us."

"The Elemental Seals are failing," Caedwyn continued. "We have time to act, but not a great deal of time. Even with the loosening that begins their failing, slumbering evil is awakening in all worlds. All manner of fell creatures are becoming emboldened and rising in Myrkur, shadows are already active in Terra, and there have been stirrings of the dark here in Ljós."

"If we do not repair the Elemental Seals," interjected Vaelwyn. "The benefits of the Great Sundering will be lost, and there will be no balance in the spiritual realm. The evil forces of Myrkur will have full freedom across Terra and Ljós." As she spoke, she looked at each council member gravely, until she reached King Delbaeth. Her eyes never faltered. "This is a terrible and terrifying prospect and it will be a monumental undertaking to repair the Seals. To complete this task, we need the assistance of a Caomhnoir of the Breacadh an Lae."

There was an audible gasp from the king's council.

"A guardian of your people," she continued, "Balance must be restored."

"There has been no formal appointment of a Caomhnoir for several generations," King Delbaeth exclaimed. "This would be an extraordinary decision for us."

"Why should we Dawn Kin involve ourselves in the affairs of the Álfur?" asked Eltaneth. "In the past, doing so has never seemed to benefit our own people. We suffer and die. The Álfur come and use us when it suits them, and then they go back to their sunny patches of forest and Fae folk while we mourn our dead."

"Yes, why indeed?" added Talendorf. "Leave this to the Álfur and their meddling. How do we even know that any of this is true? Just because Caedwyn says it is so?"

Caedwyn stood and silently gestured with his rune staff. as did Vaelwyn. The room darkened and a vision appeared at the foot of the council table.

"I will help you see with your own eyes what our council and king saw with the power of the White Henge!" Vaelwyn exclaimed. "Perhaps then, will you truly understand the evil that threatens us all!"

Delbaeth's council sat transfixed as they watched the same vision had by the Prime Adepti of the silver elves. Evil ran rampant. The room felt colder and darker as the vision played out.

There was a murky, hazy image in front of them. As it became clearer, there was smoke and fire everywhere. Hard looking men ride rough-shod through a small village in the mortal realm of Terra. Men from the village try to put up a fight but are slaughtered where they stand. Women and children run screaming through the dirty streets. Young girls are raped in the mud. Blood, smoke, and fire fill the image. Screams, cries, and the ugly laughter of hard men fill their ears ...

... a neighbor has his throat cut by his best friend ...

... large groups of bruised and battered humans are marched along muddy roads in chains. Whipped along by Dark Fae masters ...

... dead bodies hang from dead tree branches and swing madly in a howling wind ...

... dark clouds, cold winds, and gray scattered snow mixed with ash are all that the eye can see across the mortal realm ...

... Now the image shifts to Ljós, and Álfur women are screaming in their own homes as they are raped by one Dark Fae after another ...

... mass graves are everywhere, in Ljós as well as Terra, freshly dug and freshly filled ...

... and battles rage everywhere. Savage face-to-face battle. Guts ripped open, arms struck clear off, helms shattered, byrnies ripped asunder. Ugly, twisted, blood-spattered faces

of Dark Fae with evil humans battling alongside them. Thinning lines of humans and Álfur facing up against them …

"Stop!" shouted the king. "We have seen enough. We should never have doubted you, Caedwyn and Vaelwyn."

Talendorf sputtered and started to speak.

"No more!" the king asserted. "No more interruptions and second-guessing. I have given you all a chance to speak your minds. To advise me, nothing more. But the time for advice is now past. It is action that is needed now. Action and decisiveness. The decision is mine and mine alone. And I decide to help our ancient allies the Álfur against the insidious evil of the Shadow and it's Dark Fae!"

"Of course, the Breacadh an Lae will help in any way that we can," continued Delbaeth. "Not only for ourselves and our friends within the Álfur, but also for the sake of Terra's humans. We have long sought to protect them as our younger and more fragile cousins."

"You have our deepest thanks," replied Caedwyn sincerely.

"As you know," the king continued. "The appointment of a guardian as Caomhnoir is a rare and sacred undertaking for us. We do not take this lightly. There is a great sacrifice involved, which is why a Caomhnoir is only appointed once across the span of several generations. He or she bears the token of the triquetra because he is 'three-in-one.' The Caomhnoir has the strength and capabilities of the three fiercest warriors of their time but with great cost. One of the three walks the world as our Caomhnoir while the other two slumber in a deep trance in our Hall of Warriors."

"Your Majesty," interjected Talendorf. "The three are known to us all, as they always are. But how do we select the one to walk as Caomhnoir from among them?"

"Lambaeth must be our Caomhnoir," announced Delbaeth gravely.

"No!" shouted Vaelwyn. "This is my mission to lead, and I must have Emrhys as Caomhnoir."

"You astound me," replied Delbaeth. "My nephew Emrhys certainly has distinguished ancestors, but he also carries the disgrace of his brother."

"Prince Emrhys has spent most of his life seeking to atone for the misdeeds of his brother," said Caedwyn. "Even though the actions were not his. This experience has given Emrhys a humility that is rare, if not unknown, in such a fearsome warrior."

"You have seen the vision," Vaelwyn said in a strong, low voice. "You know the evil we face, and you know what challenges we must overcome. I must have Emrhys as Caomhnoir!"

"If we are to support you and your mission," replied Delbaeth. "Then we must do so wholeheartedly, despite our reservations. You must have what you see that you need. So, we will do as you request and appoint my nephew, Emrhys, as Caomhnoir. Let it be said that the Breacadh an Lae have provided the silver elves with all the aid that is ours to provide. Summon Emrhys here now," he continued. "And notify the other two warriors of the honored role that they will play here."

CHAPTER EIGHT

The Caomhnoir

Fourteen Weeks Before Winter Solstice

King Delbaeth sat in his private reception room, waiting for the others to arrive. Despite its informal nature, like most other architectural elements of Abhaile, the stone fireplace was ten feet high and twelve feet wide. The logs burning in the fireplace were the size of men and crackled with flickering flames in the space behind the king.

"Enter!" the king barked, when he heard a knock on the elaborate wooden door.

Emrhys did so. Even among the Breacadh an Lae, Emrhys was an imposing figure. He stood eight feet tall and he looked like a block of granite. Yet, despite his massive size, the warrior-prince moved with a cat-like grace, his bright blue eyes peering out from his long, shaggy blond hair. His beard was neatly trimmed, he had a dark fur collar on his cloak, and he wore a plain black tunic with black leggings. He wore a broken half mandala on a chain around his neck and a large gold ring on his left hand.

"Your Majesty," Emrhys said, his voice deep and gravelly. "You sent for me?"

"Yes, Emrhys," Delbaeth replied. "Sit by the fire with me. I would have words to share with you."

"Uncle," said Emrhys. "I am always at your service. What can I provide to you and our people?"

Delbaeth looked long and hard at his nephew. He saw the man who was probably more widely respected than any other man amongst the Breacadh an Lae. The most accomplished warrior, the most dependable friend, the most honorable countryman, and the humblest member of the royal family. And yet, a man who carried a sense of sorrow about him, a man whose family pride and sense of honor had been so deeply wounded by his brother's betrayal. Delbaeth knew that Emrhys had broken off a deep love affair years ago; solely because he thought his brother's stain on the family honor was too great a burden to lay upon his lover. Delbaeth did not know who the woman had been, but even now, he could see the broken mandala pendant that Emrhys wore on that chain around his neck. All because his brother had betrayed everyone in Ljós those long ages past. Delbaeth's respect for his nephew could not be any greater, and he knew that nobody else could make a better Caomhnoir for their people.

"You are to receive one of the highest honors that any of our people can ever hope for," Delbaeth said. "An honor accorded only once every few generations."

A look of concern was visible on Emrhys' face as he spoke, "Uncle," he said, "I believe I ought to fear what you are about to say."

"Emrhys," the king replied, sighing heavily. "I plan to appoint you as Caomhnoir, and you *will* accept the honor."

"But I am unworthy, Your Majesty," Emrhys rumbled. "My brother's conduct has tainted my entire family."

"You are the only person among all our people who believes that your brother's deeds taint you," replied the king. "And your people need you. *I* need you. You *will* accept this appointment. You will be the first Caomhnoir since your great-grandfather last wielded the fabled sword *Dawnslayer*.

"Since you command me, Uncle, I will do as you say," replied Emrhys. "Perhaps through my service, I will bring honor back to my branch of the family."

"Go to the Hall of Warriors and retrieve *Dawnslayer* from its place of honor," Delbaeth commanded. "Then meet me in the formal reception room in one hour.

Emrhys left the king's presence and walked toward the Hall of Warriors, his bearing firm and resolute. Whatever his original misgivings might have been, now that his path was clear and his king's command had been accepted, Emrhys would execute his assignment to the best of his ability, as any good warrior should.

He walked down the central entry corridor in the Hall of Warriors, past the numerous shields on the columns, the colors blurring in his peripherals. Midway down, he stopped and turned right. Framed by the largest two columns, in the position of highest honor, was an ornate metal reliquary containing an elongated violet velvet cushion. Upon this rested a two-handed longsword, borne by all the Caomhnoir that had come before him. *Dawnslayer* had last been carried by his great-grandfather Eltandyr when he had served as the Dawn Kin's last Caomhnoir.

This longsword had been crafted by elven smiths long ago. Nobody knew what alloys had been used to form its special blade, but it was stronger than steel yet light and responsive. It could be wielded in long battles without causing a trace of fatigue. It never tarnished, and the edge required no whetting. There were faint traces of swirling elven script that glimmered along the surface of the sword, visible sometimes when the blade caught the light; arcane protections and enhancements.

Emrhys bowed his head in silent recognition of the service rendered by all the previous Caomhnoir. Then he stepped forward and lifted the longsword from its resting place. As he turned to leave, he sensed another presence.

Vaelwyn stepped in from the outer edge of the corridor.

"I did not wish to disturb your silent reflection," she said. "I have a gift for you that I must deliver privately, away from prying eyes."

Emrhys looked at Vaelwyn, she looked tired. Her face was drawn but became animated as she looked into his eyes. He felt a lump in his throat.

"It is good to see you again, Vaelwyn," he replied with a soft rumble. "It has been a long time."

"Yes, too long I think," Vaelwyn replied. "The last time I saw you was the day we agreed that we would each live the best lives that we could. Each in our own way – apart from one another. You gave me a gift that day that I have treasured ever since, and now I welcome the opportunity to give you a gift."

"I would value any gift from you," he continued. "Partly because of our personal history, and partly due to your keen insight into the nature of this task ahead of us."

Vaelwyn took the bundle that she had draped over her left arm, opened it, and extended it to Emrhys with both hands.

"I had this specially crafted for you," she said. "It will look like a simple warrior's tunic to any casual observer, but it is much more." Her eyes lifted as she took him in. "The best elven smiths still living have worked on this, along with some of our best magic-wielders," Vaelwyn continued. "The tunic's true nature is concealed, and it has been imbued with spells to repel the impact of arrows or spears that might otherwise injure you. And there are also powerful spells which will protect you from the touch of shadow."

Emrhys held one end of the tunic between his large hands as he listened to Vaelwyn. His gaze lingered on her face; he thought that the special lights in this Hall of Warriors made her green eyes sparkle a bit.

"Lastly," she said. "There is a unique lightweight byrnie woven between the layers. The links were forged from the same alloy used to make *Dawnslayer*. The mail is so light you will hardly feel it but it is so strong that it will stop even the most decisive blow from sword, axe, or mace.

"A worthy gift, indeed, Vaelwyn," said Emrhys. "I offer you my sincerest gratitude."

"We will spend a great deal of time together on this journey," said Vaelwyn. "And we will be sorely tested, I fear. I would have you start this journey with all the protection that can be afforded you. After all, you are a guardian now, and not as invulnerable as you sometimes think." She smiled wryly at this, as the gift left her hands, to his.

Emrhys tipped his head slightly in a gesture of respect toward the Prime Adeptus of the silver elves. "And you will be the leader of this group," he said. "With your wisdom and arcane skills, you also protect us all." *But I will protect you at all costs, my dear. Even at the cost of my own life.*

"I must go to prepare for the ceremony," he said. "We will meet upon its conclusion. Then you must show me the hidden path to Terra."

Emrhys entered the special chamber dedicated to the Caomhnoir. He greeted the other two warriors somberly. Nerys and Theryn stood ready, each wearing a three-cornered triquetra sigil of the Caomhnoir on a chain around their necks.

Caedwyn stepped forward and pinned the large, heavy silver brooch to Emrhys' cloak. Then, each of the three warriors lay down on one of the three raised dais. The largest and most elaborate rectangular dais was aligned on a north-to-south axis, with the head placed at the southern end. This positioned the head on the outer perimeter of a small circle inscribed into the floor, its foot pointing north, away from the circle. Ornate runes ran along the inner and outer boundaries of the circle inscribed in the floor. The heads of the three warriors were aligned in symmetry with the three corners of the triquetra.

In the center of the small circle stood Caedwyn, Vaelwyn, and Delbaeth, all facing inwards, and each positioned between two of the warriors. A thick gold rope ran from one to the other, connecting them and encircling the waist of each. Caedwyn placed one hand on Emrhys' left shoulder and one hand on Nerys's right shoulder on the southwest dais. Vaelwyn placed one hand on Emrhys's right shoulder and one hand on Theryn's left shoulder on the southeast dais. Delbaeth stood between his two brave warriors with one hand on each of their shoulders.

Caedwyn intoned "Ceiliúradh a dhéanamh, Solas!" *Celebrate light!* and the gold rope began to glow, expanding to include the three figures in the inner circle.

All three of them now had an aura of faint gold that covered them from head to toe.

Caedwyn spoke again, "A dheonú, Cumhalt!" *Grant the power!* and there was a crackling of energy between the king and the two warriors. "A thógáil, Triquetra!" *Build Triquetra!*

There was a crackling of energy between the two silver elves, Delbaeth, and the three subjects. This continued for several minutes and then started to fade.

Caedwyn, Vaelwyn, and Delbaeth stood in the quiet, darkened room. The torches set into the walls flickered, casting a soft light into the chamber. Emrhys would soon awaken from the trance, but Nerys and Theryn would remain in artificial slumber until a distant time when the ceremony was reversed, its function complete. While they slept, they would be tended to so that their sleeping bodies did not wither. Their Fjör, or life force, had been temporarily transferred to Emrhys. He, the Caomhnoir of Abhaile, would now have the strength, vitality, and power of the three strongest warriors from this race of giant warriors.

Emrhys slowly awakened and rose from the dais on which he had rested. King Delbaeth approached and placed both hands on his shoulders."

"Nephew," Delbaeth said. "You bring great honor to us, and I bestow one last thing upon you." He paused to remove an object from his robes. "I had this crafted by the most talented smiths among us," the king said. "It is said that Eltandyr carried a similar weapon."

Emrhys hefted the black steel weapon. At the end of a long handle with room for a two-handed grip, a unique two-headed axe blade was nestled. Along its axis were two wickedly sharp circular axe-heads. Nestled inside the inner curve of the blades was a spherical mace that bristled with sharp steel spikes. A deadly weapon.

Delbaeth kicked a log onto the floor. "Go ahead," he said. "Try it out."

Emrhys took a few practice swings at the log with his new axe, then shifted his grip and slammed into the log with the mace. It splintered easily.

"This will do very nicely!" he said, a broad, wicked smile spreading across his face.

The weapon came with its own special baldric that he added to the one holding *Dawnslayer* on his back. Now Emrhys' breast was crossed with protection. This granite-hewn warrior was now armed with the silver handle of his elven longsword, *Dawnslayer,* protruding behind one shoulder alongside his black steel axe-mace above the other. He wore a long, wide-bladed knife on his left hip and a short-handled battle axe on his right. A thin-bladed dagger was thrust into each of his high, well-worn black boots, an enchanted black tunic wrapped his body, and the heavy silver triquetra brooch of the Caomhnoir clasped his fur-collared cloak.

For the first time in generations, a Caomhnoir ventured into the realms. Emrhys was ready.

CHAPTER NINE

Hidden Pathway to Ljós

Thirteen Weeks Before Winter Solstice

Vaelwyn walked down to the harbor front of Abhaile on a blustery day with gray skies. The rising wind blew her cloak tightly around her. She'd asked Emrhys to meet her at the ship they were taking back to the mainland, Caedwyn planned to remain behind in Abhaile and confer further with King Delbaeth. Vaelwyn and Emrhys would return to Lan Léargas on their way to the northwest corner of Ljós where they would find the hidden pathway Emrhys would use to go to Terra. They had spent almost a week in Abhaile and now travel to Lán Léargas and beyond would take yet more time. Vaelwyn felt her frustration grow; they needed to make haste.

During their stop in Lán Léargas, they would request the use of King Alderon's council chamber where they could review the large, detailed maps of Terra that Alderon kept there. Vaelwyn would utilize her magical skills and the power of her rune staff to locate the mortals who bore the amulets. Emrhys would have to be familiar with all the surrounding terrain between the end of the pathway between Ljós and Terra, and the mortals. Vaelwyn would use another charm on the brooch of the Caomhnoir to indicate Emrhys' proximity to the mortals they sought.

"Good morning, Vaelwyn," greeted Emrhys. "I hope you slept well?"

"Yes, indeed," Vaelwyn replied. "And yourself? Have you discovered you have yet more unanswered questions about our mission?"

"All in good time," he laughed. "All in good time. None for today, though."

They boarded the ship and made themselves comfortable in the bow, Vaelwyn once again marveling at the size of the two gargantuan statues that flanked the channel by the harbor.

"We will stay the night in Lán Léargas after we review the maps of Terra," she said. "Then we will leave early tomorrow morning for the far northwest of Ljós and our planned destination."

"I would like to get some input from Fjall on any strange activity in their border regions," replied Emrhys. "I have heard rumors that fallen creatures, long gone, have returned to the extreme outer borders of Ljós. This may have an impact on our immediate task as well as our long-term assignment."

"Yes, this is one of the reasons I will remain in Ljós while you travel to Terra," said Vaelwyn. "I will make sure that this end of the hidden pathway remains hidden. And guarded."

"Welcome, my friends," said King Alderon the next morning as the pair arrived with their escort in Lán Léargas.

"Thank you Your Majesty," replied Vaelwyn. "I apologize in advance for my hastiness but I fear time escapes us. May we see the maps?"

"No need for apology, you relieve me of wind bagging," Alderon said. "The maps that you requested have been prepared and await your perusal in our council chamber. I shall accompany you that we may walk and talk, a little." He smiled at Vaelwyn indulgently.

Emrhys immediately asked Alderon about any unusual activity on the frontiers of their region of Fjall.

"These are reported developments that we have a keen interest in, but we must learn more. Our rangers strive to sift fact from rumor," said Alderon. "No easy feat in a city rife with wagging tongues. Yet, if the rumors are confirmed, we shall indeed have grave concerns."

"Perhaps we could speak with your rangers after we have reviewed the maps of Terra," said Emrhys. "We may learn something helpful for our trip tomorrow."

"You have my permission," said the king. "And now I give you my leave."

Vaelwyn watched briefly as Alderon's commanding figure receded, thinking that the Álfur were fortunate to have such a strong and helpful leader with this king.

The maps of Terra were spread out on a table, one overlapping the other. Vaelwyn sorted through them and quickly identified the map that she was looking for."

"See here," she pointed out to Emrhys. "The river near the bottom of this map is called the Severn. You will be emerging from a structure on the north bank. From one of the barrow mounds. The humans call these structures

Sidhe," Vaelwyn continued. "Inside many of these barrow mounds are members of a race of powerful beings who have slumbered for many ages; the People of the Sidhe, or simply the Sidhe. They are cousins to your people, the Breacadh an Lae, of course, but they are magic wielders as well as warriors. Only the Breacadh an Lae know the answer to the mystery of why the Sidhe sleep. And only a Caomhnoir of the Dawn Kin can awaken them."

"I already know all of this, as do you," Emrhys said, "so why are we talking about it here and now?"

Vaelwyn chuckled and said, "I guess that I am thinking out loud just a bit. I was thinking about the humans and the barrow mounds and it all just started spilling out. For example, did you know that in ages past, the Fae were named 'Aos Sidhe', or 'People of the Barrows' by humans. These ancient humans knew that we Fae, or 'Aos Sidhe' as they would have it, used these structures to travel between Terra and Ljós. Most have now forgotten this, along with the true difference between the Sidhe and the Fae."

"OK, so when I stride out of the barrow the humans will really be confused!", Emrhys laughed.

"I think that you will confuse or frighten any human you encounter wherever they see you!" Vaelwyn laughed in return.

"How close will I be to the mortals that I seek?" asked Emrhys. "And what sort of human territory will surround us?"

"You will enter Terra at a location that is somewhat at the center of several warring tribes of humans," Vaelwyn said. "To the immediate northeast is one of the Saxon kingdoms named Mercia, and to the southeast is Wessex, also a Saxon kingdom. Although these two are sometimes rivals, they are generally aligned against the various kingdoms of the Britons to the west."

"The humans are constantly fighting each other even in normal times. The return of the Dark Fae's influence and meddling in Terra can only make these conflicts worse," said Emrhys.

"The kingdoms of the Britons are constantly changing their borders," continued Vaelwyn. "They war against each other constantly, as well as fighting the Saxons. From where you will enter Terra, the principal kingdoms of the Britons will be Dumnonia to the southwest and Powys to the northwest."

"All right, I understand," replied Emrhys. "I can speak their languages but what about the location of the mortals I need to find and bring back to Ljós?"

"Let's see," said Vaelwyn. She held her rune staff, rolling it back and forth between her palms while intoning, "Ceili-úradh a dhéanamh, Solas!" *Celebrate light!*

Then, she placed her open palms on the map, atop the location where Emrhys would emerge, spreading her hands out across the map, one to the west and one to the east. There were two glowing dots now visible on the map. One was a bit to the northwest of Emrhys' entry point, and the other dot was further to the northwest beyond the first dot. The first dot glowed faint green, and the second a faint blue.

"There is a topographical feature that the humans refer to as a Dyke running north to south in the area where we saw those dots," said Vaelwyn. "You must meet the mortals at the southern end of this Dyke and get them safely back to the hidden pathway to Ljós. The Triquetra will get warmer and glow as your proximity to the mortals and their amulets grows."

"The green dot shows the location of the woodland elf named Alantir," continued Vaelwyn. "And the blue dot shows the human named Bedwyr."

"I will find them both," said Emrhys. "And bring them safely back to Ljós."

Alderon had provided four of his best horses for the journey, they were fast, magnificent beasts. The horse for Emrhys dwarfed the other three that would carry smaller and lighter riders, and he sat atop his black steed with some trepidation. A small group of rangers escorted them to the northwest frontier of Fjall as the trip would take several days.

Vaelwyn and Emrhys said their goodbyes to Alderon and thanked him profusely.

As the city fell behind them, they rode hard for their destination, slowing and stopping only for short breaks. It was during one of these that Emrhys finally managed to speak to the ranger captain, Delwyn.

"What can you tell us of these rumors of strange sightings at the borders of Ljós?"

"Unfortunately, there are more rumors than hard facts," replied Delwyn. He was a thin but rugged elf. The well-worn lines on his face spoke to a lifetime spent outdoors in the sun, rain, and wind. "People claim to have seen fallen creatures that have no place here in Ljós. Rumors of goblins, even trolls from Myrkur. And there have been mysterious disappearances of some of our frontier dwellers."

Emrhys was shocked. "Trolls from Myrkur?" he said, astounded. "But no such being has been sighted in a thousand years!"

Delwyn looked at him wryly. "King Alderon has commanded us to bring back a body," he continued. "Or at least a head. We must have evidence of what we are facing."

"And in the meantime," answered Emrhys. "You patrol your frontiers aggressively. All of Ljós will be grateful for your vigilance here on the frontier of Fjall."

Several days later, the riders approached the coastline in the far northwest. A sizeable bluff that reared above the sea, there was a large peninsula that jutted out further than the rest and curved back. Several large earthen mounds were visible near the far end.

"We will remain here in this general area for the rest of the day," said Delwyn. "It would be best for you to complete your mission well before the day ends."

Vaelwyn and Emrhys continued along the length of the peninsula until they reached the last of the earthen mounds where Vaelwyn used her rune staff to reveal a hidden entrance.

"I will remain here," she said to Emrhys. "To guard this pathway and keep the way open for your return."

"You will not have to wait long," replied Emrhys and stepped into the mound in Ljós.

Emrhys sniffed the air and squinted as he stepped out of the mound in Terra. The air always felt stifling to him, unlike Ljós. The light also seemed permanently dim in Terra, even on bright, sunny days. Emrhys adjusted quickly and set off running northwest.

Alantir had been running headlong for some time along the feature her people called the Dyke. She was now very far south. As she stopped to catch her breath, she thought she heard noises behind her. It sounded like human voices yelling.

Why do they have such ugly voices? she thought to herself. *Especially the Saxons.* With her woodland skills, she knew she could investigate without being seen. And so, as she approached the source of the commotion, Alantir found a group of Saxon warriors surrounding a lone Briton. The Briton was tall and muscular, with brown hair to his shoulders and dark brown tunic and leggings. He moved with a cat-like fluid motion, unusually sure-footed for a tall man, and he brandished his sword with an air of confidence. *Stupidity,* she thought; he was heavily outnumbered by the Saxon warband.

Bedwyr turned slowly from left to right, keeping his sword extended in front of him. Eight Saxon warriors encircled him, slowly advancing. Winning this fight would be impossible but was determined to take down as many of these Saxon dogs as possible.

One of the Saxons lunged at him with his sword arm extended clumsily and Bedwyr slipped his own sword deep into the warrior's armpit, pierced his heart, and made short work of him. As he did so, his amulet slipped from his tunic and dangled in the air for a moment. Behind him, another Saxon stepped forward with a massive swing of his long-handled battle axe.

Alantir was surprised at how easily the Briton dispatched his first attacker. She was even more surprised to see he wore an amulet around his neck that looked just like her own! As if in response, hers felt suddenly warm and started to glow. Distracted, Alantir looked down and then at the young Briton. His amulet glowed too.

Suddenly, a beam of light stretched between them, blueish green, joining the amulets. The connection between Alantir and Bedwyr was clear as was Alantir. She gasped in shock as the Saxon warriors and the cornered man all turned to look at her, her position betrayed.

But Bedwyr faced a new danger from the second Saxon with the long-handled battle axe. Without even thinking about what she was doing, Alantir had an arrow nocked and released it at the Saxon. Her arrow pierced his arm and saved the Briton from the threat of the axe.

"Why did I get myself involved?" Alantir cursed to herself.

She darted past the injured Saxon and stood back-to-back with Bedwyr, facing the Saxons. Although there were now two of them, they still faced six angry Saxon warriors plus the injured axe-wielder. Given the fierce nature of these Saxon warriors, these were not good odds.

While the two young people watched the Saxons warily, the Saxons all jumped forward at the same time. Alantir managed to take one down with an arrow through the eye, and Bedwyr took another with some quick sword work, but the remaining Saxons quickly overwhelmed them.

"I say we kill 'em both now!" shouted one of the Saxons.

"And I say we take our pleasure with this sweet young thing first, while he watches," said a second as his eyes roved over Alantir's bound body. "Then we kill 'em both when we've all had our way."

"And maybe I should gut you all while your captives watch," boomed a voice from the forest beyond the clearing.

"Brave words from one who doesn't even show himself!" sneered one of the Saxons.

Emrhys stepped into the clearing. Over eight feet tall and bristling with deadly weapons, he was clad in a dark brown cloak with fur collar, fastened at one shoulder with a heavy silver Triquetra brooch, and the belt over his black tunic held a long knife on one side and a short battle axe on the other. His high black boots snapped dry branches underfoot as he stepped forward.

"I am the Caomhnoir of the Breacadh an Lae," he stated calmly in his deep voice. "And those are my friends you have tied up over there."

There was a brief moment of general confusion.

"I *will* kill you if I must," he continued. "But we who oppose Shadow should not fight against each other. We will need all who support Light to work together to restore balance."

"Dunno nuthin' 'bout no lights an' shadows," answered one of the Saxons. "But we ain't 'andin' over our prizes. 'Specially that sweet young lass." His eyes lingered on Alantir despite the turmoil.

"That was *not* the right response," said Emrhys.

In one fluid motion, he closed the gap with the warband, drew *Dawnslayer* from over his shoulder, and severed the heads of two of the Saxon warriors. In the space of a single breath, the warband advantage was lost. They had now been reduced to just two able-bodied warriors.

"I will tell you again," commanded Emrhys. "Untie my friends and retreat. Or your lives shall be forfeit."

The Saxons looked at the eight-foot-tall Caomhnoir. They looked at the headless bodies of their fallen comrades. And they ran.

The injured Saxon axe man had been left behind.

'Kill him too!" exclaimed Bedwyr. "They all deserve to die."

"I meant what I said earlier," Emrhys responded. "If we expect to be successful in restoring balance to all the realms, then we must work together with all who oppose Shadow."

The Saxon nodded enthusiastically. Understandably, he preferred his head on his shoulders.

"In fact," Emrhys rumbled on. "We will bind this man's wounds and leave him with water so that he may survive until his friends return for him."

"I don't know why I have come along with either of you," said Alantir. "My people have always avoided all contact with humans. And I don't know if you, my giant friend, are human or something else entirely."

She stared up at Emrhys' imposing figure and balked. Events had taken an alarming turn from the point when Meriel was taken by the living shadows. The devastation of Beechwood, the loss of more friends and even her family. The scenes of thrashing bodies being dragged into the light were still very vivid recent memories for her. She paled; it seemed the unpleasant surprises she encountered along the way continued to increase.

"But my new human friend has an amulet that looks just like my own, and we became connected by a vivid band of light between our amulets," she said, her left hand playing distractedly with the end of her long braid. "Also, I could not just stand by and watch that warband slaughter him without trying to help." She cleared her throat, taking a long hard look at the softly spoken man. Bedwyr was a handsome young man, and clearly a capable warrior. "I had to know … what he knows about his amulet, and if it is more than I know about my own." Her cheeks reddened at her own seeming inability to make much sense of the matter. "Besides, it seemed as if the two amulets were … calling to each other with that band of light."

"We can compare our amulets side by side once we get somewhere safe," said Bedwyr. "I don't know all that much about mine, admittedly but—well, thanks for the rescue, by the way. And thanks to our giant friend here," continued Bedwyr, his hand on the hilt of his sword as he spoke, "Maybe we can start these new friendships by exchanging names while we run south along the Dyke here. My name is Bedwyr," he stated.

"Alantir," said Alantir.

"Emrhys," boomed the Caomhnoir.

"Well met, all," said Bedwyr. "Why do you have pointy ears?" he asked Alantir.

"A rude question for a new friend," she answered mildly. "Why do you have such a big mouth?" Instead of waiting for a reply, she turned to Emrhys with a question, "And where are we going, by the way? You just told us to run after we patched up that axe-man, but we don't know who you are or where we are going. We understand you're a friend as you rescued us, but we'll need to know a lot more."

"We have already lost much of this day, but I will explain when we reach our first destination just ahead. My friend Vael-wyn will add to this at our final destination," replied Emrhys.

They slowed their pace and walked to the barrow mound on the northern bank of the Severn River where a low entry-way was framed by large gray stones.

"You don't expect us to go in there, I hope," said Bedwyr. "That just seems *wrong*. Not a place where living humans should go." He peered at the opening and then sized up Emrhys. "You'd have to bend in half to enter!"

Alantir crossed her arms, so siding with Bedwyr.

"We cannot linger here long," replied Emrhys. "I ask that you each take out your amulets. Please, trust me."

Bedwyr removed his amulet from his shirt, exclaiming, "It's warm!"

Alantir followed suit and Emrhys unpinned the Tri-quetra brooch from his own cloak. As he placed the heavy silver brooch close to the amulets, the glow of all three pieces increased, and exclamations over the emanating heat erupted from all three. Alantir's amulet glowed green, Bed-wyr's blue, and Emrhys's Triquetra had a faint golden light.

"You see," rumbled Emrhys. "We three are united in the missions ahead of us. We are all connected. The nature of reality in your world and adjoining realms is much more complicated than you perceive," Emrhys started. "Your mortal realm of Terra is just one of several related realms and has been protected for eons by powerful magic conjured by the forces of Light from Ljós—the Álfur. Their historic conjuring separated your mortal realm from the evil forces of Shadow from Myrkur."

Bedwyr interrupted. "This is all very hard to believe," he snorted. "And all I really care about right now is avenging my family and reclaiming our ancestral lands in Powys."

"These events are not unconnected," Emrhys replied. "The Dark Fae from Myrkur are behind much of the evil that you see in your mortal realm. I believe that the Alfur's work against the Dark Fae coincides with your desire for revenge for your family."

"The Álfur of Ljós are powerful and majestic beings, and their strife with the dark forces of Shadow has been waged over many thousands of years. It began long ago, before mankind walked this planet. Some of the oldest stories of all races speak to the mystery and intrigue of the struggle between Light and Shadow of the Fae. The *Darklings* were once the Álfur, but some of them … became Dark Fae."

Bedwyr and Alantir looked at each other.

"This all sounds like ancient history," said Bedwyr. "What does it have to do with my enemies?"

"Yes," said Alantir, "and what does it have to do with the living shadows that have taken my friends and family?"

Emrhys continued. "Now, in our time, the natural order of the realms has been disrupted. The evil forces of Shadow, once confined to Myrkur, have been slipping through to your mortal lands of Terra, and even into the immortal lands of Ljós, home to the Álfur and my people, the Breacadh an Lae. We are people of Light, and we will oppose the forces of Shadow with all our strength and power. In your mortal realm, these forces of Shadow are actively recruiting men that already had evil in their hearts. The *Darklings* are driving and shaping their acts and deeds, bringing them deeper into the grasp of Shadow. And they are also bringing their foul creatures from Myrkur into the other realms to spread chaos and terror."

"So, are you saying that the Dark Fae are behind the Saxons' slaughter of my family? " Bedwyr said. "And behind that foul usurper that killed my uncle and claimed the throne of Powys for himself?"

"And also behind the tragic events that I lived through in Beechwood?" added Alantir.

"Yes. These are examples of why the people of Terra must rally together to oppose the growing influence of Shadow. The two of you have been chosen as champions of Light, to rise and oppose the servants of Shadow. We must leave here now," Emrhys said. "It is time."

"Why? Where do we go from here?" asked Bedwyr.

"Our leader, Vaelwyn, awaits us on the other side. We must enter this barrow to access one of the hidden paths between Terra and Ljós," Emrhys answered, avoiding the question. "I must warn you that treading this path will be disorienting, but I assure you that it is safe."

"I find the words of our giant new friend strangely reassuring," said Alantir serenely, ignoring the look Bedwyr gave her.

"Yeah, I don't know why, but I agree." replied Bedwyr. "And I have never backed away from a fight when a friend tells me that my help is needed."

The three travelers stepped into the musty-smelling barrow, sweeping away cobwebs as they made their way toward the far end.

"I will go last to protect our group as we leave this realm," said Emrhys.

"Okay, well I guess I'll go first then," Bedwyr said. "What exactly do I do?"

"Keep pushing through, and you'll feel a prickly sensation all over your body. Keep pushing, and the portal will take over. Your head will spin, but it is safe!" Emrhys said.

Although it was invisible, they entered the portal just ahead. Walking slowly forward, they encountered a slight resistance, similar to sticking ones finger into a pot of honey.

Bedwyr was the first to push further ahead, his steps tentative at first, then stronger until he disappeared.

CHAPTER TEN

Ljós Land of Light

Twelve Weeks Before Winter Solstice

Emrhys stepped out of the earthen mound in Ljós and took a deep breath of the fresh, clean air, Alantir and Bedwyr ahead of him. This time, they were the ones squinting and adjusting to the brighter range of sensory stimulation in Ljós after coming from Terra.

"By all the holy stars!" Alantir exclaimed as she staggered forward. "I've never experienced anything like that or even imagined it!"

"All the stars whizzed by while my body hurtled through them!" Bedwyr shouted. "Did you see that?"

"Yes, and then it felt like all the stars were compressing in toward me, all around me!" Alantir said.

"Yes, yes! And then all the stars exploded and pulled me along!"

Alantir and Bedwyr were so busy comparing experiences, gesticulating and jumping about, that they had not yet seen the tall elven woman with long silver hair and bright green eyes who stood before them patiently. She held a long white rune staff that extended from the ground almost to her shoulder.

"Welcome to Ljós, Land of Light," she greeted the new arrivals. "I am Vaelwyn. You must have many questions, but I will have to fill you in as we travel. We have much ground to cover before the day ends, so let's not linger here any longer."

"What's our first destination?" asked Emrhys.

"We must meet King Baldyrien in Teilatua," replied Vaelwyn. "At the other end of Fjall."

"Even with these fast steeds that Alderon's rangers provided us," Emrhys said, "we would need several days to cover that distance. And it is afternoon now. Where can we spend this night?"

"The old Tor that sits above the cliffs of Fjall Bay," replied Vaelwyn.

"We need you to be patient with us for just a little longer," Vaelwyn said to Bedwyr and Alantir in her slightly stern voice. "We will make camp tonight at a point that gives us a good start toward our next destination but we must push hard to reach the Tor before nightfall. I can answer all of your questions once we get there."

Alantir and Bedwyr looked at each other and shrugged. There did not seem to be much alternative. Alantir marveled at the light. Everything here was so ... bright.

"I don't see any advantage in remaining here alone in this strange land," said Bedwyr. "It smells nice but Alantir and I would probably be safer if we remained with your company. That's my feeling," he said, pragmatically. "What do you say, Alantir?"

"Yes," she said. "You have the right of it, I think."

As they crossed the foothills heading south, their passage was noted by several pairs of eyes lurking in the deep fissures between some of the hills. After another few hours of hard riding, they were out of the foothills and onto the coastal plains that comprised the far western region of Fjall. By late afternoon, they were approaching the headland they sought.

The old Tor was located at the approach to the cliffs and had a broad, round top with a deep ditch and the remains of a stone wall encircling the crown of the hill. Two large, crooked standing stones marked the entry to the encampment, and a deep, long-unused fire pit was in the center.

"I will check the perimeter and collect wood for a fire," said Emrhys. "Perhaps our two visitors can tend the horses and make sure they are taken care of for the night."

"And I will see what food Alderon has provided for us," said Vaelwyn.

With a large fire crackling in the pit and some sparse food in their bellies, the four companions sat under the bright stars sprawling across the night. It was a dazzling sight to behold, but none of the constellations looked familiar to the pair from Terra.

"Let me help you get oriented by reviewing a brief history of our world," said Vaelwyn. "And some important recent events." This was met by groaning and heavy sighing from Bedwyr and Alantir who were much more interested in the sky and so she hurried on, "You know, of course, about the Great Sundering, the realms of —"

"Wait," interjected Bedwyr, his interest piqued and one hand on his sword hilt. "I don't know anything about a Great Sundering."

"All right," replied Vaelwyn. "We will start further back. There have always been three different realms, but they were not always completely separate. The lands of the Fae are Ljós, Land of Light, and Myrkur, Land of Shadow. Terra has always been the land of the mortals, yours." She looked at him pointedly. "For long ages, Light and Shadow were balanced across all of the realms. Balance is crucial. Ljós and Myrkur were both connected to Terra, but mortals were not affected too much by the comings and goings of the Fae. Shadow influenced mortal lives, but the influence of Light balanced it."

Alantir scowled a bit and said, "You talk about this as though the whole mortal realm was just about human beings. We woodland elves have always been taught, though, that Terra has always had a Fae presence. Certainly we woodland elves have been there long before the humans ever came along, and long before the Great Sundering. And there were also unicorns, and water sprites, and dryads, and many others. Most of them fled Terra for Ljós before the realms were separated. But not all!"

"You are absolutely right, Alantir," Vaelwyn said. "Actually, that is why I describe Terra as the realm of mortals. All mortals—not just humans!"

"Now, I think was describing the reality across the realms in the days just before the Great Sundering, when the evil Fae that followed Shadow in Myrkur lusted for more power and influence in Terra. And even more for influence in Ljós. Success followed success. Shadow grew stronger and deeper."

"My people, the silver elves of Ljós, realized that a drastic step must be taken to restore balance. They completed a powerful conjuring, the most powerful ever undertaken. We call it the Great Sundering. With this, all three realms were severed from each other. Balance was restored."

"Cor," said Bedwyr. "But didn't the severing cause its own imbalance?"

Vaelwyn looked mildly surprised at his question, perhaps not having expected any.

"Perceptive of you. I believe I can conjure a set of memories from the time of the Great Sundering so you may relive events taken from the memories of the key Adepti that led to this act. It protected the mortals of Terra from the Dark Fae of Myrkur, but it removed magic from your world." Vaelwyn explained. "Witness."

As they watched, seated in a circle, Vaelwyn struck her rune staff in the middle and chanted, cupping her hands around it, then pulling them up and away, as if pulling a sheet over them.

Bedwyr felt goosebumps on his arms, and watched, open-mouthed as a hazy image began to form.

Wind gusted across a snow-covered landscape, providing meager illumination from a crescent moon. Taorlyn inhaled a ragged gasp as he scrambled uphill, his breath misting in his beard in the cold air. His pursuers had moved steadily closer throughout the night and he paused now to listen carefully. They were closer than he thought, he could hear them moving through the snow on the slopes below him, their boots crunching on the ice. From the top of this peak, he could see much of the Highlands spread out below him. He must stay ahead of them just a little longer. This was the eve of the winter solstice, and dawn would come soon. He must be in position with the others before sunrise on the winter solstice, or all would be lost. The shadows were determined to prevent him.

Full-throated howls of a wolf pack echoed across the slope. A different threat from the shadows that had been drawing closer, yet they too, were closing in.

As Taorlyn turned back uphill again, he saw the first shadows moving at the edge of his vision. The shadow masters, the Vålnad, would not be far behind their minions. He leaned on his rune staff to keep his footing. The long, polished white staff was engraved with potent silver runes, harnessing and focusing the most powerful powers of his people, the silver elves of Ljós. It had always been entrusted to their Warden of the North—Taorlyn. Although, there had been many others before him.

As Taorlyn worked his way further upward, more and more shadows gathered at the edge of his vision. He could also feel another presence —a cold chill that approached, deeper than the cold of a snow-clad mountain slope, more frigid than the howling wind. A coldness that could stop a beating heart or start one that was no longer beating.

The wolf howls were suddenly cut short as they ran into the shadows, becoming blood-curdling squeals of fright and yelps of pain. Then silence.

Taorlyn needed to slow down his pursuers, but without losing time himself. The tall, cloaked, and hooded figure turned to face the shadows behind him. Some of his long silver hair escaped from the hood and blew in the wind next to his pointed ears. His cloak whipped out behind him, clasped firmly at his throat by a heavy silver brooch, an intricate and interwoven four-cornered sigil. He raised both arms with his rune staff held in his right hand and crossed his outstretched right arm in front of his left side.

"Ceiliúradh a dhéanamh, Solas! a thógáil, balla!" Celebrate light! Build a wall!

He moved his right arm slowly from left to right. Downslope, an arc of brilliant white light twenty feet high sizzled where it held back the shadows leading the pursuit.

Taorlyn, Warden of the North turned back uphill and

scrambled through the snow, using this brief respite to reach the hidden entrance to the chamber of the northern seal. He had little time left to get to his fellow conjurers and complete the critical ritual. As the last, but most important, participant here in the North, he was crucial to the success of the endeavor. Other teams were also in place at different key points around the globe. Terra was almost lost to the Shadows of Myrkur, and a Great Sundering must be completed to separate the realms. The complex ritual had to be executed by all of them at the same time. Dawn on the winter solstice in the North was approaching rapidly.

Despite having slowed the shadows, he could feel the resurgent presence of their masters; the depth of the chill could only be caused by more than one. The Vålnad were here, and he would have to lose more time to make sure that he could enter the hidden entrance to the chamber without them. Reluctantly, he turned downslope again and saw that the bright white arc was already starting to break apart in several places.

Taorlyn clasped his rune staff and raised it high in both hands, moving the head in an arc where a white arc now covered him and crackled with energy. He whispered low words as he worked, moving the staff in another arc over to the ground behind him. A second bright arc now intersected the first. A quick flourish of the rune staff, a circular motion, and a final phrase was uttered: "A thógáil, sféar!" Build a sphere! Taorlyn was now encircled in a bright white sphere that pulsed with potent energy.

A large dark mass emerged from the left side of the shadows downslope. A formless shape, wrong. And it felt wrong to all senses. It exuded a powerful sense of malignant intent. Evil. Most living things would be paralyzed just by its presence. Easy prey. Another dark mass emerged on the right.

Together, the two Vålnad approached the sphere. Behind them, they each left a trail of nothingness. Not just darkness but a trail of void, as if all existence had been erased where they trod.

The two large dark masses towered over Taorlyn's pulsating white sphere. One of them shook out a long black whip that sizzled with dark energy and lashed the sphere. Nothing happened. And so it tried again. And again. On the fourth strike, a gash opened in the surface. Now, both of the Vålnad began lashing furiously until the sphere was lost in a haze of dark and light swirling together.

When the mist cleared, the sphere was gone.

And so was the Warden of the North.

———— ◆ ————

Outside the secret entrance to the chamber of the Southern Seal, Rhedwyn, Warden of the South, breathed deeply in the thin mountain air. From this highest summit, she could see many of the other highest peaks of this southern range of mountains. The ocean that would be known as the Pacific was close to the west, and the ocean that would be known as the Atlantic was far to the east.

The shadows had pursued her throughout her long journey and had grown dangerously close as night fell. The subsequent battle had left her injured and depleted. Fortunately, her wounds were already healing, and her energy renewing over the past few hours. She would need all of it for the ritual ahead.

Rhedwyn leaned on her polished white rune staff. Tall and slender by human standards, her frame was strong and lithe. Her silver hair was worn in a long, intricate braid that hung low on her back, her pointed ears were red from the cold air, and her fur-lined cloak billowed in the strong wind near the summit. As she made her way further up the slope, she reached the hidden entrance she had been seeking.

"Ceiliúradh a dhéanamh, Solas!" she said to the east, then turned west and uttered, "A thógáil, doras!" Build a doorway!

Rhedwyn tapped the top of the staff twice in front of her, as though tapping on a door and the faint outline of an ornate carved archway appeared in a pattern of light on the stone. The interior was a mirrored surface. As she touched it with her staff, it stopped briefly, then continued through as though sinking into water. Rhedwyn followed through the mirror. She glanced behind her and, from the inside, saw nothing but solid rock. She made her way through the stone passageway to where a warm glow emanated from the smooth stone walls and slate-like floor. As she entered the high-ceilinged chamber itself, she was relieved to see all of her fellow travelers were already here. Even better, given their rapidly approaching deadline, all sixteen, including her, were already in their proper places.

The chamber was a breathtaking sight. The planes of the smooth, polished stone walls converged at a point high above the floor. Everything was illuminated by a soft glow. The Southern Seal itself occupied much of the chamber's floor; an intricate, interwoven pattern featuring four separate corners pulsed with the same light emanating from within the stone.

There were groups of four elves gathered at each corner of the Seal. The major groups of the Álfur were there to conjure the major elements they commanded. And, of course, Rhedwyn of the Silver elves, who commanded all the elements.

The Álfur from Eydimörk standing at the corner had the symbol for fire embedded in the seal below their feet. Those from the realms of Sjávar and Vatnid gathered opposite with the symbol for water. The Fjall quartet stood over the symbol for air in their corner and finally, four Álfur from Skógur stood by one for earth beneath their feet.

There was a small, round, raised platform at the center of the Southern Seal. All four symbols were embedded around the perimeter of this raised platform, with a space in the center for the Warden of the South to stand.

As Rhedwyn took her position, everyone prepared to begin the ritual. Their timing needed to be coordinated with the other teams around the globe. Sunrise on the winter solstice at the location of the Northern Seal. Each group stood back-to-back, aligned with the cardinal points of their compass and held their hands to their sides, then raised their arms together, chanting as wide, red arches that crackled with energy began to rise toward the ceiling.

A complete purplish-red dome of pulsating energy, made of four domes now rose high above the group of each of the four elements.

Rhedwyn stood at the center of all this energy and raised her rune staff above her head.

"A chur le chéile, Cumhalt!" Combine power! she sang as she moved the top of her staff in a circular motion.

The four separate domes of energy now merged into one uniform mass, circulating in a vortex around Rhedwyn at the center of the Seal. She inserted her staff into the slot at the center of the raised dais, took a deep breath and sank to one knee, gathering all her energy. The sixteen other Álfur around her continued to chant in unison.

Rhedwyn placed her hands at the base of her anchored rune staff, palms upward, and shouted one of the secret words of power. Then she stood and swept her arms upward in a strong thrust as a bolt of energy shot straight up from the top of her staff to the peak of the roof and through it.

The enormous crackling dome followed. Up to the peak of the roof.

And beyond.

—————— ✦✦ ——————

Caedwyn stood on the balcony and looked out over the hidden valley. He took a deep breath, enjoying the fragrance of the blooming flowers. The permanently balmy weather of the sacred city was ironic, since towering peaks of snow-covered mountains entirely surrounded it. Shangri-La, as humans named it in later ages.

He stood tall and proud, tucking an errant strand of silver hair behind his pointed ear. He thought back on the long history of this sacred city and the more recent history of the Elemental Seals. Caedwyn, Warden of Midgard, was the highest-ranking of the Wardens of the Silver elves. Although the Álfur were ostensibly immortal, they sacrificed some of their long lifespan every time they used magic. The life-force that they drew upon to work magic was called Fjör and the use of magic drained some of their Fjör each time. The Silver elves, with control of all four elements, also had greater reserves of Fjör than the other major Álfur groups. However, Wardens used their powers more deeply and more often than any other denizens of Ljós. Ultimately, this would leave them weaker and more vulnerable. There was a secret connection between their rune staffs, their reserves of magic and the renewal of their Fjör, which involved long and complicated rituals within the White Henge of Ljós. Caedwyn knew that the great undertaking he and his colleagues were proceeding with now would drain more energy from more of the Álfur than anything else that had ever been done in all the ages of their long history. Renewal of the life force might not be an option for all of them after this task was completed—a risk they were willing to take.

As Caedwyn walked to the chamber of the Midgard Seal, he knew that the activation of the Elemental Seals and the separation of Ljós from Terra would be wrenching but that it would also separate Myrkur, the land of Shadows, from all other lands. No longer would the vile spawn of Myrkur be able to despoil other realms. Some of the poisonous work the Shadows had already wrought would unavoidably live on in the hearts of the humans and even some of the Álfur, but the activation of the Elemental Seals would prevent deeper darkness from spreading in the Land of Light.

Caedwyn entered the chamber of the Midgard Seal, to see all of the other sixteen Álfur in their proper positions, waiting. He took his own place on the small round dais at the center and clasped his hands together in front of his right shoulder, his left hand on top of his right, palms together and began.

"Ceiliúradh a dhéanamh, Solas!" Celebrate light!

As his left hand lifted, a bright blue orb shimmered in the air between his palms. It was an accurate conjuring of the entire planet, turning slowly on its axis, suspended in midair.

The high elves began their ritual over the symbols of fire, water, air and earth.

Caedwyn was at the center of the swirling vortex of crackling golden energy. He anchored his rune staff in the slot in the middle of his raised dais and knelt down, placing his hands at the base of the staff. The image of the globe turned slowly in the air just above him and he saw a bright white bolt of energy rise up in the Northern Hemisphere, followed by an energy spike shooting down from the Southern Hemisphere. A shimmering silver aura settled over the Northern Hemisphere. From the North Pole halfway down to the *equator, there was now a beautiful silver cap on the globe, then too, from the South Pole halfway up to the equator.*

Caedwyn shouted out a series of the secret words of power as he stood and thrust his open palms upward in a single, decisive gesture. A golden bolt of energy shot out of the top of his rune staff. Up to the top of the chamber. And beyond. The large golden dome of energy swirling around him followed the bolt up and out of the chamber.

Caedwyn watched as a wide band of gold grew around the blue orb at the equator, expanded north and south, then seemed to slip under the silver cap at the top of the Northern Hemisphere and the bottom at the Southern Hemisphere, covering the sphere in shimmering gold energy.

The Great Sundering was complete.

The worlds of Ljós and Myrkur were separated from Terra. Magic had left the world of humans, and the Light and Shadow of the Fae Realms were no longer part of the mortal realm. For the most part.

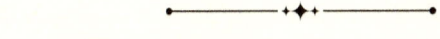

Vaelwyn finally released the image hanging before Bedwyr and Alantir, the show was over.

"Since the time of the Great Sundering, that we just witnessed, Shadow has been restricted to Myrkur, and Light to Ljós. Terra has been balanced between the two influences. Magic left Terra with the passing of the Fae," she concluded.

"So, what is happening now that changes this?" asked Bedwyr. "It sounds like this Great Sundering worked the way it was supposed to."

"Good question," answered Vaelwyn. "We Álfur used the powers of the elements to create several powerful areas of separation that we call the Elemental Seals. Their continued maintenance is what keeps the three realms of Ljós, Myrkur, and Terra separated. Recently, we sensed a shift in the balance of nature and performed a special conjuring to determine what was happening, and how balance could be restored. We learned that the Elemental Seals are failing after all these millennia. They must be repaired or the realms will join once more and darkness will flood the light."

The flames from the fire in the pit flickered on the hilltop, and Emrhys laid more wood over the embers.

"My people are the woodland elves of Terra," said Alantir. "We chose to remain in Terra with our beloved forest. We sacrificed immortality and gave up the use of magic with that choice. And what of your people, Emrhys? You don't seem to be either human or Fae."

"I am of the Breacadh an Lae," rumbled Emrhys. "Sometimes called the Dawn Kin since we have been allied with the Álfur since the dawn of time, although we are not of the Fae ourselves. We followed the Fae into existence in the early ages of the cosmos. For millennia, we and the Fae lived alongside one another before the advent of humans. Along with most of the Álfur of Ljós, we rejoiced with the coming of humans into existence. We have always viewed humans as our younger cousins, although we grieve for the shortness of their lifetimes."

"Now you are making me feel bad," Bedwyr said as he stood and walked around the others. "I never thought of our lifetimes as too short. Now I am sort of jealous of all the time that you and your people have!"

"Careful what you envy, Bedwyr," said Vaelwyn. "The long years of existence for the Álfur and the Dawn Kin weigh too heavily on some of our people. For some, the burden is unbearable and they sadly leave this world behind. We do not really understand where they go, but we call this passage The Sojourn. Our folk undertake a long and demanding trek through the Eydimörk mountains until they reach the Valley of Respite, as we call it. Once there, they complete some spiritual reflection, and then pass through the Gate of Dendalyn, never to return to this realm again."

"The Dark Fae of Myrkur, however," Emrhys continued, "along with a few of the Álfur in Ljós, have always viewed humans as fair prey for cruel tricks, capture, and enslavement. For long ages before the Great Sundering, my people were the defenders and champions of our younger cousins, the humans of Terra. However, with the separation wrought by the Great Sundering, we believed humans would be safe from the Shadows of Myrkur. Without our constant presence, we thought the time would come for humans to come into their own. We stayed in Ljós with our long-time friends, the Álfur, but we sorely miss our human cousins."

Emrhys looked downcast and his fingers stroked the half mandala pendant around his neck as he looked into the fire's flickering flames.

"Since my people chose mortal lifespans, we always need to teach every new generation about the Great Sundering and the choice we woodland elves of Terra made," said Alantir. "But our entire world has been our secret forest enclave, and we have little awareness of people or events outside our woodland home."

"My entire world has been the warring tribes of my Britons," said Bedwyr, "and the savage tribes of the Saxons. I had some vague awareness of the Gauls, the Romans and bits of the world beyond them, and of course, the Picts and the Danes and other Norse people. There were always stories and legends of the Fae, but this idea of entire Fae realms with magic and evil Shadows is ... It seems unreal."

"I can tell you firsthand that the evil of Shadow is very real, and it is back in Terra in our age," said Alantir, her voice breaking slightly. "I lost my family and my best friend to these living shadows. Maybe all of my people are now lost. That is what I was running from when I met you."

"I am very sorry for your loss, Alantir," comforted Vaelwyn. "But if we do not succeed in our task, this may be the fate that all of Terra suffers. Both you and Bedwyr must help us repair the Elemental Seals and restore the Great Sundering," she beseeched them. "Let me share what I know of each of your own stories."

"I will gather some more wood for our fire while you tell these tales to our new companions," Emrhys said. "I would like to stretch my legs and check our perimeter. It's a beautiful night with a light breeze and a sky full of starlight. I will be back soon."

"Let us start with Alantir's story, since we already know that she is one of the woodland elves of Terra, a noble people who made brave decisions many ages ago," Vaelwyn resumed. "They were formerly part of the Skógur tribe of Ljós, known as the green elves of the dense forests, with control of the elemental magic of Earth. They bore a great sadness that their cousins in Terra would be lost to them forever. One of these woodland elves was a princess of Skógur and she and her sisters made a pact. They vowed to maintain a connection with their sister in Terra and somehow found a way to have their spirits meet, although their bodies could not. This connection was passed from mother to daughter, generation to generation. A magic amulet bearing the Tree of Life was the key part of this connection."

Alantir gasped. "My amulet!" she exclaimed. "Given to me by my mother and to her by her mother. But that would mean …"

"That you have latent magic within you," stated Vaelwyn, nodding. "And that you are a distant part of the royal family in Skógur."

There was a stunned silence around the fire. Then Bedwyr burst out laughing.

"So, I was saved from a Saxon warband by a Fae princess!" he guffawed. "My brothers would never let me hear the end of that!"

They all shared a laugh at that—even Alantir.

"All right," Alantir said, sobering. "So now let's hear Bedwyr's story. With those short, round-top ears, I don't think we have any secret Fae prince here!"

"Bedwyr, you know, of course, that your mother was your father's second wife. He married your mother after his first wife passed away," said Vaelwyn. "But did you know that you are the only one of your brothers to whom she gave birth? She stepped into their lives early and acted as mother to all four of you, but blood mother she is only to you."

"I guess I did know that," Bedwyr said, "but it was never anything that me or my brothers spent a lot of time thinking about. She was mother to us all; it was as simple as that."

"Your mother's family had a history outside of Powys," Vaelwyn continued. "Many generations earlier, one of your mother's ancestors had a love affair with an Álfur warrior from Teilatua in Fjall. This determined elf found a way to fly his giant war-hawk from Fjall to Terra despite the separation of the realms. In Terra, he fell in love with a human woman. A child was born in Terra but the Álfur warrior's king discovered the violation of the Great Sundering, and he was forced to end the affair and never return to Terra. Before he left, he gave his lover a magic amulet that had been in his own family for many ages. An amulet with the Tree of Life. Your mother was a descendant of that child of

Ljós and Terra. Although very distant in the past, you do have a faint trace of Álfur ancestry yourself, and a distant relationship to the warriors of Teilatua who ride the giant war-hawks and wield the elemental power of air."

Again, there was stunned silence around the fire.

"Ah, I don't mean to offend anyone," Bedwyr exclaimed, "but I am human! One hundred percent human!"

Vaelwyn smiled and placed her hand on Bedwyr's forearm, "Nobody doubts that you are fully human, Bedwyr," she said gently. "You have only the faintest trace of distant Álfur heritage and a very small amount of personal magic, or "talent" as we call it. For the most part, your talent is limited to what can be imbued to your amulet."

Emrhys had returned with a new stack of firewood which he laid out next to the fire.

"Magic is overrated anyway," he laughed. "On a beautiful night like tonight I am more than satisfied with the strength of my limbs and the sharpness of my blades!"

He clapped Bedwyr on the shoulder as he finished, and Bedwyr nodded and chuckled in agreement as he rubbed his shoulder.

"We know that you both play a central role in restoring the Elemental Seals," said Emrhys. "But the final details of the task ahead remain obscure to Vaelwyn and her people. We know only that first, we must travel to Teilatua in Fjall, which will take us several more days, where we must activate the elemental power of air that resides within Bedwyr's amulet."

"Then we must travel to Garmoniya in the Skógur realm," continued Vaelwyn. "And there we must activate the elemental power of earth that resides within Alantir's amulet."

"Will we have full use of our magic once our amulets are activated?" asked Alantir.

"No," said Vaelwyn. "For that, we must journey to the White Henge of my people where we will complete an ancient ceremony to awaken any latent magic that exists within each of you. This will be more significant for Alantir with the great amount of latent magic she holds within herself."

"And then ..." she paused and looked sharply at Bedwyr, "... then you must gain the approval of your Elementals. And they can be very demanding! You will have to hold your temper and be very diplomatic. Do you think that you can do that, Bedwyr?"

"Okay, okay," he said. "Why are you looking at me like I am some sort of miscreant? I can behave very well ... sometimes ... when I want to."

"In this case, Bedwyr," Vaelwyn said calmly, "there is no room for human jokes and misbehavior. All of the leaders of the Elementals are ancient and powerful—they are not generally amused by humans. Or very fond of them. And the leader of the Air Elementals, King Aeryn, is the most skeptical of them all. So you must be on your best behavior with him. Do you understand?"

"You will not be successful without gaining the support of your Elementals," Emrhys rumbled. "Your amulets will be much less powerful—and have much more limited reserves of power."

"We will not let you down," Alantir said flatly. "Bedwyr and I are both completely dedicated to this quest—and to striking back at these Dark Fae! And we will do whatever is necessary to succeed. Right Bedwyr?

"Absolutely! And then what?" asked Bedwyr. "Our amulets are activated, the latent magic within us is awakened—and we are accepted by our Elementals. What then?"

"Well, education," Emrhys said, shrugging. "You both need a crash course in understanding the magic of the Álfur before you can begin to use your powers. The standard ways of learning take a lifetime, which we simply do not have." He sighed disparagingly before continuing, "However, Vaelwyn and I will be here to help you understand the basics, at least. And we will make plans for deeper training later—as time allows."

"For now," interjected Vaelwyn, "let's get some sleep. We have given you a lot of new information to digest for now."

"Yes," said Emrhys, "I will tell you about the magic of the Álfur in the morning, when we resume our travel toward Teilatua tomorrow morning"

Alantir and Vaelwyn bedded down for the night, while Bedwyr and Emrhys went for a short nighttime walk.

"It feels good to walk a bit after sitting for so long," Bedwyr said. "So much in my life has changed in such a short time. I still don't know if I am more sad or angry about what happened to my family—and I am not even sure "angry" would be the right word. Mostly, I am filled with a murderous rage whenever I think about them. But now, here I am in the Fae realm! How could this be? I am a capable enough warrior, and a stalwart friend, but a champion of Light? It all just seems so unbelievable."

"Aye, Bedwyr, twouldn't be normal if you did not have a confusing whirl of thoughts and feelings," said Emrhys. "You are a solid lad, just give yourself time to soak it all in. You will do just fine once you adjust."

"Do we need to set a watch at night around here?" Bedwyr asked.

"No, not you anyway," Emrhys replied. "I sleep lighter than any human possibly could, and I'll be on guard while you get some rest with the others."

It seemed like it had been no time at all before the morning came with cooler weather. It was gray and cloudy, but no rain. Alantir took care of the horses while Bedwyr packed up their few belongings. Once the horses were packed and the companions had swallowed a few bites of their meager breakfast, they started out for Teilatua.

Alantir still marveled at the sights, sounds, and smells of Ljós. Even on a gray and cloudy day like this, the grass, wildflowers, and trees all seemed to glow with an evanescent inner life. The morning birdsong was more joyful than Alantir remembered hearing for quite a long time.

"Emrhys," Alantir said, "you promised last night that you would tell us more about the magic of the Álfur today."

Bedwyr rolled his eyes and Vaelwyn smiled.

"To start," Emrhys said, "you should understand that not all Álfur can conjure magic; it is uncommon among their people. Those who do have magic abilities are referred to as having the *Talent*. And there are two broad categories of Álfur with the *Talent*. The most common form is control over a single element. Air, earth, fire, or water. And the element controlled is tied to the tribe, or realm, from which the Álfur originates. Fjall is the realm of air, Skógur is the realm of earth, Eydimörk is the realm of fire, and Vatnid and Sjávar together are the realms of water. An Álfur with limited *Talent,* is talented. Álfur with more advanced capabilities are mages. And those with advanced skills are masters."

Like Alantir, Bedwyr was noticing the enervating vitality of this realm.

No wonder these Álfur want to be separated from us in Terra, he thought, *I mean, look at their world, it is incredible. The remarkable scents as well as the beautiful sights. I don't even know how to describe how good some of these scents are—or what they are!"*

"Now, the less common form of *talent* is control over all four of the elements," Emrhys continued. "This is the *tal-*

ent of the silver elves and their Adepti. There is a long and complex training regime to become an Adepti, and few silver elves succeed in achieving even the lowest level of this order. All Álfur respect the silver elves, but the Adepti are feared as well as respected. They are mysterious and powerful, limited in number, exotic. Their highest orders are more powerful than the royalty of the Álfur, and most know them more from legend than from personal acquaintance. Yet, even within the small number of Adepti of the silver elves, there is a ranking of training and talent.

"Álfur, at the first stage, having achieved the status of Adeptus but demonstrating limited training besides their strong *talent*, are referred to simply as Adeptus. They use simple, unadorned rune staffs made of brown wood. Álfur, at the second stage, demonstrating deep expertise after many years of intensive training, along with their powerful gifts of *talent*, become Adeptus Major, and are awarded a polished black rune staff. A very select few, the Adepti elite, are elected to join the senior order Prime Adepti, of which there are only twelve at any one time. The five Wardens are chosen from this select group. Prime Adepti carry polished, white rune staffs engraved with powerful silver runes. Their power is intimidating."

Vaelwyn edged her horse up alongside the two Terrans, held up her own rune staff and said, "Many of the runes on our staffs are shared by all Prime Adepti, but we each choose a few special runes that are unique and whose powers are known only to us."

"And the Dark Fae of Myrkur mirror these levels of capabilities," Emrhys concluded. "We are very fortunate to have Vaelwyn as the leader of our group. She is one of the Prime Adepti and the Warden of the North. Although young by Álfur's standards, she is considered the most powerful Prime Adeptus the silver elves have seen in thousands of years."

"All magic is drawn from Fjör, the life force of all living beings. And magic users must be careful not to exhaust their own Fjör, or they will die. It is as simple as that. Use up all of your Fjör with your magic, and you die. There are ways to store one's own Fjör for later use, or even to store Fjör given by others for one's use, but we will discuss that later. Silver elves have a much greater reserve of Fjör than the rest of the Álfur," Vaelwyn began. "When elemental magic is drawn from Fjör while maintaining one's balance, the user feels as 'one' with all Fjör. This is energizing, euphoric, and empowering. But one must be careful not to get lost in the rapture of drawing Fjör. I will talk more later about how the skilled user achieves balance while drawing Fjör."

Alantir reached her hand over and touched Bedwyr's thigh as their horses trotted alongside each other.

"This is all so interesting," she said, "don't you agree?"

Bedwyr rolled his eyes again—and then looked up sharply, shaded his eyes with his hand, and broke out into a big grin.

"Is that an eagle that I see?" he asked.

"Yes, Bedwyr, it is," Emrhys rumbled. "But you need to pay attention to Vaelwyn right now."

Bedwyr scowled and the only sound from him for a while was the jangling of his horse's harness.

"The elemental magic of the Álfur can be drawn down quickly if the user does not first seek a balance. But this snatching of Fjör is less powerful, and the lack of balance makes the user vulnerable to the taint of Shadow. The forces of Shadow love chaos and instability, and the unbalanced use of strong elemental magic creates a great opportunity for chaos to ensue. This is the fatal flaw of the Dark Fae. They have become tainted by Shadow, and their magic is quicker to deploy than the Álfur, but less powerful," Vaelwyn continued. "They wield their power using different elements to practice their dark, evil magic."

"If these Dark Fae can deploy their magic quicker than the Álfur, doesn't that give them a big advantage?" asked Alantir as their horses slowed down to climb a steep rise.

"In the use of our own Álfur elemental magic, the deeper you draw upon Fjör, the greater the struggle with chaos to maintain balance. For the basic level of use, which is what most of our Álfur experience as they use their talent, achieving and maintaining balance is not too challenging. They hold an image in their mind and fight to maintain it with practice and discipline. This basic image is the rising sun balanced with the setting moon, and stars above balanced with the earth below. An image of all nature in balance between day and night, and between earth and sky."

"We Álfur believe strongly that this balance, in all things, is essential for all life. Balance must be maintained at all costs. Loss of balance can result in loss of life. For civilizations as well as for individuals," Vaelwyn observed. "Higher levels of magic require deeper and deeper use of Fjör, and fiercer struggle with chaos to avoid the taint of unbalanced draw. At the highest levels of our magic, the fight against chaos to maintain balance is tremendous. It is like fighting raging winds and fearsome lightning while poised on a narrow ledge high on a mountain.

We advanced users also have an image and feeling that we hold firmly in our minds and hearts to maintain balance. For us, it starts with the same image of rising sun balanced with setting moon, with stars above balanced with the earth below. However, we add important aspects to what we feel in our visualization. We concentrate on the warmth of the earth below and sense a connection with all life on earth, and we let that warmth rise and envelop us. This is the anchor for our material selves. And we concentrate on the beauty of the stars above and sense a connection with the boundless cosmos. This is the anchor for our spiritual selves. With this advanced level of balance achieved and held against the raging storm of chaos, we are powerful indeed. The most powerful among us is more than a match for any one of the Dark Fae. But, as you have pointed out, the time we take to achieve this perfect balance is our vulnerability."

Bedwyr shifted in his saddle and as their horses emerged from a copse of trees onto a wide open plain he moved his horse closer so that he could hear them better.

"So, how do you protect yourselves from this vulnerability?" he asked.

"There are ways for Adepti to offset this vulnerability, like storing Fjör in various forms and objects. Balance is achieved in this manner, and it need not be repeated when it is deployed. This allows us to deploy some of our magic immediately while we are working on achieving balance to draw deeper upon our reserves of Fjör in the moment. This magic is limited and is less powerful, but the speed of use does provide some advantages."

"The rune staffs of the Adepti are the principal object used to store Fjör, along with various jewels, brooches, and other small ornamental pieces. The Adepti can infuse their rune staffs, or jewels, with their life force, a bit at a time over long periods. This slower approach avoids leaving an Adeptus in a depleted state from a sudden drain of Fjör too large for future storage. Fjör may also be drawn from allies in the Light, the Elementals themselves. This is only done with the full knowledge and consent of the Elementals, and a small amount of Fjör is typically pulled from each one of a large number of these beings so that even a powerful 'draw' has a limited impact on each individual. The Elementals are largely uninvolved with events on Terra, Ljós, and Myrkur, but they have always been aligned with the Álfur and with Light over Shadow. They are very dependable allies," Vaelwyn continued.

"I am going to ride ahead a little way," interjected Emrhys. "I want to see if there is a good place for us to make camp for the night. If I remember right, there is a large forest not too far ahead."

"Here, though, is another important difference between the Álfur and the Dark Fae. They also draw extra Fjör and store it in various personal items that they keep on their person. When they draw from outside their own Fjör, they typically draw from Daemons—evil beings aligned with the Dark Fae and Shadow. The Dark Fae have advanced magic-wielders that we call gölge yürüteç, or Shadow Walkers. As we talked about earlier, these are the agents of the Dark Fae that we believe were behind the personal tragedies that you each experienced back in Terra."

"What?" Bedwyr exclaimed. "Explain that again!"

"As I told you before, these Dark Fae often work through human agents that they have under their control. This is one of the many ways that they sow chaos and terror throughout the realms. We believe that the gölge yürüteç manipulated the humans that slaughtered your family and stole your kingdom, Bedwyr; as well as unleashing the living shadows in Beechwood that took Alantir's friends and family from her."

"Damn them!" Bedwyr shouted. "I have been seeking my revenge in the wrong place. It's not Saxon blood that I want then—it's these Darkling bastards!"

"Not so fast, Bedwyr. These are fearsome foes, even for we Prime Adepti. These gölge yürüteç also draw Fjör from humans. Unlike the Alfur's voluntary use of Fjör drawn from other beings in small quantities, though, the gölge yürüteç rip the life force from their victims involuntarily. Sometimes they rip almost all of it out, leaving their human victims as drooling, mindless slaves for their Dark Fae masters."

"That sounds a lot like what happens to the victims of those living shadows that I saw back in Beechwood," said Alantir. "It is all just so evil and so far beyond any of my experience. My days enjoying the peaceful calm of the forest seem so far away now – and so unlikely to return."

"You also need to know that there are a few special amulets and rings that not only store Fjör, but actually create a direct connection with the users, as well as with the kings and queens of the Elementals. The power that these special amulets and rings can channel is truly awesome, and few things can stand before it."

"There are ten rings for the ten Lords and Ladies of the Álfur realms, and these rings control the alliance with the respective Elementals associated with each realm. Air for the two Fjall kingdoms, earth for the two Skógur kingdoms, fire for the Eydimörk kingdom, and water for the four kingdoms of Vatnid and Sjávar," Vaelwyn continued. "The tenth ring is for the king of the silver elves, and he holds secret what powers it controls."

"And there are four amulets for the four champions of Light, one for each group of Elementals. And there are two secret rings. One is said to align with both earth and air Elementals, and one that is said to align with both fire and water Elementals."

"Wait," said Bedwyr, "isn't this part about our amulets?"

"Yes," she replied, "we will get to that in just a minute."

"There is another aspect of Elemental magic that is more fable than known fact. Few, if any, Álfur alive today have any personal experience with Spirit. But there is a secret belief that there is a special member of the Prime Adepti, in addition to the twelve that are known, that is chosen once in a millennium to serve as an Adeptus D'Or, or *Golden Adeptus*. This special Álfur is rumored to receive deep training by the Spirit Elementals and is taken to dwell in their celestial city. And apparently, to have a third secret ring that draws on the power of the Spirit Elementals. Now," Vaelwyn said forcefully, "let us discuss your amulets, and the journey ahead to gain your magic and wield it safely and effectively."

"First, each of you will go through a ritual within the respective realm of each amulet. This will link your amulets to each of your own Fjör, giving you some basic strength in your elemental *talent*. You will not be able to access deeper strength or power until the second ritual, and until then, your use of magic will likely have erratic, undisciplined results. Even after the second ritual, you will need to undergo extensive training to wield your magic powerfully and dependably."

"The second ritual will take place within the White Henge of my people. This is a sacred and powerful location in the center of Ljós. This ritual will link the amulet and its bearer to the deep powers of your respective Elementals. This power is given voluntarily to champions of the Light who have undergone this ritual. The king or queen of each Elemental kingdom is present at the ritual and acts as the critical link between amulets and Elementals. These Elemental kings and queens are fierce and foreboding, and they do not enter into this link with amulet bearers lightly."

Emrhys had circled back and rejoined the group.

"There is a good spot for us to make camp a little deeper into this forest, I found a good level spot close to a good size stream."

"By all the stars," sighed Alantir, "this is all so complicated and overwhelming. But also exciting."

"It is exciting," said Bedwyr, "and I am interested in exploring all of this. But I still attach more importance to my skill with a sword than to any Álfur magic mumbo-jumbo."

"Careful, Bedwyr," rumbled Emrhys, "remember to treat this Prime Adeptus with the respect she is due!"

"Okay, okay, easy, my big friend," Bedwyr replied. "I did not mean to give offense. But, Vaelwyn," he continued, "do you also store Fjör in some of your jewelry in addition to your rune staff? Although they are subtle, I could not help but notice the different jewels that you wear."

"If I may ask, with all due respect," he quickly added, with a sidelong glance at Emrhys and his hand on the hilt of his sword..

"Yes, Bedwyr," Vaelwyn replied. "I store Fjör in the large green emerald in my gold necklace, in the red ruby in my gold ring, in the blue sapphire in my ivory bracelet, and in the iridescent pearl in the brooch for my cloak. All four elemental powers."

"Before our detailed discussion about the magic of the Álfur, Bedwyr asked about what happens after we complete the second ritual," Alantir said.

"The four of us will return to Terra," continued Emrhys. "And we will return by another one of the hidden pathways that runs from the White Henge itself."

"Once we have returned to Terra," Vaelwyn interjected. "We will have to make our way through hostile territory to Northern Gwynedd. We must be on the summit of Yr Wyddfa for the dawn on the winter solstice. Two important aspects of our task will happen on Yr Wyddfa at that time," she continued. "One is a ritual that we will perform that will begin the repair of the Elemental Seal in the north. This is clear. However, what comes next is not. The timeline is part of the lore regarding the Elemental Seals, but we do not know why these deadlines have been set. All we do know is that after we complete our first task, whatever comes next must be done by the mid-winter festival of Imbolc. Or we will fail."

CHAPTER ELEVEN

Lord of Teilatua

Eleven Weeks Before Winter Solstice

Several days later, the morning broke with bright, golden sunlight highlighting the plain where their party had made camp the night before.

Bedwyr's head was still spinning with all of the new information he had absorbed over the past several days, including the revelations about himself and his family. He still had trouble believing that he had a secret ancestry with the Álfur of Ljós. Truth be told, it was more interest than alarm. He was particularly intrigued by his ancestral connection to the warriors of Fjall and their giant war hawks. He had heard Emrhys and Vaelwyn describe these majestic birds, but he could not wait to see them himself.

Alantir seemed less overwhelmed by the new information, Bedwyr thought, but at least she had already known that she was a woodland elf. She was more saddened by her recollections of the living shadows in Terra and her loss of family and friends. He had heard her weeping in the night but did not know what to do or say about it.

They continued their trip to Teilatua in the Fjall realm, the horses were well-rested and made riding easy. Bedwyr rode a bay stallion that bore him easily and maintained a steady pace. Bedwyr loved horses and they had always responded well to him. Teilatua lay far to the south of Lán Léargas, although it was the second main city of the blue elves of Fjall. It would take them most of the day to travel to Teilatua from this most recent campsite. They would be riding through the heathlands and moors that lay between the coastline to the west and the mountains to the east.

"Are the rest of your people as large as you are?" Bedwyr asked Emrhys. "You look very intimidating even by yourself. I can scarcely imagine the sight of an entire war band of your people."

"Yes, for the most part," laughed Emrhys. "I am slightly larger than most of our warriors but not dramatically larger. We are certainly all much larger than you humans."

"And larger than our Álfur as well," added Vaelwyn.

"I don't know exactly how to describe how I am feeling about what I see, hear, smell, and taste here in Ljós," said Alantir. "But my senses almost feel overwhelmed. In a good way!" she hastened to add. "The sunlight seems warmer and brighter, and the colors of simple grass and flowers of the heathland seem so deep and vibrant. It makes the colors of living things in Terra seem like just a painting of the real things here in Ljós."

"And the simple sounds of the wind blowing and the birds singing," Bedwyr said, agreeing.

"Yes!" Alantir looked at him, smiling, seeming relieved that she wasn't alone in all her thoughts. "It feels like I hear these sounds in my heart instead of my ears. They bring a sense of deep peace and harmony."

"Yes," Vaelwyn replied. "Ljós is the Land of Light. You are sensing the Light without the filter of Shadow. It is beautiful on its own here in Ljós, but across all of the realms, it must be balanced with Shadow. That is an essential part of Terra's unique beauty, the balance of Light and Shadow within the same realm.

———— ✦ ————

The approach to Teilatua from the coastal plain was similar to the approach to Lán Léargas. There were numerous twists and turns and fortified defensive positions built into the crags above. As they began their final approach into the city of Teilatua itself, however, it was a breathtaking sight. Unlike Lán Léargas, which had a large, consolidated city built into the mountainside from the valley floor, Teilatua was an entire ring of buildings surrounding the valley, built on top of the mountains.

The valley floor was a verdant plain of grasses, flowers, small trees, and a meandering river. The city was an elegant blend of carefully crafted white columns and balustrades set against the hand-carved gray granite of the mountains. The city was poised like a rooftop above the valley floor. There were two waterfalls entering the valley, one to the north and one to the south. And there were two large open structures with their own peaks that rose above everything else in the valley and the city. One structure to the east was where the people of Teilatua celebrated the elemental power of Air. This was also where they invoked that elemental power when needed. The other large structure to the west was where the special warriors that rode the giant war hawks were based. As they watched from the valley floor, they could see one of these majestic birds gliding in for a landing, the late-afternoon sun highlighting the warrior on its back.

The small group of weary travelers made their way across the valley floor to the eastern side. Another week had passed since they had left the Ljós end of the hidden pathway to Terra. When they reached the east side, they found a large rectangular channel that had been carved into the side of the mountain from the valley floor all the way up to the building, dedicated to the element of air.

Emrhys guided them to a large wooden platform on the valley floor near the side of the mountain, which resembled a ferry with rails around all sides to prevent anyone from falling into the water. Once the entire party was settled, he closed the gate where they had entered and the platform started to move. As Bedwyr and Alantir watched in amazement, the large platform began to rise into the air; straight up the channel carved into the mountainside.

"They use the elemental power of air to raise and lower the platform," said Vaelwyn when she saw their faces. "This is how they come and go here in Teilatua. There are hidden stairways as well, but it takes quite a bit of time to reach the city that way."

"This is amazing," exclaimed Alantir. "Look at the valley, Bedwyr!"

The two friends clutched at each other in wonder and delight.

Alantir's plait had finally come undone over the days of their travel, and, Bedwyr thought, probably with all her twisting of it. She looked very pretty just now, the loose tresses blowing in the breeze as they rose. "I can just imagine how this would look from one of those giant war hawks," he added, suddenly uncomfortably aware of how close they were standing. The thought brought back memories of his brothers, with Griffin's happy banter about Glynis. A shadow passed over his features then, dousing his lightness of spirit.

"Everything here is designed to be complementary to the element of air," Emrhys said. "The arms of King Baldyrien show a white hawk in flight against a light blue background, and he rules from the Sky Throne here in Teilatua."

"We will meet King Baldyrien at his palace," said Vaelwyn. "At the south end of the valley, it straddles both sides of the river that feed that waterfall," she said, pointing. "His palace has breathtaking views of the waterfall itself, with the valley stretching out below and his city encircling the peaks above." She sniffed thoughtfully, enjoying the heights.

They soon saw that beautiful view firsthand as they were escorted in to see the king, passing through several reception halls. The first was narrow, with large, slender columns rising high above them. Colorful banners and pennants fluttered in the breeze from open windows high up on their columns. The second was slightly wider than the first, but with a ceiling just as high, walls lined with paintings, statues, and weapons. Every twenty feet or so, there were torches burning, seemingly for atmosphere more than light because the far end of the hall was wide open, and sunlight flooded in, even in the late afternoon. Finally, they reached the elven king of Fjall's reception hall.

An expansive balcony overlooked the waterfall as well as the entire valley below and the city all around them, open to the air and celebrating the open blue skies all around them.

King Baldyrien himself, like his fellow Fjall ruler to the north, was an extremely gracious host. He had thinning blond hair, a high forehead framed by the tips of his pointed ears and piercing blue eyes. His silk tunic and leggings were elegantly cut, and he exuded a reserved grace and power as he strode forward to greet his guests.

"Vaelwyn and Emrhys," he said. "It has been far too long since I have seen either of you. And you have brought a pair of mortals from Terra, I see. Most unusual. There is more to them than meets the eye, I wager." He smiled broadly, revealing a set of perfectly pearly-white teeth.

"Allow me to introduce Alantir, of the woodland elves of Terra," said Vaelwyn, "And a Briton warrior, Bedwyr ap Cynfor."

"Well met, both of you. Well met indeed," responded King Baldyrien. "I sense a special connection to both of you; yet it is surprisingly strong with you, young Bedwyr."

"There is a story to tell there, Your Majesty," replied Vaelwyn. "Perhaps over dinner this evening?"

"of course, of course," Baldyrien said. "Let me have you seen to your rooms for now. I will see you again in an hour for dinner."

After the four companions had freshened up in their rooms, they met back in the second entry hall. With the arrival of nightfall, the torches that lined the sides of this hall were now providing light as well as warmth. They were escorted to a table where they would dine with the king. This was located at the other end of the large open balcony from the king's reception area. It seemed that in Teilatua, the celebration of air and openness was not limited to daytime and sunshine.

A vast array of bright stars twinkled above them in the clear mountain air. Dozens of candles burned on their table, and the flames of many torches flickered at the edges of the balcony. A mild breeze wafted by, carrying the faint scent of grass and flowers from far below.

"This is breathtaking," said Alantir. "I never thought that I would see or feel anything that made me feel as warm and content as my forest home. But here ...although it's very different ..." she trailed off.

"I am a warrior and a human," replied Bedwyr. "Neither poet nor elf. Yet, the beauty ... the visual splendor here ... it moves me greatly."

"And the warmth of new friendship," interjected Emrhys. "Don't forget that."

As the group enjoyed their dinner, Vaelwyn spoke at length with the king. He snorted when she told the story of Bedwyr's ancestors.

"I knew there was something special about this human," said Baldyrien. "However distantly related, you are one of my people. I welcome you to the home of your ancestors."

"I am deeply honored, Your Majesty," Bedwyr said graciously.

"As a warrior yourself," continued the king. "You must be very curious about our warriors who ride the giant war hawks."

"Yes, Your Majesty," enthused Bedwyr excitedly. "I am very curious about them indeed!"

"Well, we shall arrange for you to meet their captain tomorrow," concluded Baldyrien. "A complete introduction to his team."

———— ◆ ————

There was a knock at Bedwyr's door early the next morning. Captain Raynor was somewhat short for an elf, with an unusually dense thicket of close-cropped hair on his head. Known for being gruff, with limited patience, in his many years of service he had never been asked to nursemaid a guest before. *One of my superiors must really be enjoying my discomfort with this assignment*, he thought. *But I'll show them. I will be more polite and patient than anyone ever imagined that I could be.*

"Captain Raynor, and a jolly good morning to you!" said the man as Bedwyr tried to flatten his bed hair. "Are you ready to meet my warriors?" asked the captain.

"Yes sir," answered Bedwyr.

"Well then, let's get over to the aerie then," Captain Raynor said.

As they approached a large, open structure on the west side of the circular city, Bedwyr saw several of the giant war hawks take flight. They looked so peaceful as they spread their wings and glided away on the thermal currents. Below them, riders were scrambling here and there to prepare their mounts, strange leather harnesses with crisscrossing ties that fastened over the bird's breast with a giant buckle. The riders were dressed in a royal uniform of sky blue, with double rows of brass buttons on their jackets, and a thin, double gold stripe down the outside of their trousers. And they wore unusual-looking helmets. Up close, the birds towered over everybody, their backs as high as Emrhys, and their heads and beaks unnerving. Bedwyr gulped inwardly. He hoped he would never be anywhere near the receiving end of those beaks.

"I see that you are trying to figure out why we wear what we wear," laughed the captain. "Our helms are uniquely designed because we have more to fear from talons and teeth than swords or axes. Most of our battles are fought in the air against other warriors astride other mounts that fly, and their mounts also have talons and teeth, just like ours. Not that we cannot also fight on the ground like other warriors, with sword and shield or bow and arrow."

"What about those leather harnesses that all your warriors wear?" asked Bedwyr.

"Some of those straps are to fasten to the saddle, although experienced riders seldom use them," replied Captain Raynor. "The straps in front are used for carrying inexperienced passengers. For their own safety."

"I'm Maltrin and this is Heribert. Would you like to touch him?" asked one of the hawk riders standing nearby.

Bedwyr didn't need asking twice. He was surprised at how different the feathers felt on different areas of the giant bird. The feathers on his back felt smooth but hard, but under the throat were downy soft to the touch. His eyes flicked nervously to Heribert's large, sharp beak and his hand dropped away. And those keen eyes with their unblinking stare...

"Can I take our guest for a ride?" asked Maltrin.

"I suppose it will be all right if you keep it brief," replied Captain Raynor.

Bedwyr put on the special harness and one of their helms, then stepped up on the platform next to Heribert. "I'm Bedwyr by the way," he said, sticking out a hand.

Maltrin shook Bedwyr's hand. "You climb on first, in front," he said.

A few minutes later, Bedwyr was whooping with delight as he glided out of the aerie and into the blue sky on the back of the giant war hawk. They climbed above the peaks of Teilatua and circled the elven city. It looked just as beautiful up above as it did from the king's balcony. Bedwyr loved the feeling of weightlessness and freedom with the giant bird's wings flapping, outstretched. As they climbed to a higher altitude, he thrilled at the feeling of a headlong dive downwards, swooping and curving around the mountains with the wind whistling by.

"I would never get bored if I lived in Teilatua," exclaimed Bedwyr. "How long did you have to train for this?"

"It only takes one or two months of full-time training to be able to handle the basics with any mount," replied Maltrin. "But after you master those, it's a year or more of constant flying with the same mount to create a solid bond between bird and rider."

Bedwyr and Maltrin took a long flight north of Teilatua. The sunshine brightly illuminated the snow-capped mountains all around them and the sensations of rushing air and dizzying views were exhilarating. After flying north for a long time, they banked right and executed a long, graceful glide, then flew east for a while where the sparkling waters of Lake Solas shimmered in the distance. This was the largest lake in Ljós, more like a great inland sea, and the island home of the Breacadh an Lae, Abhaile, was located in its waters.

As they approached the edge of the lake, they glided down to a landing on the open plains at the south end of the lake.

Bedwyr and Maltrin dismounted and left Heribert to rest on the ground for a while where he promptly fluffed out his feathers and began to preen. The two young men walked to the edge of the lake to stretch their legs and began skipping stones across the lake's surface—this soon turned into a friendly competition. Bedwyr was working hard to skip his stones further than his new friend, but Maltrin finally skipped one so far that they could scarcely see it at the end of its run. Bedwyr laughed and acknowledged defeat.

They sat on the waterfront of the lake and ate the light lunch that had been packed for them. Maltrin told Bedwyr stories about riding his giant hawk that Bedwyr simply could not get enough of. As Maltrin said, with Teilatua comprising the larger southern half of mountainous Fjall, their territory could not easily be protected by troops on the ground. So the riders of the war hawks were the elite corps of their kingdom. They were able to cover all of the vast mountainous terrain and keep watch on all the deep valleys crisscrossing their kingdom. Maltrin spoke of how they trained intensively for solo flights as well as formation flights. With dozens of riders sometimes flying together in their formation flights.

On their way back west, they crossed over the foothills at the southern end of the Fjall mountains, flying in a large circle, with Teilatua at the center. As they flew, Maltrin spotted activity on the ground below them and suggested they double back for a closer look. As they got closer to the ground, they could see it was a band of goblins. Bedwyr, although never having previously seen a goblin, was still able to identify them. It was obvious; their misshapen hunchbacked forms, dark marble eyes and curved, taloned hands, pointed noses and ears, all fit an image he knew only too well from childhood stories.

As he looked, he watched the band as it scrambled under rocks and into crevasses to escape the hawk's eye and its rider. Bedwyr took Maltrin's word that this was what they were seeing. He also took Maltrin's word that there were simply too many for them to confront alone. The best thing they could do was to return to the aerie as soon as possible and report. The aerie would dispatch a proper war band to take care of the goblins.

"Thank you very much for sharing that experience with me," said Bedwyr as he dismounted once they landed back in Teilatua. "I envy your ability to spend every day doing that!"

"My pleasure. Thank you for accompanying me," Maltrin said. "You'll have to excuse me, though. I must report to Captain Raynor about the goblins."

Bedwyr returned to his rooms, and Alantir, who had been watching for Bedwyr's return, was outside in the corridor—smiling at the sheer joy on his face.

"I am delighted for you!" she said, running to him and grabbing his arm. "And I want you to tell me all about it. But we are to attend another dinner with Vaelwyn and Emrhys." She grimaced, crossing her eyes. "They will review this ceremony about restoring the power within your amulet. Tomorrow, the ceremony will be held on the other side of the city and we're both supposed to be dressed and in place on the eastern side before the sun is at its height, midday tomorrow." She dropped his arm, gesticulating indignantly.

Bedwyr laughed at her complaint. "It's just a bit of dress-up. It won't last long and besides, we'll learn more about ... everything we're supposed to be doing."

The smile crept back over Alantir's features and she sighed. "You're right, I'm just ... I feel awkward, not knowing my place and I miss my ... parents, Meriel."

The shadows returned, clawing away the smile Bedwyr was beginning to yearn for.

"You'd have liked her, Meriel," Alantir continued. "She was so bright, so full of life." Her face crumpled and tears sprang to her eyes.

Bedwyr took his hands in his. "It's ok to miss them," he said, comforting her as best he could. "I miss my brothers. You'd have liked them, too, I think. One day, if we're lucky, you'll meet one of them. Dylan. He's very ..." he struggled to describe his bull of a brother as Alantir's tear-stained face rose to his. "He's very, um, brash. Likes his food." He hurried to raise her spirits, thinking to talk about something, anything, to distract her. "Anyway, you'll have to ride one of these war hawks with me when I get trained. There's nothing like it. And I definitely plan to get trained!" Bedwyr said, deftly changing the subject. "But wait, what d'you mean about us getting dressed? I am already dressed."

Alantir sniffed, taking a deep, gulping breath. "Well, first of all, you probably smell like bird feathers now after spending all that time on that giant hawk," she pointed out. "And secondly, they have some sort of special white tunics they want us to wear for tomorrow's ceremony. We ought to try them on this afternoon. I thought maybe we could do that together." She looked at him hopefully, biting her lower lip.

Bedwyr realized he would probably be quite happy doing anything she suggested, even putting on tights, but he thought to keep that to himself for the time being.

"OK, although I don't see why it's important what we wear. I thought this was all about our amulets," he replied.

Magwei was watching and listening from his vantage point in the astral plane. The gölge yürüteç had unearthed new uses for this arcane dimension that was seldom used by any others.

These idiots, he hissed to himself, *prattling on about total nonsense.*

I will be there for their precious ceremony tomorrow, he continued to himself, *and I will make sure that no magic flows to this so-called champion of the Light!*

I am surprised, he mused, *almost disappointed in Vaelwyn's stupidity. I thought I would have a worthy adversary here. But she has chosen half-grown mortals as her champions – foolish! And one of them is human no less!*

The next day, Alantir and Bedwyr stood to the side with Emrhys to Bedwyr's right, as Vaelwyn and King Baldyrien stood back-to-back in the center of the wide-open structure, their arms outstretched. They were dressed all in white and faced to the east and west. Bedwyr could not hear or understand everything that was being said, and instead, let his thoughts wander. A breeze had sprung up and was growing gradually stronger, it seemed, with the elven chanting.

He looked over at Emrhys, studying the gigantic man and noticed for the first time that he wore an ornate ring on his index finger. It was heavy gold with a green emerald set in the center, and smaller sapphires around the emerald.

As the midday sun stood directly overhead, Vaelwyn murmured a few arcane words, and placed her right hand on Bedwyr's shoulder. She had an ivory bracelet that Bedwyr had barely noticed before, featuring a transparent blue sapphire set in the center. And now it was glowing.

Then, Emrhys placed his left hand on Bedwyr's other shoulder, the blue sapphires in his ring also glowing blue. Then Alantir stepped closer to him and placed her hands on his lower back, and King Baldyrien stretched out his hand. Bedwyr was now fully unsurprised about the faint blue glow.

As instructed, Bedwyr reached out with his amulet and touched it to Baldyrien's glowing ring and waited.

"*Solas, thoir soir! Aer, Cumholt!*" Light of the East! Power of Air! the king commanded.

The growing breeze now formed a column of air that began to solidify in front of the king. Small bolts of lightning flared within it as the amulet glowed brighter and brighter. They could all smell the crisp clear scent of ozone.

"*Aer, a dheonú, Cumholt!*" Grant the Power of Air!

The amulet began to spin impossibly fast, now drawn into the center of the air column, and was struck again and again by the small lightning bolts. When it finally stopped, the king reached out for the amulet and started to place it around Bedwyr's neck.

Unseen by the others, hidden in the astral plane, Magwei twisted his hands and muttered some foul utterances.

The chain around Bedwyr's neck tightened as the king's hands dropped away. And then the chain tightened even more.

"What the—" Bedwyr exclaimed.

He grasped at the amulet's chain and struggled to pull it away from his neck.

"I don't underst—" Bedwyr gasped, struggling now to catch his breath.

He pulled at the chain with all his strength then, and it broke apart in his hands.

Oh, you think you are safe now, do you? chortled Magwei.

Everybody else had removed their hands from Bedwyr and taken a step back as the wind grew stronger, twirling around him and twisting his tunic. His amulet now pulsed blue, and the wind was so strong that it was pushing him off balance. The amulet and its chain were slipping out of his hands. The amulet seemed to have a life of its own, struggling to escape Bedwyr's grasp and fly into the air.

Yes, yes! Magwei exhorted, *fly away, fly to me, my pretty. Magwei will put you to good use!*

"Stop!" shouted Bedwyr, raising one of his palms without thinking, and thrusting it downwards. At the same time he grasped the chain tightly in his other hand and twirled the amulet above his head. The amulet pulsed wildly as it circled through the raging wind.

"Once again," Bedwyr shouted, "I say STOP!"

The raging wind seemed to calm for a moment, then to his surprise, the wind turned to a gentle breeze. The chain in Bedwyr's hand loosened, and the amulet dropped into the palm of his hand.

Damn! from Magwei

"Nicely done Bedwyr," the king said. "I sensed some touch of Shadow for a moment, and I thought that the amulet might be lost to you. I don't know how we were touched by Shadow here in our own realm, but you were strong Bedwyr! And you cast them out. Now, through your amulet, you have some limited ability to control the element of air. Once your own latent magic is activated as well, and the Air Elementals accept you, the power you wield through the amulet will make you powerful indeed."

Very surprising, Magwei muttered to himself, *and very disappointing. I have failed here, and I'm sure that I'll pay a heavy price for my failure. But I'll not underestimate these foolish mortals the next time that we meet!*

———— •◆• ————

King Baldyrien greeted the new day with considerable enthusiasm. He would be spending it with his hawk warriors at the aerie, and there were few activities that he enjoyed more. He had a hearty breakfast of wild boar sausages and poached eggs (he had to watch his belt buckle, after all) and then walked briskly over to the aerie.

As he did so, he was greeted by his senior commanders who called the hawk warriors to attention, and then King Baldyrien followed them onto the flight deck of the aerie. A vast area with high ceilings and a spectacular view of the mountains to the west from the large, open bay, it housed many scores of mounted warriors comfortably.

The hawk warriors of Teilatua stood to attention in neat ranks to the left and right with their riders before them. The magnificent birds all had their groomed wings swept back and tucked in close, ready for inspection. Baldyrien walked the line, stopping to banter with and ask personal questions of each and every one of his hawk warriors. They were friendly, animated conversations as he took time to know them and their families. Equally, the warriors clearly held their king in high regard.

After pleasantries had been exchanged, a group of eight riders mounted their giant hawks and flew out of the aerie, leaving the rest lined up at the edge of the flight deck. Those already airborne put on a great show of flying in formation and forming complicated patterns in unison and demonstrating aerial combat maneuvers.

The morning was a great success and later on, all the riders joined King Baldyrien for a celebratory luncheon, their mounts treated to the finest collection of extra-large grubworts. Large tables and serving boards had been brought out onto the flight deck after the giant hawks had been taken back to their roosts where fortunately, their eating trough was far removed from everyone else. The flight deck echoed with the joyous sounds of warm laughter, quiet conversation, and shared camaraderie.

The king stood and called for quiet. When he had the attention of all, he called Maltrin to come forward to be heartily commended as the 'Rider of Distinction' for this year amid thundering applause.

Baldyrien enjoyed the final amount of time spent with his hawk warriors as the luncheon concluded. And then he had a brisk walk back to his quarters, already looking forward to next year's event.

Alantir was surprised to hear a knock at her door the morning after Bedwyr's amulet ceremony. A friendly-looking female elf stood standing on the threshold. She had a big smile on a very round face with flushed, apple cheeks, and her blue eyes twinkled as she smiled.

"Good morning, my name is Lyndelle," she said. "I am sorry to surprise you, but my uncle, King Baldyrien, suggested you might like to join me today."

Alantir was still staring at Lyndelle, with her big smile and wavy blonde hair tucked behind her pointy ears. She caught herself, blushing. "Oh, pardon me," Alantir said. "What is it I would be joining you to do?"

"Oops, my turn to apologize," laughed Lyndelle. "I completely forgot to say!"

She snorted, which sounded like a fart, and then choked, her eyes bulging. Alantir began to laugh. Then they both began laughing.

"I'm going for a long climb up ... the stairway next to ... the north waterfall," Lyndelle said between splutters. "And then taking a hike above the city!"

"That sounds great!" said Alantir, wiping her face. "Thank you for the invitation. Let me get ready and I'll grab my bow and arrows."

"No, it's too steep for that," said Lyndelle. "Just put a knife on your belt and bring some water."

Alantir felt like she had been climbing forever. They had taken the airlift down to the valley floor and walked to the north waterfall where an entrance was hidden behind a rock outcropping, far enough to the side to remain dry from the water spray. It was every bit as steep and narrow as Lyndelle had said. Lyndelle, though, was like a tireless mountain goat, clambering her way up the stairway at a challenging pace. Alantir found she was pushing hard to keep up.

When they finally reached the top, Lyndelle stepped back, spread her arms wide, and gestured all around them. The peaks above the north and south waterfalls rose a bit higher than the rest of the mountains comprising Teilatua. It was a beautiful vista with bright blue skies providing the backdrop for a range of snow-capped mountain peaks, extending as far as Alantir could see in every direction she looked. The warmth of the sun warmed her cheek and she felt suddenly better than she had in days.

"I thought we could hike to the east from here," Lyndelle said. "That way, we can circle around the city and end up at the Temple of Air. That's where your friend Bedwyr had his amulet ceremony yesterday."

Alantir blushed despite herself, at the mention of Bedwyr. She enjoyed Lyndelle's company as they hiked together along the heights above Teilatua and asked her many questions about Ljós and the Álfur. In return, Lyndelle peppered her with questions about Terra and the woodland elves—and Bedwyr! Before they knew it, they were more than halfway to the Temple of Air. They were so preoccupied that they did not notice the threat creeping up on them until they heard the snarl.

"Get down, Alantir!" shouted Lyndelle. "This is one of Fjall's rare snow leopards!"

"I can't believe I left my bow and arrows behind!" shouted Alantir.

The snow leopard paced slowly around the pair, muscles rippling below her fur. Her fangs bared as she snarled and her body tightening as she poised to spring when suddenly, Lyndelle leaped onto the snow leopard, a knife in her hand already stabbing the big cat.

The creature was not going down fast, however, and it shook Lyndelle off angrily. Then, it attacked her with a swipe of its long claws.

Alantir saw her bloody friend lying on the ground with her limbs askew. As the leopard prepared for a killing blow and Alantir prepared to leap into the fray herself, she saw Lyndelle move. She had her knife ready at her side, and as the big cat pounced, Lyndelle rolled over and thrust the knife right into its heart.

"Lyndelle, Lyndelle!" Alantir shouted as she rolled the dead leopard off her friend, to reveal Lyndelle blood-soaked and grimacing. "You were amazing! I thought that leopard would be the end of you!"

"She just about was," groaned Lyndelle. "My back feels like it's on fire where she swiped me with that paw."

"I will try to stop the bleeding," said Alantir. "And bandage it somehow. But we need to get you some real help from the healers."

"I am sure that I have been hurt worse than this before," Lyndelle said, "but I just can't remember when."

Alantir tore strips from the bottom of hers and Lyndelle's tunic and used them to bandage the wounds as best she could. Then she gave her some water and helped her climb unsteadily to her feet.

"Let's just put one foot in front of the other for now," encouraged Alantir. "We'll make steady progress and get back to the city before we know it." *I will never go anywhere without my bow and arrows ever again;* she vowed to herself.

The two friends made their way across the heights above Teilatua. The beauty of the view was now lost on them. They just wanted to get back and take Lyndelle to the elven healers.

"Hang on, Lyndelle!" Alantir exhorted her friend. "I can see the Temple of Air just ahead."

As the pair stumbled down the last snowy slope, someone rushed out to help.

"My friend needs the healers!" Alantir barked out.

"Yes," she was answered. "And so do you!"

There was a fire blazing warmly behind her back as Alantir continued to sit by Lyndelle's bedside while her friend recovered.

"You really don't need to sit with me nonstop," Lyndelle admonished. "I feel much better after getting a good night's sleep."

"You saved my life!" Alantir exclaimed. "The least I can do is sit here."

"It's not anything that I thought about or planned," Lyndelle said. "I just attacked that snow leopard before she could finish us off."

"Well, I will be forever grateful to you," said Alantir. "And I will come back to visit you here when I have completed this mission with Vaelwyn and Emrhys."

"It's a deal!" laughed Lyndelle. "And I will hold you to it!"

CHAPTER TWELVE

Journey from Fjall

Ten Weeks Before Winter Solstice

Bedwyr turned around on his horse to look back at the way they had come. Despite their early start, the day was well underway by the time they emerged onto the heathlands beyond the foothills.

"This southern area of Fjall looked so different from the air," he said. "And it seemed so easy to get around the mountains astride a giant hawk. Much easier than on horseback."

"Tell us about the realm of Skógur we're traveling to now," asked Alantir. "Garmoniya is one of the two major kingdoms there, isn't it?"

"Yes, Garmoniya in the northern region of Skógur is ruled by King Mandáron," replied Vaelwyn. "All of Skógur, north and south, is the most heavily forested region of Ljós. Garmoniya stands closer to the open heathlands and the mountains of Fjall. King Mandáron ..." Vaelwyn looked like she was about to say more but closed her mouth instead.

"Tishina, though, is located deep within the southern forests, far from any plains or mountains. Some of the forests around Tishina include the oldest trees in all the realms. There is a stand of trees there that have stood since before the Álfur came into being. Tishina in the southern region of Skógur is ruled by Queen Dalamyra. These are the two kingdoms of the green elves of Skógur, who control the elemental magic of Earth."

"What about the other realms of Ljós?" asked Bedwyr. "We know so little about this land."

"Yes, Bed is right," said Alantir, not noticing how Bedwyr's face lit up at the use of his nickname. "What about your own people, Vaelwyn? What about the realm of the silver elves?"

"Well, Álfur history stretches back tens of thousands of years," said Vaelwyn, getting comfortable in her saddle. "The origins of our ability to wield magic have been lost in the mists of time and many of our Álfur have allowed pride to become arrogance, and their speed, strength, and prowess with arms to make them warlike."

Bedwyr shook his head as he looked around the surrounding heathlands.

"I definitely met elves in Teilatua with pride and with strength in arms," he said. "But I did not get any sense of arrogance or any warlike nature from them—as long as they were not provoked."

Emrhys looked back as he started to ride ahead of the group to reconnoiter the surroundings ahead of their group's path.

"Aye," he said, "'tis true that the Fjall elves north in Lan Léargas and south in Teilatua are leaders among the Álfur in many respects. Their pride becomes confidence, not arrogance. Unfortunately, many others of the Álfur do not share the fine qualities of the Fjall elves."

"But the silver elves do share these qualities," Alantir said. "Don't they?"

"Yes, they do." Emrhys shouted back as he rode forward. "Vaelwyn can tell you more about her people."

"Silver elves have the most fully developed magical powers, and with our expanded powers comes an additional sense of responsibility and a need for restrained behavior. With our command of all the elemental magics, we wield power that other Álfur cannot even dream of," Vaelwyn continued. "My people live in a secret city located in the same region as the White Henge but hidden from all outside visitors. We silver elves control all the magic elemental powers of air, earth, fire, and water, and our Prime Adepti have arcane knowledge and powers beyond the imagination of other Álfur. The discipline and training of the Adepti of the silver elves is legendary but remains a mystery to all other Álfur."

"I see," said Bedwyr, although he didn't entirely. "But what about the other Álfur? We have met one of the high elves of Fjall who control the magic element of air," he began, "and we are on our way to meet one of the high elves of Skógur who control the element of earth. But what about the rest?"

"Yes, what can you tell us about the fire elves and the water elves?" Alantir asked. "We are eager to learn everything that we can."

"The high elves in the Eydimörk realm control the elemental magic of fire," Vaelwyn explained. "Their kingdom of Tulipesä is deep in the middle of a hot desert in the far southeast region of Ljós. Their ruling house features a red scorpion on a tan background as its emblem. A king and queen rule them. King Kalderion and Queen Löswellyn, and they rule from the Sun Throne of Tulipesä. The Álfur

167

of Eydimörk are more isolated geographically than the other realms, and their culture and traditions are more unique."

"What about the water elves?" asked Bedwyr. "They sound like the most complicated realm."

"Yes, even more complicated than you think," laughed Vaelwyn. "Because the water elves are divided into two separate realms. Sjávar in the south and Vatnid in the north. Both have as much water as they do land, which is appropriate as theirs is the elemental power of water."

"Why don't you start with the southern realm of Sjávar," suggested Emrhys.

"Yes, that's a good suggestion," agreed Vaelwyn. "There are two major cities in Sjávar, both close together, both seaports, but with access to two different seas. Ekaitza is a port that opens to the southern sea, whereas Vilnis is a port that opens to the northern sea. There are only a limited number of miles between these two seaports, but the cities are very different from one another. Vilnis is ruled by King Tendoryn and Ekaitza is ruled by Queen Valrexyn. Both cities are saltwater seaports, and their citizens are all experts at long sailing trips and familiar with wind, weather, and currents."

"The northern realm of Vatnid also has two cities, and both are also ports," continued Vaelwyn in her strong calming voice. "But Vesë to the east is a saltwater port, while Rélegur to the west is a freshwater port."

Vesë," she continued. "is ruled by King Talyrien and Queen Selmaryth. Rélegur, on the other hand, is ruled by Queen Látellyn."

"There is just so much to learn," said Bedwyr. "All the names and places are getting mixed together in my head."

"It is a lot to absorb," agreed Alantir. "But what about Myrkur? Does Myrkur have the same variety of people and places? Terra has at least as many types of people and places as Ljós so probably Myrkur does too."

"No," Emrhys said flatly. "It does not."

Bedwyr looked at Alantir, his eyes widening. Emrhys was quite imposing even when he wasn't aggravated. Which … seemed to be much of the time.

"Myrkur is a dark, cold, and forbidding realm," he continued. "It is a land littered with the lifeless remains of trees that used to be green and alive long, long ago. Lakes, ponds, now swamps all full of putrid water. Desolate."

"Sounds very un-tempting," Alantir said, trying to lighten the mood.

"There are many creatures that live and thrive in Myrkur," Emrhys rumbled on. "One large city where the Dark Fae live, which is built into the ring of jagged mountains surrounding the Dark Henge, located at the center of their lands. Forbidding towers and dungeons infest the city where fissures split the ground. Below them, endless fires that burn, blowing noxious fumes above. Yet the land is cold. Those fires bring no warmth; everything there is soulless."

"The Dark Fae have many fell creatures that serve them in Myrkur," interjected Vaelwyn. "Hordes of goblins and trolls, pursuing their blood lust together. Both detest humans, but they have a special hatred for the Álfur. In turn, we view them as vermin that should be exterminated, like rats or roaches."

"The most dangerous things that live in Myrkur, however," Emrhys said. "Are the living shadows and their masters, the Vålnad. Fortunately, there are only a limited number of Vålnad, but they are protected by vast living shadows. We believe they are the shades of former victims; scant spirit remains of humans and Álfur now condemned to serve their Vålnad masters."

Bedwyr shuddered at the thought of how the living shadows came to be. Horrific.

"And let's not forget those damned gölge yürüteç," spat out Vaelwyn. "The Six. Traitors to the rest of Ljós. Once the most honored and talented of the Álfur, now serving at the right hand of Shadow. They disgust me!"

"What of the Dark Fae themselves?" asked Alantir. "Were they always evil?"

"It is said that they were much like the Álfur at the dawn of creation," said Vaelwyn. "But they were more interested in rocks and gems and exploring the dark spaces beneath the ground. Soon, the sunshine began to matter less, fresh air, and green things growing on the surface were taken for granted, then dismissed, and finally ... reproached."

"Even on a warm and sunny day like today, these stories of Myrkur send a chill down my spine!" Alantir said as she pulled her horse up alongside Bedwyr.

"Aye, I feel it too," Bedwyr said as he shared a sad smile with Alantir. He wished he could give her a hug although that was not an easy feat while riding on horseback together. "As we ride through this beautiful scenery and enjoy the sunshine and fresh air ourselves, it is so sad to think that a whole race of elves turned their back on all this. And then drove themselves deeper and deeper into darkness and evil."

"They are said to have been weaker in nature than the Álfur," she continued. "And they became infatuated with the gems and shiny metal objects they crafted from those ores mined from the earth. They went so deep, they encountered dark spirits that had been locked away from the beauty of the surface in the early days of creation."

"These dark spirits had no personal identity," Emrhys said. "They were the disembodied voice and will of Shadow.

170

Shadow always retreats before Light but also eagerly awaits the opportunity to return."

Bedwyr's horse whinnied and shook his mane, rattling his harness.

"Look," said Bedwyr, "even my horse is chilled by these stories of Shadow while we ride through this beautiful landscape. How can anyone be unaffected by these stories of dark spirits deep beneath the earth?"

"Just waiting there," said Alantir as she shivered, "since the early days of creation!"

"The power of Shadow made the Dark Fae more powerful than they had been," Emrhys said. "They were now equal rivals to the Álfur and became a beacon for all the fell creatures of the world, fostering the growth of the living shadows under their servants, the Vålnad. The Vålnad are controlled by the gölge yürüteç who draw dark magic from the Shadow, its use often wounding the mind and spirit, as well as wounding the body."

"There are other unknown dark creatures that thrive in the cold and dark of Myrkur," Vaelwyn stated firmly. "It is not a place you would ever want to visit."

"How do you know all of this?" questioned Bedwyr. "How can you stand to even think about all of these dark things? I am more comfortable thinking about flesh and blood enemies, like the Saxons I plan to hack apart with my sword!"

"Aye, young Bedwyr," said Emrhys. "Easy for you humans to avoid the hard truth of even thinking about the Dark Fae for long ages now. Because Vaelwyn's people have protected you from them and created an existence for you that has been separated from all the darkness of Myrkur!"

"That time has now passed," Vaelwyn said firmly, "and you and Alantir will now know more about the Dark Fae and the evil that dwells with them in Myrkur than you ever imagined."

———— ◆ ————

Emrhys' thoughts returned to his meeting with Vaelwyn and King Baldyrien just before they had left Teilatua. The king had pulled the two of them into his private study along with Captain Raynor of his hawk warriors. There was a large map of Fjall on one side of the fireplace and a map of all of Ljós on the other.

"We've had scattered reports of unusual activity in our part of Fjall for some time now, as you know," Baldyrien said. "As have Alderon's people in the north, but without being able to confirm what we are facing." He paused and looked at them seriously. "All that has now changed," he said. "One of our hawk riders brought back the head of a goblin. From a group he chased down just to the west of Teilatua."

"Goblins are certainly disgusting, hairy little creatures," said Emrhys in his deep rumbling voice. "And large numbers together can be dangerous, but we have seen them here in Ljós before. One or two are not much of a threat."

"This time may be different," said Baldyrien. "We've also received reports of trolls, which concern us far more than goblins. Although smaller in number, each one is large and fierce; a real warrior. Goblins are like other, smaller vermin. Where you see one, there are always many more that you have not yet seen. There may be large numbers of goblins building up here in Ljós, and we just do not see them yet. Perhaps the start of a large-scale effort from Myrkur to penetrate Ljós in a way not seen since the Great Sundering."

"Hmm," pondered Vaelwyn, "confirmation of trolls here in Ljós would certainly be a great concern. But I also would not discount the significance of goblins here in Ljós if they are starting to build up large numbers. They could do a lot of harm to your common elves out in the countryside. Terrorizing our populations, destroying crops and stealing livestock. Not to mention widening murder and mayhem."

"Your Majesty," said Captain Raynor. "Scattered sightings are reported by our cousins, the riders of Lán Léargas, to the north, near the coastline," he said. "As well as to their far northeast, in and around that dense tangle of wildwood forest. A few reports included trolls in the northeast foot-hills. They found troll scat in that area, but no other hard evidence so far."

"Do we have any idea about how they are getting into Ljós?" asked Emrhys. "Or where these vermin are gathering once they enter our realm?"

"Our hawk riders have reported sightings in these areas around the north of Teilatua," Captain Raynor said as he indicated several points north of the city on the map of Fjall. "And one of our riders finally brought one down in this area just to the west of Teilatua."

"How much of this activity is also going on elsewhere in Ljós?" Baldyrien asked as he stepped toward the map. "In Skógur, Vatnid, Sjávar and Eydimörk? We don't know if these are a limited incursion from Myrkur up here in Fjall or part of a larger pattern across all of Ljós." He swept his hand across the entire map of Ljós.

"It does make sense that Myrkur can penetrate Ljós more easily with the weakening of the Seals," Vaelwyn said to Emrhys. "We find it easier to travel to Terra from Ljós, after all."

"Do we have any information on these activities from the other Lords of Ljós?" asked Emrhys. "Perhaps the Shadow Fae of Myrkur have simply found a previously unopened pathway in the far north of Fjall and are sending in goblins and trolls."

"Alas," replied Baldyrien, "No such thing is known. I have heard nothing from any of the other kings."

"I will ask my fellow Adepti of the silver elves to reach out across all the realms of Ljós," replied Vaelwyn. "I can reach them by means of the spirit connection, even though we are spread all across Ljós."

"And we will be in Garmoniya soon enough," said Emrhys. "We can ask King Mandáron about what they are seeing in Skógur when we get there."

"Be wary on your trip to Garmoniya," Captain Raynor replied. "Your path will take you through that same area where we retrieved the goblin head."

"I will ensure we make it safely to Garmoniya," Emrhys flatly stated. "And I would love to obliterate some of these damn goblins along the way!"

CHAPTER THIRTEEN

The Realm of Skógur

Nine Weeks Before Winter Solstice

The further the group of travelers went into the forests of Skógur, the more Alantir felt at home. The gentle sunlight filtered through the canopy of leaves far overhead, the sounds of small animals moving through the brush, and distant birdsong echoed through the hushed silence of the forest. All of it felt achingly familiar to Alantir.

They had already spent a few days riding and today, when they stopped to rest their horses, Alantir took a walk on her own through the trees. She let her hands move over the bark of the sturdy trunks, feeling the same affinity she would have felt back in her woodlands in Terra, but she also felt more. Alantir felt some faint energy or spark within each plant, perhaps something unique to all of Ljós or only to the forests of Skógur; either way, it was definitely there.

Alantir had moved a little bit further from her group of fellow travelers when she heard the sound of light laughter. The voices were very high-pitched but joyous. She made her way forward, deeper into the forest, until a clearing with a small pond came into view. A shaft of sunlight shone directly on the far side of the pond and there, frolicking in the water, was a group of water sprites.

They were small and slight. Much smaller than the Álfur. Where the Álfur looked like tall, slender humans with pointed ears, these sprites looked far too small to be mistaken for humans or Álfur. If one stood next to an Álfur, they would probably not be taller than her knee. They had the same pointed ears as the Álfur, but unlike them, had small, gossamer wings.

They were clearly enjoying themselves, their lilting song dissipating often into laughter and splashing; it was joyful but also mysterious in some deep way, not exactly like birdsong nor the poetic laments of the Álfur, and not at all like the clumsy songs and simple melodies of the humans.

"They bring a certain lightness to one's spirit," said Vaelwyn as she joined Alantir. "I could spend an entire day listening to the sprites in a sunlit clearing like this."

"I have never seen or heard anything like this before," replied Alantir. "It is enchanting."

"Yes," laughed Vaelwyn. "It is indeed. You have been transfixed for several hours already by this enchanting song and lay. It could easily have been long days instead of a few hours."

"We will need to select a good location to make camp for the night," Vaelwyn said. "Once we get settled I'll seek entry to the spirit plane so that I can communicate with my fellow Adepti Prime despite the distance."

"I believe that there's a good location up ahead," Emrhys said. "As I recall, there's an area with a low rise within a small area of meadow—and a spring on the far side of that low rise. We can make camp there for the night."

"We must take care about using a campfire," Vaelwyn pointed out. "Even though our fire will be using old wood that has fallen long ago, the trees are understandably displeased about any fires burning in the midst of their forest."

The group of travelers gathered fresh water and prepared a meal after taking care of their horses and settling their gear. They sat and chatted amiably as they watched the sunset through the trees off to their west. As the dark of the night took hold, they huddled close to their small campfire.

Vaelwyn crossed her legs and arms, clasping her right hand with the heavy gold ring over the Adepti brooch pinned to her cloak over her left shoulder. The red ruby in the ring began to glow a faint red as Vaelwyn muttered quiet words, her eyes closed.

To the others, it looked like she was sleeping. Alantir played with her braid nervously.

Vaelwyn herself was acclimating to the spirit plane. No matter how many times she did this, it was always an adjustment at first. Everything appeared misty, with no apparent landmarks, which made it very disorienting. She could always sense where the White Henge was located, as could all Prime Adepti. This was where they met in the spirit plane.

It was a simple matter of willing yourself to be there and, although the travel itself took no time at all, it was always a bit of a shock to see her fellow Adepti. They appeared as vague clouds of white wisps with nominal facial features, and it was easiest to recognize them when they spoke.

"Caedwyn," Vaelwyn asked. "Is that you?"

"Yes, Vaelwyn," he answered. "I am here most nights at this time unless an urgent matter calls me elsewhere. I don't believe that we have anyone else with us this evening though," he continued.

"There have been developments in Fjall," Vaelwyn replied. "A number of goblin sightings near Teilatua, and trolls. The other Adepti should be made aware. Are similar things happening elsewhere in Ljós?"

"This is a concern," mused the spirit form of Caedwyn. "And we have other reports that raise even greater concerns."

"What reports?" Vaelwyn asked sharply. "And what concerns?"

"The gölge yürüteç are active again after all these long ages," he paused, "and outside of Myrkur."

"Not here in Ljós!" Vaelwyn exclaimed. "Surely that is not possible. The Elemental Seals could not have weakened that much!"

"The nature of our existence is changing before our eyes, my friend," Caedwyn replied. "But no, I don't believe that the gölge yürüteç can be physically present in Ljós. Not yet at any rate."

"So what is it that you are concerned about?" asked Vaelwyn.

"These Shadow Walkers have always been very clever at using the astral plane in ways that even we Prime Adepti can't understand," he said.

"Yes, so what?" she replied.

"Queen Dalamyra of Tishina reported a disturbing dream that she had a few nights ago. One of the gölge yürüteç had penetrated her dream—the Shadow Walker had become a Dream Walker."

"I thought that Dream Walkers were just a matter of myth and legend," Vaelwyn said. "Something from the ages before the Great Sundering—if ever at all. Not something that could actually be done in our age."

"He was using this unique access to her mind through her dreams to try and seduce her to join the Dark Fae!" Caedwyn reported. "You know that the legends have always said that Dream Walkers can have undue influence on anyone once they enter their dreams. If true, with such a rare type of assault only a few of our strongest Álfur would be strong enough to resist. And fortunately, Queen Dalamyra is one of those few."

"Yes, but ..." Vaelwyn muttered, "who else could these Dream Walkers seek out and try to seduce to their evil schemes?"

"Indeed ..." Caedwyn replied.

Vaelwyn felt the warmth of the fire as her awareness returned to the camp. Her companions all looked at her with concern on their faces. She was grateful for the presence of Emrhys as the Caomhnoir. *It could have gone very differently,* she thought to herself. *And I might have been assigned someone who made me feel all alone on this mission instead of having the company of Emrhys—my former lover..*

"Vaelwyn," Alantir gently asked. "Are you all right? That did not last too long, but it felt like you were truly gone, not just sleeping."

"It is a very deep trance that our physical bodies enter when we send our essence into the spirit plane," answered Vaelwyn. "I am sorry if I caused concern."

"I think that it would be best if all of you got some sleep now," Emrhys rumbled. "I will keep watch and awaken Bedwyr just before dawn to serve a short watch."

As they drew closer to their destination, the nature of the path they followed began to change. Similar to the approaches to the two mountain cities of Fjall, the path here started to twist and turn. The areas around some of the sharpest switchbacks were accompanied by large fortified wooden outposts built into the upper reaches of the trees. Any enemy attempting to approach in force would be decimated by scores of elven archers firing volley after volley from these fortified outposts. And the forest was too thick now for a large force of intruders to force their way through off the path, with larger, older trees and fewer glades or meadows between.

"As the earth elves of Skógur know very well," Vaelwyn spoke. "Each tree in this forest has its own spirit. If you know how to speak with them, you can communicate, after a fashion."

"What does that mean?" asked Bedwyr.

"Well, it is more like an exchange of thoughts and feelings," Vaelwyn explained. "Not specific words said aloud." For a moment, Vaelwyn looked flustered, perhaps having temporarily reached the limit of her explanations.

"Show us, please!" asked Alantir. "I used to feel faint traces of something like that with the trees in my own forest back in Beechwood. But I would be thrilled to know how to enter more deeply into such an exchange!"

Vaelwyn dismounted from her horse and approached one of the largest trees that stood a slight distance from their path. She closed her eyes and placed both palms on the trunk of the majestic old tree. The others heard the faint sound of rustling leaves and tree boughs rubbing against each other in the wind. Vaelwyn started slightly as she looked up and withdrew her hands.

'What did she share with you?" asked Emrhys.

"They are uneasy," Vaelwyn replied. "Not frightened or angry, but uneasy. There is a presence here that does not belong, it is unwelcome. But the trees do not know exactly what it is or where."

"Let us be wary as we continue on to Garmoniya," said Emrhys. "The trees are slow to stir, but they are never wrong about what goes on in their forest."

The next day, as the group continued to draw closer to Garmoniya, Alantir found a spot in the forest that called to her. It was a woodland glade with a pool of water fed by a small waterfall. It reminded her of where she and her friend Meriel used to swim and she was overcome by the urge to stop.

"Can we please stop for a quick swim in that glade?" she asked. "We've been traveling for a long time now, and I would like to wash off before we meet the ruling Álfur of Garmoniya. After all, they are apparently my distant relatives, and I must look like a dirty wreck."

Bedwyr whooped with delight as he stripped down to his undergarments and jumped right into the refreshing water. Alantir was almost as quick, stripping down to a short, thin under-tunic that highlighted her long legs while providing some modest privacy for other parts of her body. Secretly, they admired each other. Bedwyr, her lean, toned body as she entered the water and Alantir, his warrior's physique, dark wet hair falling on muscular shoulders.

She is more attractive than any human girl that I have ever met, Bedwyr thought to himself. *But she is just a friend, I suppose. And she would probably never want anything to do with a human.*

Back on the banks and sitting in the sun to dry, they sat very close together. Bedwyr could feel the heat of Alantir's body right next to him, and he wanted to reach out to her. When he looked at her, she held his gaze for several long moments, and he felt a stirring that was entirely new to him. Then she turned away, seemingly nervous.

As they dried, the end of a heated conversation between Emrhys and Vaelwyn could be clearly heard.

"...but we could learn more than we now know," Vaelwyn was finishing. "And what we learn could be important."

"I would be dazed afterward!" Emrhys thundered. "And not much use as a Guardian for some time."

"That's something we can manage," protested Vaelwyn. "The risk seems small this close to Garmoniya, and the information we gain may be worth a small risk."

"What are the two of you talking about?" asked Alantir, not wanting to eavesdrop.

Emrhys looked at Vaelwyn, and she shrugged. "My people, the Breacadh an Lae, have an unusual ability. We can enter the spirits of certain animals and share their awareness. It can be useful, but it is very draining. We were just discussing," he looked at Vaelwyn pointedly before continuing, "whether gathering information from animals ranging long distances away is worth the risk."

"Sometimes I think that I am dreaming," said Bedwyr. "You Álfur have your magic and your talking trees—and those damn gölge yürüteç—and now my giant friend here is going to enter the minds of some animals? It's just all so unbelievable—it makes me feel that I must be dreaming!"

"Vaelwyn would like me to try, to find out what is making the trees uneasy," Emrhys answered.

"We will protect you while you are in the trance," Vaelwyn rasped. "I feel it is important."

After much hemming and hawing, Emrhys reluctantly agreed. He lay on his back with his head in Vaelwyn's lap, her hands placed gently on his forehead. Emrhys breathed deeply but was otherwise completely still for a long time. Then his body began to twitch slightly, and his lips drew back from his teeth in a silent snarl. After a time, he became still again.

Time passed and Alantir and Bedwyr fidgeted. Bedwyr plucked a daisy and threw it at Alantir when she wasn't looking. It stuck in her hair. Getting it out would require touching her and so he hesitated, instead, he got caught staring. Alantir looked at him, questioning *what?* with her eyes but Bedwyr just shook his head awkwardly. Both of them blushed.

Emrys's blue eyes suddenly opened wide and he gulped loudly drawing in air.

"Dark creatures! Here in the forest!" he said. "The awareness of animals is not always advanced enough to identify or distinguish specifically. But there are creatures here that ... feel *wrong* to the wolves I was with. The wolves are ..." he struggled to explain, "they are very territorial."

"Where?" Vaelwyn asked simply.

"Between Garmoniya and Tishina," Emrhys answered.

Emrhys thought back to the first time he had forged this special bond with an animal. His people, the Breacadh an Lae, separated boys from their families at a young age to raise them as warriors. It was a harsh and disciplined life for the young boys but also thrilling. Their young bodies grew hard, their minds disciplined, and their skills with weapons became second to none. All weapons.

They became as deadly with long knives and short axes as they were with longswords and arrows. Two-handed battle axes and maces were also in their training, as was deadly hand-to-hand combat.

On selected days, the boys fought matches against each other from dawn to dusk.

When their seniors determined them ready, the boys were sent out into the wilderness on their own. One at a time. They were given unusual instructions to carry out. They were not told to bring back wolf pelts or bear claws but stories of what the wolves and bears were thinking. They were not instructed on how to accomplish this unusual task; they were simply to get it done. And, despite all their weapons training, they were permitted only a short knife and some water. Nothing that would help them take on a pack of wolves or a towering bear.

When young Emrhys was sent out, he was unsure. After the first few hours on his own, he set about crafting his own spear. He found a long, sturdy piece of wood, and carved one end into a sharp point. He started a fire and used that fire to harden the point of the spear, proud of himself for his skill and ingenuity; he felt better with a familiar weapon in his hands. With newly restored confidence, young Emrhys strode into the deeper part of the wilderness.

It took him a long time to find the trail of a bear, but he finally did it. He tracked behind it, careful to remain downwind as they moved through the forest together. Then, Emrhys stopped to drink some of his water and lost sight of the bear. He looked all around but could not see it; he had lost track of his prey.

He was startled by a roar right behind him. He grabbed his spear and spun around. The bear was even bigger than he'd thought, towering over him. How had it furtively snuck around behind him without making any noise? It was terrifying, its arms upraised with massive paws, each razor-sharp claw at least six inches long. Its gargantuan slobbering jaws widening as it bellowed only feet away from Emrhys.

Emrhys was glad that he had armed himself with a spear as he thrust it at the bear. But the bear shattered the pointed stick with one swipe of its massive paw, bellowing even louder. Emrhys backed away slowly as the bear advanced. Now, he was trapped against a tree and could go no further. Desperately he sought an escape but there was none. Saliva flew from the bear's maw and Emrhys was more terrified than ever before in his young life. Yet, amidst his stress and anxiety, unfamiliar thoughts were starting to bubble up in his mind.

Images of young bear cubs huddled together, sleeping in their den, the taste of raw honeycomb, fresh from the tree where the bees lived, anger at this man-cub intruding on her territory.

He was sharing the bear's thoughts! He did not know how, but he was! Struggling against his own fear, he tried sending thoughts of reassurance to the bear, trying to ensure the bear knew he meant no harm to her cubs and would leave its territory immediately.

The bear backed off.

Emrhys scrambled away. As far from the bear as he could get and, as he wandered through the forest, he tried to remember how he had done it. How had he entered the bear's thoughts? He vaguely remembered the feeling that had preceded it but couldn't recall any specific steps he had taken. How would he be able to recreate that feeling? But he still needed to bring back the thoughts of the wolves in addition to the thoughts of the bear.

As night fell, he could hear a wolf pack in the distance. As much as he wanted to successfully complete his challenge, the thought of facing wolves with nothing but a short knife was not reassuring. However, he was determined to give himself whatever advantage he could, and so, he headed off for a rocky hill that he had passed by earlier. There, Emrhys wedged himself into a rocky crag where he was protected from all sides. The wolves could only approach him from the front, and he had his knife in his hand, small though it was.

He did not have to wait long. A small group of wolves advanced toward him. Slowly, with a stiff-legged gait, their fur raised on their backs. Their yellow eyes held him in baleful glares. The lead wolf sounded a low growl, its lips pulled back and fangs bared. Despite his cleft position, Emrhys would not be safe for long. And without any conscious effort, it happened again. Suddenly, he was sharing the thoughts of the wolves.

Hunger. The thrill of the hunt. Warm flesh and blood from a recent kill.

Emrhys projected his own thoughts; he was a friend, not a foe and the wolves halted their advance, seeming as surprised as he.

The next morning, young Emrhys strode back into the barracks he shared with the young warriors. He was the first one to return and report success with this unusual challenge.

• ———— •◆• ———— •

Emrhys's thoughts returned to the present. His three companions were all staring at him with looks of concern.

"What …" he sputtered. "What is it? Why are you all staring at me like that?"

"Because you were sort of gone again," Bedwyr said.

"Yes, you were in that deep trance at first," Alantir said. "Then you came out of that and told us what you learned from the wolves—but then you were sort of in a trance again for the past few minutes."

"Okay, enough resting now," Vaelwyn said sharply. "I am pleased that you feel yourself again, but we have to pack up and move on to Garmoniya now. Quickly. We gained some useful insights from both trees and wolves—and they both tell us that there is danger in these forests of Skógur!"

CHAPTER FOURTEEN
Lord of Garmoniya

Eight Weeks Before Winter Solstice

Alantir and Bedwyr gaped at the view. The path they had been traveling on had widened as it entered the elven city of Garmoniya and the two travelers from Terra stood and stared. The city was completely integrated into the majestic trees that surrounded them. Buildings that were in the tre-etops themselves, as well as archways and stairways that ran between the trees and up into them. A multi-level city of wood, rope, and stone that rivaled the city of Teilatua in size and scale. There was something intrinsically warm about the city; perhaps the wood construction or the leafy green branches integrated into its every part. There was some activity, but it was relaxed. A few elves here and there going about their business, but not the widespread rushing about they had seen in Teilatua.

There was one group of elves, though, that seemed animated and moving quickly together in the same direction.

"Hey Alantir," Bedwyr said, "I think that I heard one of them say something about an archery contest. Have you ever watched elven archers compete?"

Alantir stopped in her tracks, crossed her arms, and gave Bedwyr a frosty stare.

"What!" he stammered. "Oh yeah, you are a good archer yourself ..."

Alantir arched one eyebrow and continued to drill into him with that frosty stare.

"... So ..." Bedwyr finally spit out, "... you must have competed in archery contests yourself, right? And uh, ... done pretty well ... That is ... I mean to say ... well, you are really good, Alantir, and I would love to see you actually compete someday!"

Alantir laughed and said, "I was just teasing you. But yes, I was actually the best champion archer that ever drew a bow back in our woodland realm of Beechwood."

Bedwyr laughed in return and said, "Modest too, aren't you!"

"Well, I must admit that I have a fatal flaw as an archer," she replied. "I have to be calm—very calm—to do my best. When I am rushed or nervous and can't concentrate, I'm just not as good. This is something that I really have to work on. Maybe you can help me practice, Bedwyr, so that I can learn how to shoot better when I'm nervous."

"Sure, I would love to help you any way that I can," he said. "Let's start by following these elves and watching this archery competition. Maybe you can learn ... uh, maybe you can teach them something."

"Wait a minute, my impetuous young friend," Emrhys rumbled. "Don't you think that you should check with our leader before you go running off in a new kingdom?"

Bedwyr snorted and rolled his eyes at Emrhys.

Alantir sighed heavily and rolled her eyes at Bedwyr.

"He is right, Bed," she said, "we can't just go running off wherever we want whenever we want. And Vaelwyn is standing right here, by the way ..."

Vaelwyn smiled and said, "I had forgotten how impatient and impulsive humans can be—especially the young men! I think that it's perfectly fine to go to this archery contest. After all, judging from the crowds we see, it must be some sort of major event for this kingdom; which means King Mandáron will likely be there instead of in his hall anyway."

"If that's the case," Emrhys said, "then we can greet the king there."

"Yes!" said Bedwyr as he hooked his arm in Alantir's and started off to follow that animated group of elves.

•———— •◆• ————•

"Okay," Alantir said. "I have talked to a number of these elves and this is not really a competition today. It's more like a demonstration. Their leading archer is going to shoot a few rounds to entertain the local crowd."

"Well," mused Bedwyr, "even though you make it sound like it's not a big deal, I think it is."

"Oh," she said archly, "and now you think you are an expert on elven archery exhibitions?"

"No," he laughed. "But I am becoming an expert on Vaelwyn. And I think she is talking to the king over there. Can't be too trivial an event if the king is here."

Emrhys came striding over to them, towering over everyone else in the crowd.

"Vaelwyn wants Alantir to come and meet King Mandáron," he said. "Just Alantir."

Bedwyr started to sputter.

"I will explain later, my friend," Emrys said with a hand on Bedwyr's shoulder. "The reason will be very clear soon enough."

Alantir joined Vaelwyn and was introduced to the king. The king was very gracious in an exaggerated and supercilious sort of way.

"So pleased to have yet another special guest join me here along with my Prime Adeptus friend and her hulking bodyguard," he said. "And my other special guest is the current champion of our formal archery competition," the king said. "As we all know, Garmoniya prides itself on the prowess of our archers, and our champion here holds a special honor. Tallendal is the current holder of the Golden Arrow award."

"Oh, my goodness," exclaimed Alantir. "I was also a champion back in my woodland home. I won the honor of the Ash Arrow several years in a row!"

"An award made from ash wood sounds very rustic, my dear," said the disdainful archery champion. "Perhaps you'd like to show us an example of your woodland style with some of our junior archers, just to make it fair." He smiled dazzlingly.

His rudeness took Alantir aback and she almost stuttered in reply; her attention caught on the elf's glittering teeth.

"I would welcome the opportunity to shoot here today," she replied. "But let's make it a head-to-head match between ourselves. Allow me to provide you with a first-hand opportunity to critique my rustic style."

"All right then," replied the unabashed champion. "We will meet just over there in a few minutes."

Alantir stalked over to where Bedwyr stood with their horses and supplies. He knew enough to stand back, as she rummaged angrily through her gear.

"Easy, my friend, easy," he said softly. "Don't let him get you so rattled that you can't shoot straight."

Meanwhile, Tallendal stretched side to side and back to front, bending first one knee and then the other. He looked like a spoiled cat who'd gotten accustomed to cream. Everything about him was bronze, from his chestnut-copper hair to his marigold tunic, all the way to his aventurine-capped teeth. As the awarded Golden Arrow champion of Garmoniya, he had developed a haughty air, becoming ever more arrogant with every successive win. His company was arduous and his manner unpleasant. He had few friends but remained in King Mandáron's favor as a trophy, the city's pride and pleasure. As supercilious as he was, his aim was religiously revered.

"There is something about that arrogant elf that I just don't like," grumbled Bedwyr, watching Tallendal's gymnastics. He frowned in thought, his hand on the hilt of his sword. "I hope you're a better shot than he is."

"I am very good," Alantir replied. "We will just have to see."

A match had been arranged, partly to welcome the visitors and partly to show-off Garmoniya and underscore its prowess in the Pan Ljós Archery Games. These were a much bigger deal in the Skógur realm than anywhere else in Ljós and had garnered a loyal following. Compared to Terra, archery here was taken very seriously.

Tallendal sauntered over and greeted Alantir, joining her at the shooting line.

"Not too late to change your mind, my dear," he said. "After all, you're not just competing in front of your granny and a few other simpletons. This is Garmoniya!"

Alantir took a deep breath, making an extra effort to remain calm. She exhaled sharply and said sweetly," Thank you for your concern, but I am sure that we will all learn something new here today."

Tallendal looked at a loss for words—for once—and sauntered back to his position.

There were a series of stations with different target arrangements along the line where they would take turns drawing their bows and shooting. They both had to complete three shots successfully at each station.

The first was fairly simple and they each split the willow wand with three shots.

The second had a metal ring the size of an outstretched hand suspended from a rope in front of the willow wand. The arrows had to pass through the ring before splitting the willow wand. Once again, they each split the willow with three shots.

The third had an additional ring, hanging between the first ring and the willow wand, the size of a clenched fist. Each shot had to clear the rings and then split the willow wand. These rings swayed in the breeze. The fletching on one of Alantir's arrows grazed the inner ring, but she still managed to split the willow wand with three shots. As did Tallendal.

The fourth and final station added yet another ring, only half the size of the second, and the breeze was picking up.

Alantir completed her first two shots without a problem. On her third, she concentrated closely as the three rings swayed in different directions in the breeze. When she released her third arrow, it sped through all three rings and split the willow wand.

Tallendal looked nervous as he stepped forward. He completed his first shot without a hitch, concentrated closely on his second, and when he released, his arrow scraped the inner edge of the third ring and failed to split the willow wand.

There was silence from the onlookers.

Alantir heard clapping behind her, and as she turned, she was surprised to see that it was King Mandáron.

"Bravo," the king said. "Well done, young Alantir. The Ash Arrow trumps the Golden Arrow, after all. Tallendal is lucky that this was an informal match and not a formal competition or you might have claimed his Golden Arrow for yourself."

He laughed, his broad grin widening and Bedwyr noticed the smile did not reach his eyes. As the king and his retinue moved away from the open field and back toward the trees the king said, "Please join me for dinner tonight so that I can welcome you properly. Meet me in my reception hall shortly before dinner."

Tallendal threw his bow on the ground and stalked off in a huff.

Alantir gave a brief bow of thanks and then pulled Bedwyr close for a huge hug. She lingered a bit, enjoying the feel of his muscular form pressed firmly against her. He moved his hands down to her lower back and pulled her in tighter.

"Congratulations, Alantir," boomed Emrhys, thoroughly pleased by the whole event. "You made that arrogant elf eat his hat!"

Bedwyr and Alantir broke off their hug, laughing at Emrhys's outburst, and each glanced curiously at the other, each a bit short of breath and slightly flushed.

King Mandáron's hall was built on suspended supports between two of the largest trees in Garmoniya and was open along both of the long sides. One side opened back to the east and looked over the treetop city of Garmoniya.

The other side opened to the west, looking out through a thin scattering of trees to the coastline and the western sea. The stairway that led from the forest floor up to the king's hall was in the form of a wide spiral that wound around the outside of a very large tree at the far western end of the city. Just when Bedwyr thought they could not get any higher, they reached the landing.

The king himself was splendidly attired in a dark green silk tunic with a pattern of interwoven tree leaves subtly worked into the dark green silk. His long, thin blond hair was pulled back into a long ponytail. The pulled-back hair highlighted his pointed ears. He wore a gold circlet on his brow and very soft brown leather boots. He had a vaguely imperious air as he greeted the travelers again.

"Greetings to you, Vaelwyn," he greeted them. "And to you, Emrhys." And then he stepped back, looking a bit startled.

"You have brought a human to my halls now," the king said sharply. "You know, of course, that I used to delight in hunting and trapping humans before the Great Sundering. There was not much sport in the hunting, because they are all so slow and stupid." He eyed Bedwyr as he spoke, sizing him up in a calculated fashion. "We enjoyed ourselves far more trapping them or tricking them, often holding them captive in our Fae realm to serve and entertain us. In the best of these entertainments, we would pit them in fights against each other and place wagers ..." He smiled nastily, "on which of the creatures would win."

Bedwyr was visibly bristling, and Alantir glanced worriedly between him and King Mandáron. Emrhys placed his large hand on Bedwyr's shoulder in a calm and reassuring fashion.

"You always were unusually cruel for an Álfur, Mandáron," Emrhys rumbled. "Particularly for one of the ten kings here.

Ljós is fortunate that your cruelty toward humans is so unusual amongst the royalty of the realm."

"Ah, my friend, I see you don't fully understand," Mandáron replied. "First, don't mistake the kindness and understanding of some of my peers for enlightenment. It is naiveté. Nothing more. Many of my fellow Álfur kings and queens are simply soft and weak, as well as misguided." The king did not look abashed or defensive as he spoke. In fact, he looked relaxed and supremely confident.

"Second, don't be so sure that my own views and attitudes are really so unusual among Álfur royalty. There are more who share my opinions about the natural supremacy of the Álfur than you may think. Some share my belief that humans must be our subjects, not our equals. Our history is tens of thousands of years older, and our knowledge and wisdom far superior, as is our culture. The magic we wield is a dramatic example of our natural superiority This is not an unpopular view."

"Your Majesty, let us not sidetrack our meeting with unpleasant discussions," Vaelwyn smoothly interrupted. "As we introduced earlier, this is Alantir of the woodland elves of Terra."

"Well, certainly more interesting than a human," replied the king. "And an excellent archer! Is this the one referred to in the dispatches from the silver elves?"

"Yes, Mandáron," Vaelwyn replied. "We believe Alantir is a very distant relative of your own royal family, based upon ancestry dating back to before the Great Sundering."

"Step closer, my dear," Mandáron instructed Alantir. "You are a lovely young elf, although your dark hair is very unusual for our royal family. Mixture with other bloodlines, one supposes. And your amulet," he said, light dancing in his small, rounded eyes. "Might I examine it before we move to the dining hall?"

Somewhat reluctantly, Alantir held it out for him.

"Yes," he said greedily. "This is Skógur workmanship. Now, that is interesting."

<hr/>

The dining hall was located one floor below the king's reception hall and was also open along the long sides on both the east and the west. The view to the west held their attention initially, with the setting sun over the western sea visible through the trees. As the dark of night settled in, however, the view to the east captured more of their attention. As the torches and candles were illuminated throughout the scattered, multi-level city, it looked like countless fireflies interspersed within the branches of the trees. There was a small, warm glow in every group of branches wherever they looked. A unique and lovely panorama that literally filled their entire view to the east.

The candles and torches were lit inside the dining hall as well. One delicious course after another was served. The travelers had not realized how hungry they were until all of this marvelous food was placed in front of them. Just when they reached the point where they could not imagine eating another bite, the king raised his glass to make a toast. As everyone else also raised their glasses, the king exclaimed, "Hail to Skógur! The bright green gem in the crown of Ljós!"

"I have invited some special guests to join us in addition to you travelers from Terra," said the king. "One is my cousin, Fallyrin, who we believe to be our closest living relative to the woodland elves in Terra that were once a part of our tribe."

A lovely older female elf with golden hair stood and bowed her head slightly. "I welcome you, Alantir, as a long-lost member of our royal family." Alantir nodded in turn as a respectful acknowledgment of this warm greeting.

"Yes, the stories of our long-lost cousins, the woodland elves of Terra, have been passed down from mother to daughter for many generations," Fallyrin said. "A tragic story really. Those poor woodland elves loved their trees so much, you see, that they chose to remain in Terra at the time of the Great Sundering, losing their magic and their immortality. Why, it is even said ..."

"My dear Fallyrin," the king interrupted, "would you be good enough to tell us the part that pertains to Alantir?"

"Oh yes," she replied, "of course, of course. I do so easily get off track, you see. Now where was I ... oh yes, our family that remained in Ljós felt so badly about their cousins in Terra that they gave them a priceless gift to ease their lives in the darkness of Terra, cut off from all magic. And mortal now as well! Oh, the poor dears ..."

"The gift, Fallyrin, the gift," the king interjected.

"Of course, of course," she replied. The gift was the beautiful amulet that Alantir is wearing right now. It can embody a powerful concentration of the elemental magic of Earth that is our unique birthright here in Skógur. This link to our powerful Skógur magic was meant to be a comfort to our lost cousins in Terra—cut off from the Light of Ljós and the magic of Earth—forever. Very sad, really. Poor dears ..."

"And that, my guests, is our confirmation of Alantir's heritage," the king concluded. "And her rightful place here amongst the Álfur of Skógur."

The king turned to look directly at Alantir and scowled as he noticed that she sat next to Bedwyr. Very closely next to Bedwyr.

"If you two are not too busy," Vaelwyn broke in. "We need

to prepare for Alantir's amulet ceremony tomorrow. We need to be in place when the sun is at its midday height."

"Which means," she said as she glanced back at the king, "that you two need to leave now—separately—and get some sleep!"

— ◆ —

The next day found Alantir and Bedwyr dressed once again in white tunics and leggings. This time, they had been directed to a wide clearing right on the coastline that ran along the western boundary of the forest near Garmoniya.

They completed the ceremony, Emrhys once more placing his hand on Alantir's left shoulder and Bedwyr on Alantir's right. When Alantir had placed her amulet over the king's ring, he called out, chanting the spell:

"*Solas, an iarthair! An chré, Cumholt!*" Light of the West! Power of Earth!

Large tree roots burst through the soil and entwined in front of the king. He placed the amulet on top of the column of tree roots as they descended into a churning mass of soil. The ground trembled, and in their place a large flower emerged. The flower opened in front of the king, and he removed the amulet, now glowing a bright and luminescent green. Then, the king stepped forward to place the amulet back around Alantir's neck ...

"*Now you fool,*" hissed Uulwei. "*You are going to miss your chance to take the amulet! Again!*"

"*Shut up, you idiot!*" Magwei hissed back. "*Our ability to reach into Ljós from here in the astral plane is very limited – which you would know if you weren't so stupid!*"

"*I can't get there physically,*" he continued, "*so I have to use what few shadows I can find in that damned land of Light to do my work for me. Fortunately, these foolish Álfur*" *cannot see me while I conjure the shadows in their realm from here in the astral plane."*

Magwei scowled as he concentrated, muttering some arcane words in a strange tongue and gesturing with his gnarled and twisted hands.

A shadow fell across the king's hands as he moved the amulet toward Alantir's neck. The amulet suddenly felt very heavy and started to slip from the king's grasp.

"Mandáron!" yelled Emrhys. "Careful there, the amulet is falling from your grasp!"

"It is not just slipping!" the king shouted. "It is being pulled! How is this possible?"

The king now had both hands on the amulet's chain, tugging hard. But it was being inexorably pulled deeper into the shadow.

Back in the astral plane Magwei smiled broadly and increased his muttering and his gestures.

Bright white light and warmth suddenly flooded the struggling figures as Vaelwyn held her rune staff aloft and it pulsed with the power of Light.

"Quickly you fool!" she shouted. "Clasp the amulet around her neck! Complete the ceremony!"

The king finally clasped the amulet's chain around Alantir's neck and the shadows were no longer to be seen in the bright white light from Vaelwyn's conjuring.

Magwei cursed loudly.

Then the earth at Alantir's feet trembled slightly. There was a strong scent of fresh, dark soil as the ground beneath her feet began to churn. A large circle surrounded her, growing and continuing to churn more quickly as Alantir started to sink into the soft soil.

When she reached her knees, Alantir outstretched her arms and commanded, "Stop!"

The soil ceased its churning and began to restore itself.

Bedwyr started to run to Alantir's side, but Emrhys put his arm out to restrain him.

"Easy lad," he said softly. "Don't step in front of the king—certainly not this king."

King Mandáron stepped forward and said, "You have moved further down the path that will return you to your people. Although the magical powers within you have not yet been fully awakened, your amulet now possesses strong power to control the elemental power of the earth."

"I am humbled, Lord King," she replied. "But resolute against Shadow."

"Yes, yes. You better guard that amulet well, my dear," the king said slyly with a sidelong look at her amulet. "Many there are who would take it from you.

"There is something else that I would like to discuss with you later," the king continued. "In my reception hall late tomorrow—just before sunset."

Bedwyr and Alantir sat next to each other on a large fallen tree trunk that overlooked the sea, enjoying the afternoon sun and the faint scent of salt in the air from the sea below.

"I have never known a human," said Alantir as she played with the end of her long braid. "But you have become my closest friend during our travels here in Ljós."

"And you mine," Bedwyr replied as he wrapped his arm around Alantir. "I think both our friendship and adventures are just beginning."

"What do you want to do in the future, Bedwyr?" asked Alantir. "Once we have completed whatever we must do here."

"It may sound crazy," he replied. "But I would like to return here to Ljós and train to be a hawk-warrior. First, I must make sure my brother Dylan is well. I must return to Terra, but then, if they will have me here, then I would return."

"As would I," Alantir replied. "I, too, must first satisfy myself if I have any remaining family that are alive and safe, but then I would also like to return to Ljós."

Bedwyr tightened his hug and felt her warm body against his. Alantir turned to look at him, and he was lost in her gaze for a moment. She looked so beautiful right now, framed in the sunlight. And her back and shoulders felt warm and strong under his arm. His mouth felt dry, and his palms felt damp. In this moment, Bedwyr wanted nothing more than to fully embrace his friend and kiss her passionately. But he did not want to ruin their friendship if she did not feel that same way. Bedwyr could feel the warmth of her affection for him, but he could not be certain that she would welcome his kiss.

"It is probably getting late enough for us to start walking back," Bedwyr said suddenly.

He thought that he saw a look of annoyance flicker across Alantir's features.

"Yes," she snapped. "Of course. Why would we want to keep sitting here alone? And I suppose that I do not want to be unprepared for my audience with the king tomorrow."

Bedwyr suddenly hugged her in his arms, throwing caution to the wind. He touched her face tenderly as he brushed his lips against hers. Alantir buried her hands in his hair and kissed him tenderly—and then passionately. They eagerly exchanged kisses and increasingly passionate caresses.

"Wait ..." she mumbled. "Oh, I want you so much Bedwyr. But not here, not now. I want something more special for us—not a log in the woods."

Bedwyr reluctantly pulled himself away, his hair disheveled, and looked at her with a warm, soft look in his eyes.

"I want you too, Alantir," he said. "More than I have ever wanted anyone else. But I want you without hesitation or reservation. So I can wait until you feel the time is right."

They looked at each other intently for long moments. Then she threw herself back into his embrace and his passionate kisses and they rolled onto the forest floor, lost in each other's arms.

Alantir was dressed in the fine silk clothes that had been left in her room for her. Dark green, of course. She and her companions waited for the king's arrival. They admired the view of the setting sun from the western side of the hall. Through the trees, they could see the sun beginning its descent towards the horizon of the sea, with an increasingly deep red glow starting to spread across the sky.

King Mandáron, Elven Lord of Ljós, entered the hall. He carried himself, as always, with a regal air. Where the two kings in Fjall were sometimes more relaxed and informal, this king of Skógur was always formal and aloof. He looked every bit the elven lord, with his impeccable attire, his regal bearing, and his hall held open and aloft among the treetops of Garmoniya.

The king stepped in front of his throne and commanded, "Alantir, please approach."

As Alantir stood in front of the king, he said, "Please kneel."

Alantir was a bit confused about what this was all about, but she knelt on the soft, thick rug in front of the throne. One of the king's courtiers stepped forward, bearing a velvet cushion. The king lifted a small gold circlet with a deep green emerald set in the front.

As he settled the gold circlet on Alantir's head, he said, "In recognition of your distant ancestry, I confirm you, Alantir, as a princess of the High Elves of Skógur. Welcome back to your people!"

Alantir was stunned. So was Bedwyr.

"I... I don't know what to say," she stuttered.

"Don't say anything right now," said the king. "Just enjoy the moment. With your new status, you will also face an important decision.

The hall had been buzzing with excitement, but the king raised his hands and signaled for silence. Once the hall was quiet, the king said, "The decision that you will now have to make, Princess Alantir, is whether you wish to remain mortal or to reclaim the immortality that was the birthright of your ancestors."

The hall remained quiet. Alantir and Bedwyr looked at each other. They both looked stunned. And confused.

CHAPTER FIFTEEN

Shadows in the Forest

Seven Weeks Before Winter Solstice

After almost a week in Garmoniya, it was time to leave and a palpable sense of relief combined with trepidation infused the group as Emrhys led them eastward through the forest. They were traveling to the White Henge but had to make their way through a long stretch of forest deep within Skógur before reaching the open plains.

Emrhys thought back now, to a previous encounter many years ago with King Mandáron in these same forests.

He was hunting wild boar with the king and a small group of the king's hand-picked favorites. Tracking the boar through dense underbrush up to rocky outcroppings around a hillside where their small group had spread out. A shout of surprise rang out, and a pair of royal elves emerged from the underbrush with something between them. But it was not a wild boar, it was a goblin.

The goblin looked injured as it staggered forward and fell on its face in front of the king.

"Well, well," said Mandáron. "We've not seen your kind in Ljós for a wide span of years. Are there any more of your disgusting friends hiding around here?"

The goblin seemed too weak to muster anything more than mumble in the negative. His head hung and there were angry red patches on his skin. Short and spindly with sallow skin, he had sharp teeth and sharp claws. Emrhys still remembered the creature's horrible smell, like carrion. Suddenly the goblin raised his head, snarled at the king's elves around him, and spat.

The king yelled, "I want every dark crack and crevice searched for any more of these vermin. If you find any, drag them out or kill them where they cower! Stab them, spear them, burn them!"

Emrhys shared the king's powerful revulsion for goblins. And he was puzzled and concerned that this creature of the Dark Fae was here in Ljós. But he also knew the extreme nature of the king's brutal interrogation techniques.

After hours of fruitless searching and many rounds of unproductive interrogation, the king became frustrated.

"My king, you tax yourself too much. It is not worth getting so impatient and annoyed. If the creature has companions nearby, your elves will find them," Emrhys said.

But Mandáron was a stubborn and arrogant elven king.

"String it up by its thumbs!" the king commanded. "And light a fire underneath it. Then light torches from that fire and set the underbrush on fire. If there are any more of them in hiding, we will smoke them out or burn them alive."

Emrhys remembered the concern he saw amongst the king's

elves that day at the prospect of setting fire to their beloved forest. They grumbled and dragged their feet uncharacteristically. To Emrhys, these elves clearly seemed concerned about the cost of destroying scores of trees that were centuries old.

The hillside was soon engulfed in flames, and the bottom of the goblin's feet were blackened where the smaller fire had burned them. It had stopped screaming and struggling a long time ago, but it was not dead yet. Emrhys was sickened. He had no love of goblins and no hesitation to take their lives in battle, but he had no tolerance for unnecessary cruelty. And for no discernible purpose, since no other goblins were discovered.

"Cut it down!" ordered King Mandáron. "And drag what's left of it over here."

The king's company dutifully cut down the miserable goblin and dragged it over to the king.

He kicked at the half-conscious creature viciously. "So," the king said to its unresponsive form, "you hope to keep your secrets from me? I think not. I will have my elves carve the skin from your living body, strip by strip until you tell me what you know of your goblin kind here in Ljós."

Emrhys wrinkled his brow in disgust. Not for the first time, Emrhys felt that there was something very dark about King Mandáron. This feeling made him uneasy in the king's presence.

"Start with its toes and feet until you reach its knees. Then shift to its fingers and hands, up to the elbows. Perhaps it will talk while being flayed alive."

Hours later, the king's elves came forward to tell him that there was no life left in the goblin. And he had never offered any new information.

"Throw that disgusting sack of bones on the fire," said the king. "We return home. I have lost interest in hunting wild boar today."

Emrhys' thoughts returned to the present as Alantir pulled her mount alongside him and looked at him strangely. He felt as though he could still smell the smoke from his memory.

"What do you think of my last meeting with the king and his offer to return me to full status as one of the Álfur?" she asked.

He knew very well that this king never offered anything to anybody unless there was something in it for him. Emrhys took a minute to look around, warmed a bit by the sunlight filtering through the tree branches. Something seemed off, but he could not place it. He drew a deep breath, savoring the smells of the forest.

"Have you considered all of the implications here?" Emrhys asked her. "Including any secret agenda of his own that the king might have?"

Alantir looked surprised and gave Emrhys an apprising look.

"And, have you also considered the implications of the prospective immortality that goes with being restored to existence as a full Álfur? For example, how would you handle watching any of your remaining family grow old and die while you remain forever young and healthy?"

"And what about Bedwyr?"

As Alantir considered his words, Emrhys noticed the silence. That was what seemed unusual. There was no bird-song on this pleasant sunny afternoon in the forest. Just the jangling of the tack, the sound of the hooves on the packed dirt, and the occasional snort from the horses carrying their group. He stopped on the path ahead and swiveled his head to the right. Suddenly every part of his giant body tensed and he was fully alert. Emrhys continued to look to his right, due south into the heart of the forest. With surprising speed, he darted from the path, crashing into the foliage.

As he moved, he pulled his longsword, *Dawnslayer*, off his shoulder and shouted back to his companions, "Prepare yourselves!" he shouted. "An enemy is upon us."

Vaelwyn and Bedwyr stood back-to-back on the path. Vaelwyn had her rune staff raised in her right hand, and it was crackling slightly with silver flashes of energy. Bedwyr held his sword firmly, crouched in a ready stance. Behind them, Alantir had drawn her first arrow. Then Emrhys was back with them.

"Form up with a half-circle now!" Emrhys barked, taking the point position. "A large band of goblins is coming!"

"What!?" gasped Alantir, her eyes round with shock.

"Sharp teeth and claws, and their stone spears, axes, and clubs can kill as easily as a man's sword," Vaelwyn said calmly. "Be on your guard."

"Killing frenzy like a human berserker," continued Emrhys. "Fifty or sixty goblins like this can easily overwhelm a smaller group like our own."

"How do I kill the nasty little things?" asked Bedwyr.

"Just cut their bloody heads off," thundered Emrhys. "Or slash them to bits."

And then they were in it.

Bedwyr was stunned for a moment when the frenzied pack of goblins burst from the woods but Emrhys had bought them some time to prepare. The giant Caomhnoir wielded his longsword in one hand and his black axe mace in the other, cutting down goblins like he was scything wheat. Instantly, he'd cut down a dozen or more.

Bedwyr's blood boiled, his muscles tensed, and a red haze obscured his vision. He could see the goblins easily enough—and they were everywhere. He immediately started hacking them down with his sword.

The first goblin was right there in front of him. Mouth agape, sharp jagged teeth hissing at him. Bedwyr rammed his sword right down its throat. He could feel the sword hesitate here and there as it slashed through goblin flesh. Bedwyr found that feeling strangely satisfying. And then he was truly lost to his bloodlust.

He spun to his right side and thrust his sword into the guts of another goblin. He relished the feel of his sword pushing through the tough outer skin and then sliding smoothly through the goblins guys inside. Blood spurting everywhere delighted Bedwyr. He deeply inhaled the iron tang of fresh blood that hung in the air.

Bedwyr howled with joy—lost in his bloodlust.

Alantir heard him howling and she glanced over for just a moments with concern on her face—then nocked another arrow and drew—goblins were scrambling to reach her from every direction.

Bedwyr slammed the flat of his sword into the back of another goblin's head knocking him to the ground. He thought to take his time with this one, pinning it to the ground with his boot. But the bloodlust consumed him completely now. It drove him to kill this one quickly and move on to the next. So Bedwyr grabbed his short-handled battle axe in his other hand and hacked off the goblin's arm at the shoulder. He loved the feel of his axe slicing through goblin flesh—and then crunching through bone. And then he spun to pursue his next target—howling with glee again.

"Bedwyr!" Alantir called. "Bedwyr! I need you!" She was trying to bring him out of it.

The tall and muscular young warrior was lost to his blood-lust and barely heard Alantir's calls as he punched his sword through the side of another goblin. He relished the spurting blood and the goblin's dying cries.

Finally, Alantir's calls started to penetrate his awareness.

Bedwyr shook his head a few times, breathless from his exertions. Dead, stinking goblin carcasses lay slaughtered all around him.

He blinked his eyes a few times and shook his head again.

"Bed!" Alantir called out. "Are you all right? Are you back in control of yourself?"

"Aye ..." he stammered. "Aye! All good here. Look to yourself!"

As Bedwyr regained awareness of his surroundings, his eyes widened as he saw Emrhys.

Bedwyr watched as one goblin rolled on the ground in front of Emrhys. Once below Emrhys feet, the goblin leaped up mightily and stabbed his stone spear into Emrhys' gut with savage force. The stone spear was deflected by some magic in Emrhys' tunic and the goblin's head was rolling on the ground in the blink of an eye.

In another instant, two goblins attacked Emrhys at the same time, one from the front and one from the back. Emrhys moved to the side so fast that Bedwyr only saw a blur of movement. Before he could draw another breath, Bedwyr saw the longsword, Dawnslayer, hew down both goblins in one fell swoop from the side.

Another moment of time and there was a goblin leaping down from a branch above Emrhys, stone axe swinging for his unprotected neck. The black steel axe of Emrhys whirled around at blinding speed and clove the goblin's arm off at the shoulder. Goblin, severed arm, and loose stone axe all clattered to the forest floor and lay still on that blood-soaked ground.

"You forgot to tell us about the smell!" Alantir shouted. "Disgusting! Like rotten eggs!"

She loosed one arrow after another as she spoke and had a dozen or more down quickly.

Bedwyr had several goblin heads rolling on the forest floor at his feet, and Vaelwyn was putting them down two at a time with each thrust of her rune staff. There must have been thirty goblins fallen already. And then Emrhys really went to war.

Bedwyr looked on in astonishment at Emrhys the killing machine. He was not just big; he was also blazingly fast and ruthlessly efficient.

He whirled through the remaining pack of goblins and one could hardly identify where the sword or axe mace was at any point in space; it all blurred together in a hazy, fast-moving trail of death. The individual scenes of carnage and slaughter all blurred together.

One-minute Emrhys was running a goblin through with his longsword. A moment later and Emrhys was whirling his black steel axe-mace and striking off the heads of one goblin after another. The shrieks and screams of slaughtered goblins were ringing in Bedwyr's ears.

Alantir and Vaelwyn easily picked off the few remaining goblin stragglers as the space around them gradually transitioned from a noisy, frenzied slaughter ground to the quiet space of only moments before.

Emrhys calmly cleaned the goblin blood from his weapons.

"Oh, by all the stars in the sky!" Alantir said. "They smell even worse when they're dead! I'd not have thought that possible!"

"Alantir, retrieve your arrows and clean them," Emrhys instructed. "Bedwyr, pack up all of our gear as soon as you clean your sword."

"I'll burn the bodies," Vaelwyn said. "It shouldn't deplete too much of my reserves."

Emrhys nodded gratefully. "Do it," he answered. "We need to be well away from here before another band of goblins gets the scent."

Bedwyr calmed the horses. The brief but savage battle had left them terrified. These were well-trained horses but encounters with the creatures of Shadow apparently spooked them more than normal battles. Once the horses were calmed, Bedwyr loaded up all their gear. Alantir helped him once she had finished with her arrows. The woodlands around them were calm and quiet now. The old growth trees were majestic. With enormous trunks and the lowest branches high above their heads. The top of the forest canopy seemed impossibly high. On a normal day, this would be a beautiful stretch of forest.

"I think I know what you are feeling," Alantir said. "These trees inspire reverence, don't they. They are even more awe inspiring than the trees back in my woodland home. And I never thought that I would feel that way about any other trees."

Soon enough, their group was moving quickly down the path and away from the grisly battle scene. Vaelwyn had incinerated the goblin bodies, reducing their lumpy forms to ash with a few simple words as brilliant white light flashed from her rune staff.

"It's too soon," the others heard Emrhys say to Vaelwyn. "I don't even know if it will work again this soon."

"We must take advantage of their extended range," Vaelwyn replied. "The bears will be easier to bond with as the animal totem of your people. We need you to enter that trance state again and merge your consciousness with any bears in this area. Then you will be able to tell us if there are any other threats ahead of us in this forest, and which path will be the safest."

"I'll try," Emrhys said, giving in. "But we must be fast! I must quickly recover before another band finds us."

As before, Vaelwyn stood by as Emrhys got into position, then helped him ease into the necessary trance state.

His companions watched the surrounding forest while Emrhys drifted deep in his bond with the bears. He snarled and twitched his arms. His fingers were tightly curled as though he were swiping at something. Slowly, Emrhys emerged again from his bond. He looked concerned.

"The bears are restless. There are more large goblin bands between here and Tishina but they seem to be heading to the small mountain range beyond the Skógur forests and—" he broke off, frowning.

"What else, Emrhys?" Vaelwyn urged, her brow furrowed in concern.

"There's something else ... Something that bothers them more than goblins, but they cannot identify. A darkness spread along a stretch of the border where the open plains begin."

"We must pass that border and cross the plains to reach the White Henge," said Vaelwyn. There is no alternative; we will just have to be wary."

"Trolls?" asked Bedwyr.

"No, the bears could identify trolls," answered Emrhys. "Whatever this darkness is, the bears have no words for it. Not in their language. They just project images of shadows moving amongst the trees."

"Oh no!" Alantir gasped. "Not here! Not again!"

Everyone turned to look at her, questioning the sudden outburst.

"I'm afraid that this darkness they see is—are—those awful living shadows," said Alantir. "They killed my friends and family in Terra. These are terrible things, and they are almost impossible to see in the dark spaces between the trees."

•————— ◆ —————•

"What is it that you think this 'darkness' could be?" Bedwyr asked Alantir as they continued their passage through the forest.

"I don't know for certain," Alantir replied. "But it does not sound good at all. It sounds like those living shadows that killed my friends and family back in Beechwood."

A sense of paranoia and alarm came surging back, filling her with fear. She turned, thinking she saw a flicker at the edge of her vision, but there was nothing there.

Vaelwyn watched her carefully, finally speaking, "We will have to watch for anything at all out of the ordinary. If these are the living shadows of Myrkur, they will not bear contact with iron or direct sunlight. We must use this to our advantage."

"What is it about iron?" asked Bedwyr. "Why does iron keep them away?"

"The touch of iron is fatal to all Fae," answered Vaelwyn.

Alantir saw another flicker, and the sudden certainty the shadows were here triggered a flash of terror. Vaelwyn saw it, too.

"Emrhys! Bedwyr!" Vaelwyn called. "You both bear iron. Form a circle around Alantir. Now!"

"Up ahead to the left," Emrhys called out. "I see a larger clearing—sunlight. We must get there!"

They carefully moved forward, with Alantir in their midst, brandishing naked steel before them. Vaelwyn protected the rear, her rune staff illuminating bright white light to keep shadows at bay. Their horses followed behind at a distance, but that is not what the shadows wanted.

The group reached the large, sunlit clearing and huddled in the center.

"This may work for now," said Emrhys. "But we still have a good bit of dark forest that we have to pass through, and we cannot stay here forever."

"The day is fading, and the shadows grow larger the longer we wait," Bedwyr said, his eyes always checking on Alantir.

The group recreated their formation and carefully moved forward, slowly. They made good progress, though they could see the shadows flickering just a short distance from their path as they went. As the day lengthened, the shadows continued to grow.

"Sacred oak trees!" Bedwyr exclaimed, "What is that!"

"That looks like one of the gölge yürüteç," said Emrhys. "But how can that be? They should not be able to enter Ljós. The Elemental Seals have not failed completely."

"My horse does not like this," Alantir said. "She is going wild. And so are all the other horses."

Magwei's tall dark silhouette on the path ahead menacingly blocked their path forward.

"He is not actually here. He cannot be," Vaelwyn stated. "This must be an avatar that he is projecting into Ljós. I have heard that this thing is possible from the astral plane, but I have never actually seen it done before."

Magwei drew himself up to his full height and threw back his cloak. A ball of dark energy spun wildly between his hands. Miniature black tornados and small bright lightning flashes roiled within.

"Even my avatar can draw enough power to challenge you in your own realm, Adeptus," Magwei sneered. "I had heard that the highly vaunted Adepti had admitted a ridiculously young woman as one of their Prime members. How far the mighty have fallen in these later ages."

Then he hurled his dark spell toward Vaelwyn.

Vaelwyn raised her hands quickly and spoke a few words in the elven tongue. A circular shape fashioned from filaments of bright light appeared. It looked like an illuminated spider web. Vaelwyn gestured with her hand. Magwei's ominous black globe of dark magic was caught in her net of light.

Vaelwyn flicked her hand contemptuously and her net tossed the dark globe back at Magwei. He pulled his cloak in front of himself and the dark magic was absorbed by his cloak.

"Let's see if you can protect your precious companions as easily as you protect yourself!" Magwei shouted.

And he threw both hands toward Bedwyr and Alantir. It looked like two clouds of tiny black needles were hurtling toward them. Each cloud had dozens of small black icicles traveling very fast. Right at them.

"Drop to the ground!" Emrhys shouted. "Now!"

"Those black icicles are conjured with elemental magic of the Dark Fae," he said. "They are highly poisonous. No medicine can cure a wound caused by ice or magma magic wrought from the bones of the Earth."

A wall of fire sprang up in front of them before they could drop to the ground. And the black icicles were vaporized. A red glow was fading from Vaelwyn's ring as she lowered her hand.

"You are really making me angry now!" shouted Magwei.

Vaelwyn and Magwei faced each other on the forest path, and Emrhys held the horses back with Bedwyr and Alantir.

A silver glow surrounded Vaelwyn. A faint hum could be heard as the glow grew.

A dark shadowy aura surrounded Magwei, and a crackling sound could be heard. It sounded like bacon frying, but it smelled like rotten eggs.

Bedwyr felt the hair rise on the back of his neck. Some memory was stirring in the back of his mind. *What was it?*

"You know that you cannot protect yourself and your companions at the same time, child," Magwei growled at

Vaelwyn. "Prepare yourself for a dark magic assault like you have never seen!"

Something about iron, Bedwyr mused. *But what exactly?*

The silver glow around Vaelwyn expanded and strengthened. There appeared to be a tangible sphere around her now. And the shadowy aura surrounded Magwei with an irregular pulsing boundary.

Dark clouds and flashes of small jagged lightning bolts raced across the surface of the dark aura around Magwei. The warm glow of moonlight and sparkle of starlight flickered from the sphere around Vaelwyn.

Magwei visibly moved his hands inside his dark cloud.

"I remember now!" exclaimed Bedwyr.

Magwei raised his hands above his head and the dark shadows around him roiled and pulsed madly.

Bedwyr threw his steel battle axe at Magwei. It spun end over end as it hurtled toward the head of the avatar within the dark cloud.

"No!" Magwei screeched.

The dark shadows were split asunder by the iron in the axe tumbling through them. The avatar of Magwei was broken into pieces and started to fade.

"You have made a terrible enemy today, boy," Magwei shouted at Bedwyr. "You will regret your interference someday. This I promise you!"

"Brave words from a wisp of smoke!" Bedwyr shouted back.

And Magwei's avatar dissipated back to the astral plane.

"Nice work Bedwyr," Emrhys said as he clapped him on the back. "You were smart to remember the effect that iron has on the Fae, and quick to act."

"You were really brave too Bedwyr," Alantir added. "You did not hesitate to confront one of those gölge yürüteç."

"Aye," Bedwyr growled. "That was one of those bastards

behind the slaughter of our families. I only wish that he had been here in person so that I could sink my sword or axe in his actual flesh!"

"Look around us now, though," Emrhys interrupted. "We still have to get out of this forest."

The living shadows had continued to encroach on them from both sides. The path ahead had continued to narrow, and now a solid wall lay directly ahead of them.

Emrhys surged into action, both of his weapons whirling as he cut into the dark with black steel and *Dawnslayer*'s bright blade. The wall shuddered, and great rents appeared where Emrhys' weapons struck. The shadows pulled back and then surged and closed again.

"There are too many!" he thundered. "We can keep them at bay, for now. But we cannot force our way through. This will only get worse as night falls!"

Vaelwyn took a deep breath, shook off her weariness, and tapped her rune staff on the ground, bending on one knee. Her right hand was clasped at the base of her rune staff, touching the ground, and her ring glowed with a faint red light.

"Ceiliúradh a dhéanamh, Solas!" she cried, and then slid her hand up her rune staff as she stood.

Her right hand shot up from the top, and a bright red sphere surrounded her and her traveling companions. The sphere expanded. Beyond it, a blinding white light spilled into the dark, banning it. The surface of the sphere crackled with energy.

"Begone evil spawn of the Shadow!" she shouted, straining. Her voice reverberated in an echo into the night as she struggled to stand, the power draining her rapidly. Then she turned to look at the others. "Run!" she screamed.

CHAPTER SIXTEEN

Potent Magic Awakened in the White Henge

Six Weeks Before Winter Solstice

Bedwyr and Alantir were anxious. Vaelwyn had always seemed like an invincible tower of strength. She had certainly saved them all from the living shadows in the Skógur forest. But she had collapsed into a deep sleep after they had gotten safely away from the forest and its shadows. Battling Magwei and then maintaining the sphere around them as they fled had come with a hefty price and she had been sleeping for a full day. It was now more than a week since they had left Garmoniya.

Emrhys sat on the ground with his legs outstretched, and Vaelwyn propped up in his lap. He gently stroked her long silver hair.

"The Prime Adepti must sleep deeply when they have quickly used a great amount of their magic," he explained. "Without friends to take care of them, it leaves them very vulnerable when this happens, no matter how powerful they might otherwise be. It is good to have friends."

"It may be a strange time to ask this question but why did Magwei keep referring to Vaelwyn as very young, or as a child?" asked Bedwyr, his hand rubbing his sword hilt. "I mean, to me she looks old enough to be my mother."

Emrhys chuckled a bit as he responded, "Yes, I understand that she does not look young to your eyes. But the Álfur age very differently than you mortals. Vaelwyn has already lived for many hundreds of years which is very old by your mortal standards. But for Álfur, Dark Fae, or my own people, the Breacadh an Lae, who live for many thousands of years, Vaelwyn is quite young indeed.

"Alantir, in my saddlebag, you will find a small glass vial," he continued. "Please bring that to me."

Alantir found the small glass vial and was surprised to see that it was glowing with a slight golden glow. She pulled the stopper for Emrhys as he squeezed open Vaelwyn's mouth and shook a few drops of golden liquid onto her tongue."

"It is called Uisce na Beatha," he explained. "Literally, the Water of Life. There is a small spring in the center of my people's island where it is found. It has powerful restorative qualities. This will help rejuvenate her health and energy while her body rests and help prepare her spirit for its travel on the astral plane later."

Somewhat later, Vaelwyn stirred slightly and her eyelids fluttered a bit. She stretched and opened her eyes. When she saw Emrhys and felt his arm around her, she looked visibly more relaxed. She sat there with Emrhys for a few more minutes and then stood up. Still a bit unsteady, she took a few steps and then paced off a large circle and walked around it several times to shake off her mental haziness.

"It looks like we might have another hour or so before sunset," Vaelwyn said. "I might feel better if we rode the horses for a while until we find the right spot to make camp."

"As you know, I have to attend another meeting of all Prime Adepti on the spirit plane tonight," she added.

They kept the horses' pace to a trot so that Vaelwyn could complete her recovery more easily. They found a good location to make camp and then set up for the evening.

———— ✦ ————

Vaelwyn was back in the spirit plane and making her way to the White Henge. She could see that all of the other Prime Adepti were there already, occupying their compass positions.

"Greetings, Vaelwyn," said the wispy puff of white mist with Caedwyn's voice. "We are waiting for King Aneirin to join us, and then we can start our meeting."

Vaelwyn saw that the other Adepti Wardens were in their designated positions, east, west, and south, with Caedwyn in the center. Her spirit form hovered in its own position in the north. They all greeted the king as he arrived and settled into his own position.

"I have communicated with all of you individually," Caedwyn began. "But this will be the first time any of us have heard a complete summary of everything happening across all of Ljós."

"Vaelwyn," he continued. "Will you please begin by sharing what has been happening in the north?"

Vaelwyn shared everything that she had seen and heard in the north. On Abhaile with the Breacadh an Lae, in Lán Léargas with King Alderon, and in Teilatua with King Baldyrien.

Although Garmoniya was in the region typically covered by the Warden of the West, Vaelwyn continued on to recount her more recent experiences with King Mandáron, especially the experiences that she and her companions had as they left Garmoniya.

As expected, there was a rumble of agitation in the group as Vaelwyn recounted the large number of goblin attacks that they had encountered and their disturbing encounters with an empowered avatar of one of The Six as well as living shadows in the forests of Skógur.

Taorlyn, Warden of the West, spoke after Vaelwyn had finished.

"I will follow Vaelwyn's reports on Garmoniya and the forests of Skógur with what I have learned. This is, indeed, troubling," said Taorlyn, Warden of the West, "Queen Dalamyra in Tishina reported a number of similar encounters with large bands of goblins, yet thankfully, no living shadows. I am especially shocked to learn that one of the gölge yürüteç was able to enter Ljós and successfully launch an attack."

There was general muttering in the mists as the details were deliberated.

"Tishina also reports," he continued. "That the goblins appear to be moving toward the small mountain range on the northeast border of Skógur's forests. In ancient legends that area was said to be the home of some unspeakable evil in the distant past long before the Great Sundering separated Ljós from Myrkur and Terra."

Neldorin, the Warden of the South spoke next, and she reported that there had been no unusual activity reported from the southernmost realm of Eydimörk nor from the southern seaport city of Ekaitza in the Sjávar realm. However, she did confirm that there had been sightings in the forests to the north of the other Sjávar seaport city, Vilnis. More goblins, and this was echoed by Aldorthyn, the Warden of the East who said that Queen Látellyn in the freshwater port of Rélegur had sighted goblins moving around their lakefront and down the peninsula that connects connected their north with the southern region of their realm. One of their ship captains did manage to attack a goblin war band on the shores of the lake, and he brought back a goblin head as proof that they were there.

Caedwyn's spirit spoke from his place at the center of the group, "We have ample reasons to be concerned, yet we do not seem to have an immediate crisis to respond to. The forces of Myrkur are clearly present again in Ljós," he continued. "Sightings in the south of Fjall, to the northwest of our White Henge, and in the forests of Skógur, north of Vilnis and south of Rélegur."

King Aneirin's spirit stirred, and he spoke to the gathered Prime Adepti of his Silver elves.

"For the first time since the Great Sundering, Shadow has established positions in Ljós," King Aneirin said. "Converging on various points around our White Henge. There must be a new vigil for the Lords of Ljós to monitor their borders more strictly and dispatch these vile creatures of Myrkur wherever they are found. The lords in all your regions must be notified immediately." He spread out his fog-covered arms expansively and the outline of his body wavered.

"When our mission to repair the Elemental Seals begins to take its first tangible steps," Caedwyn said. "This should stop any further penetration by Myrkur into Ljós and Terra. But the longer it takes us to do this," he continued, "the stronger Myrkur grows."

"We must activate the potent magic that slumbers within the two mortals from Terra," Vaelwyn said in her strong, resolute voice. "First we complete the White Henge ceremony, and then we will return to Terra where we will make our way to Gwynedd and reach the summit of Yr Wyddfa by dawn on the day of the winter solstice. Only then will we have a chance at repairing the Elemental Seals."

"Whatever forces Shadow has stained our realms with by then will remain," Caedwyn said. "And even a little evil is a lot while Vaelwyn and her companions work to complete the steps of their task."

"What will your task involve after Yr Wyddfa?" Taorlyn's spirit asked Vaelwyn.

"All of the Elemental Seals must be completely repaired. North, South and the Seal of Midgard as well." she said. "We will not know the fullness of our task, however, until we get started."

"I fear that we will have much work to complete," Taorlyn emphasized. "But balance must be restored."

• ⬩◆⬩ •

Vaelwyn's companions out on the heathlands had been watching her carefully. She had been in a trance much longer this time than when she had simply gone into the spirit plane to speak with Caedwyn before. And even after waking this time, she had still not completely recovered from the massive burst of magical energy she had expended to protect them from Magwei and his living shadow creatures.

She was gazing into the east, looking in the direction of the White Henge. Finally, she turned and walked back toward her companions.

"I have learned from my fellow Adepti that the forces of Myrkur have crept into the dark dens and hidden fissures throughout Ljós. It must surely be the same in Terra. Their numbers are still limited," she continued, "but we must hasten to stand ready at the White Henge by the time of the full moon in less than a fortnight from now."

"So when do we leave?" asked Bedwyr.

Dawn was now far behind them as Emrhys led their group across the heathlands on his large steed. Clouds of butterflies dispersed in flutters among the grasses and flowers of the heathlands as they passed. The violet hues of their wings were mixed with dark red and bright yellow, making Alantir laugh softly in delight. As the sun rose higher in the sky, Bedwyr enjoyed the feel of the warmth of the sun on his face.

"I was worried about you," Bedwyr said. "You were so frightened by those living shadows—and after what they did to your friends and family back in Beechwood."

"You saw them," she replied, "they are terrifying!"

"And now we know that those damn gölge yürüteç were behind that!" he said, his face red and his eyes half closed in anger. "And now that we know, we will both avenge our families!"

Bedwyr relaxed then and looked her in the eye as they rode side by side, "You know that I would do anything to protect you from all of this," he said. "Anything."

Alantir gave him a warm smile in return. "I do know that, Bed," she said. "And that means a lot to me."

"Not that I need a man to look after me," she hastened to add. "But it does comfort me to know that I can always depend on you."

Clearly, she and Bedwyr were once again on more affectionate terms, any minor annoyances forgotten.

"How long until we reach your people, Vaelwyn?" Bedwyr asked.

"We should be in the area of the White Henge by midday," replied Vaelwyn. "We will have lunch with my king, Aneirin, and rest for a few days. Then we must begin the ceremony that will be held in the light of the full moon."

———— •◆• ————

The various Prime Adepti of the White Henge were all assembled. They all wore long, white cloaks, their white rune staffs carried at their sides. Bedwyr and Alantir wore white tunics, as before, their amulets visible around their necks.

Taorlyn began the ceremony by entering the towering ring of roughly hewn white stones from the east. The full moon added to the illuminating glow of the twelve white stones. And there was flickering light from the flames of torches planted between some of the stones.

As the ceremony came underway, a glowing green sphere hovered in the air in the center of the White Henge, then moved to where Alantir stood, gradually expanding. Then a blue one plinked into existence. It too, began to slowly expand as the green one had done a few moments earlier. In the span of a few heartbeats, the blue sphere had expanded to completely envelop Bedwyr.

What – what is going on here? What in the name of the sacred oaks is going to happen next? Bedwyr thought to himself.

And the green sphere likewise with Alantir. Both spheres pulsed with energy, and small crackles of sparks coursed across the surfaces.

Caedwyn invoked another arcane phrase at the center of the circle and pointed his rune staff at each sphere. All of a sudden, both spheres collapsed into the bodies of Alantir and Bedwyr.

A faint resulting glow emanated from each of the two Terrans, and their eyes shone brightly. A deep green from Alantir's eyes, and a bright, dark blue from Bedwyr's.

And now this blue aura is inside of me? It must be—look at that green glow inside Alantir!

Bedwyr gestured in a swirling motion with his hand, and a strong wind circled inside the stone circle.

Okay, that was interesting! Much easier than before—and the magic feels stronger.

Alantir gestured after him, pointing to the ground and then crooking her finger upwards. New blades of grass poked up through the ground in a rapidly thickening circle around the center dais.

Look, Alantir is stronger too.

"Now that the latent magic within has been awakened," said King Aneirin. "The Elementals must be summoned to accept or reject a connection with these new champions of the Light."

Caedwyn first summoned the king of the air elementals by using his rune staff to create a large circle of light between the towering, roughhewn white stones to the east. Rare words of power were used once the circle was completed and Caedwyn continued to intone his chants in a low, measured voice until everyone felt a soft wind enter the White Henge.

The soft wind circled the interior of the White Henge and grew stronger. And stronger. The robes of the Adepti flapped as the circling air rose above their heads in a column of strong wind. A large white cloud appeared above their heads at the top where a face began to form.

"Who summons me!" the face in the cloud shouted.

"King Aeryn," said Caedwyn, "I am sure that you remember me. I am Caedwyn, Prime Adeptus of the silver elves."

"Aha!" boomed the cloud, a smile emerging from boiling areas of cumulus fluff, showing curved lines. "Long has it been since the silver elves have summoned me. Why now?"

"I know that you must feel the weakening of the great Elemental Seals as much as we do," said Caedwyn. "The influence of the Shadow is once again moving out of Myrkur. After all these eons of balance, evil is growing strong again."

"Yes, yes," King Aeryn said, his mouth down turning. "We Elementals feel this. It is a terrible thing."

"Our small group of Prime Adepti, leaders of the silver elves, have undertaken the task of repairing the Elemental Seals to restore the balance between Light and Shadow," Caedwyn said.

"But why have you summoned me? I do not understand."

"Oh Noble King," Caedwyn replied. "We need your support and acceptance of a new champion of the Light for the elemental magic of air. We have sought out the first two of the long-lost amulets that connect champions of the Light with the respective Elementals," continued Caedwyn, "and tonight, their own latent magical abilities have been awakened."

King Aeryn dissipated and reformed, his shape shifting as he listened. His expression remained earnest as Caedwyn spoke, though his eyes roved disconcertingly.

"In order to make full use of their powers, they must be able to access the vast stores of elemental magic through their connection with your fellow Elementals," Caedwyn said. "This is Bedwyr, a human from the Britons of Terra, a great warrior among the humans, with some faint and distant ancestry of Álfur. He will be a fierce defender of the Light!"

I hope that I am ready for this. My new companions are all counting on me. What is this creature anyway? Some sort of demi-god or something?

"A human!" exhaled King Aeryn, his face billowing in surprise. "This has never been done before! How can I ask my air elementals to link their reserves of magic with a puny human?"

Wait a minute! Is this demi-god insulting me? Saying that I don't measure up? Well …

"I don't know much yet about your world of magic, Great King," Bedwyr broke in, "but I know a lot about good and evil, and I welcome any chance to help fight these forces of Shadow. I cannot offer you much, and I cannot promise you much, but I can promise to give you and your people every bit of fight that I have within me in these battles ahead. You will not find a fiercer defender of Light nor a more dependable ally for the air elementals than you will find in me!"

King Aeryn's large cloud face came down through the column of air and faced Bedwyr directly, several times the size of the human. He blew onto Bedwyr and inhaled. He repeated this several times, frowning in intimidating concentration.

I hope that my temper has not caused me trouble here— once again.

"Indeed, I sense the champion within this man-child," King Aery said. "I like the fight within him – it is like a boiling storm, ready to spill out at any time. And I accept him! His expression once more broke into a beam. "Your amulet will connect you directly to me, boy. You will be able to draw the full power of the air elementals into your amulet. Use it wisely!"

With that, King Aeryn retreated back up through the column of air, his rolling laughter heard like thunder in the sky above. The air slowly dissipated until only a residual breeze was left inside the White Henge.

I am so glad that I did not fail my new companions!

Caedwyn did not wait. He immediately created a second circle of light, this time between two towering white stones to the west. Once again, rare words of power were used once the circle was completed and once again, Caedwyn continued to intone his chants in a low, measured voice until everyone felt a rumbling in the ground that continued into the interior of the White Henge itself.

A woody shoot emerged from the ground, growing rapidly until a large oak tree towered over the inner circle of the Adepti Prime.

"Why have my friends, the silver elves, summoned me?" a deep, warm voice asked. "It has been many, many years since Queen Sylvane has received such a summons."

"Welcome Queen Sylvane! We know that you must feel the weakening of the great Elemental Seals as much as we feel it,' said Caedwyn. "Evil is growing again, and the Shadow once again slithers out of Myrkur.

"Why do you disturb my slumber to tell me what I already sense in my roots, my leaves, the very bark of me!" exclaimed Queen Sylvane.

Uh, I had started to think that Alantir might have a friend-lier demi-god than I had – but now I am not so sure ...

Caedwyn told her, as bid.

"This is wonderful news, my friends," said Queen Sylvane. "And how can I help? Where do you need my assistance?"

"Your assistance will be critical in many ways as we move forward, my Queen," Caedwyn replied. "Tonight, we are pleased to introduce a new champion of the Light for the elemental magic of Earth. We ask that you support and accept her so she may gain full use of her magic."

"Who!?" asked Queen Sylvane, her branches rustling like a sea of shells. "Who have you chosen as my champion?"

"Alantir," Caedwyn told the queen, bowing low. "A woodland elf from Terra. She had strong residual reserves of latent magical ability despite her tribe's decision to forswear magic all those ages ago at the time of the Great Sundering. She is a talented archer, a champion among her people. She will be a fierce defender of the Light!"

Hey, don't forget that she is also a royal princess of Skógur, the forest realm!

Queen Sylvane extended two of her branches, growing them long enough to touch each temple on Alantir's head. Then the queen closed her eyes with heavy bark eyelids and hummed for several minutes.

Alantir glanced nervously toward Bedwyr as they waited and Bedwyr smiled and nodded briefly in encouragement. She also glanced at Emrhys but saw that he stood stiffly upright in stone-faced silence. And Vaelwyn and all of the other Adepti had their heads slightly bowed in deference to the queen's deliberations.

"I like you, child!" the queen suddenly said as she opened her eyes again. "Why are you so kind but also so strong? What a wonderful combination. And I feel your love for my trees. How could I expect any less from a child of the tribe who chose their love for my kin over the use of their magic? A child of the tribe that traded their immortality for long, mortal lives amongst their beloved trees!"

"Thank you, my queen," said Alantir reverently.

"I welcome you, dear, as the Champion of Light for the elemental magic of Earth. Your amulet will now connect you to me and, through me, to the almost limitless power of all my earth elementals. You will be strongest when you use these powers as a defender of the earth elementals and all other allies of the Light, and weakest when you try to use these powers to attack and not defend."

The queen closed her eyes once more as the tree slowly returned to the earth, and the trail of rumbling soil retracted from the White Henge.

"The connection with the first two Elementals has now been completed, following the earlier activation of the first two amulets. Potent magic has now been awakened within our first two champions of the Light," said King Aneirin.

All right then—we are both prepared for whatever comes next. Whatever that is ...

Alantir let out a small nervous laugh. Bedwyr responded with a hearty full-throated laugh. Then he looked sheepishly at the gathered Adepti, concerned that he had not shown proper decorum. But he was greeted with hearty smiles and friendly nods from all around the circle. Even Emrhys had a huge grin on his usually stern face.

◆

Emrhys stepped into the stone circle from the east. He nodded to both Bedwyr and Alantir and waited respectfully, towering over the silver elf king as Aneirin clasped arms with him in greeting.

Caedwyn was still in the center of the circle and surrounded by the other Wardens. He raised his rune staff again and uttered another arcane phrase. He pointed his rune staff at the empty northwest point within the circle and began to raise the tip. A line of silver light was traced in the air. When he was done, a doorway limned in silver light stood at the northwest point within the White Henge.

Caedwyn nodded to Emrhys, and Emrhys stepped forward. He moved to the glowing silver doorway, stopping to clap Bedwyr on the shoulder as he passed him and gesturing to Alantir on the other side of the circle. She, too, stepped forward and received a nod from Emrhys, and then they all stepped up to the light-limned doorway with Vaelwyn behind them. Emrhys raised his hand in salute to the Prime Adepti, and the companions all stepped through the luminous portal to a different realm.

CHAPTER SEVENTEEN

Wessex

Five Weeks Before Winter Solstice

Emrhys stepped through the other side of Caedwyn's light-limned doorway. Alantir followed directly behind him, then Bedwyr and finally Vaelwyn. Once Vaelwyn stepped through, the doorway itself faded, no longer visible.

"Where are we exactly?" asked Bedwyr as he looked around him. "This ring of stones around us is not white, and although they're large, they're not as high as the White Henge. Of course, after spending a week around the White Henge, everything seems smaller and less impressive."

"We are in the Saxon kingdom of Wessex," answered Vaelwyn. "This is the kingdom of their tribe called the West Saxons. We are on an open plain in the west of their territory, the Salisbury Plain."

"We are standing inside an ancient stone circle that was

here long ages before the Saxons ever were," Vaelwyn said calmly. "There is residual magic here that we use to create a connection between this smaller stone circle and our White Henge in Ljós."

"We plan to move northwest from here," said Emrhys. "And return to the point where I met each of you at the southern end of the Dyke between Saxon Mercia and Powys of the Britons."

"Give me a minute," Alantir said. "I am still a bit muddle-headed from that magical traverse from one realm to another."

"Yeah, me too," Bedwyr said. "And stepping into the dark and cold of Terra's nighttime is a big change too."

Alantir shivered. "The cold damp of this winter rain just goes right to my bones."

"We are on foot," Emrhys rumbled. "So, we cannot move as fast without horses. But fortunately we are traveling light, with scarcely more than our weapons and water."

"It will be dawn soon," said Vaelwyn. "Best for us if we can move off this open plain before the sun rises. The large hoods on these cloaks will hide our ears from the humans for me and Alantir, for the time being. And also give us some shelter from this damp drizzle."

They shouldered their weapons and moved out of the huge stone circle; they were preparing to head northwest at a rapid pace.

"As much as I want to be well away from all the Saxon tribes, I am not sure where things currently stand with my own tribes of Briton," he said. "The unexpected betrayal of Eluad ap Glast, the renegade king of Dogfeiling, was stunning. And he's now acting as the ruler of my kingdom of Powys, controlling the central region of the land of us Britons."

"Aye Bedwyr," Emrhys grumbled, "I have questions about that and more. Let's have a talk after we cover some ground."

This land of the West Saxons looked to be fine, fertile land. Well-tended fields dotted the landscape through which they walked. They were heading in the direction of the bridge that they would need to cross to enter the Saxon kingdom of Mercia. From there, they could get back to the land of the Britons, cross Powys, and enter Gwynedd.

Before they could get close to the bridge, though, they started to see large groups of Saxon warriors also traveling in the same direction. So they detoured, deciding to travel through farmlands, meadows, and forests to avoid the more heavily traveled roads and paths. In this indirect fashion, after a few days, they finally moved within eyesight of the bridge. Mercifully, the cold winter rain had finally stopped, leaving cold, gray skies in its wake.

"Is this usual for the humans in this area?", Alantir asked.

"I am actually surprised to see such a large number of Saxon warriors on both sides of the bridge," Bedwyr answered. "I am accustomed to seeing war bands of twenty or so warriors at a time, but here, it looks like there are hundreds."

The Saxons from Mercia and Wessex seemed to be at odds with one another. Angrily facing off and shouting across the bridge at the other side.

"I know these Saxons are your sworn enemies," Emrhys said. "But what is your honest assessment of them as warriors?"

Aside from his hot temper, Bedwyr begrudgingly respected the fighting forces the Saxons assembled, and he said so.

"Well, I guess I would give them some respect in that regard," he said slowly. "They can always expand their number of fighting men by calling out the *fyrd*, but that is mostly field hands with little to no fighting experience.

Most times, the Saxon fighting force is spearmen, equipped with shields and spears, and some tough, seasoned warriors with leather helms, swords, and shields. If they have armor at all, it's typically made of hardened leather."

"So there are some hardened warriors among them?" Emrhys said.

"Aye, and there's lots of them here by all looks," he answered.

Given this angry standoff between the two groups of heavily armed Saxons, it was clear they would not be able to slip across the bridge unnoticed. The next bridge was many miles upstream, with no guarantee that it would not also be crawling with large numbers of Saxon warriors. They would have to devise an alternative plan.

"I suggest that we travel south, and once we reach the coastline, we can follow that west until we reach the Briton territory of Dumnonia on the western side of Wessex," Emrhys said. "From Dumnonia, he reasoned, we can easily get passage north across the Channel to the Briton kingdom of Dyfed. From there, we can travel north to Gwynedd more easily than we could have from the southern end of Mercia."

"Yes," Vaelwyn said. "This is good thinking Emrhys. Let's move on now."

As they moved south, an opportunity presented itself in a small, wooded area well away from the bridge. After another night spent sleeping rough, Bedwyr had stepped away from his companions to wash in a stream nearby, but as he was just getting dressed again, a small group of Saxon warriors came upon him. It looked like they had been planning to water their horses in the stream.

"An' what marvel is this?" the Saxon leader said. "A wandering Briton. Deep in our Saxon territory."

"Mebbe 'e wandered from the lands once held by 'is dear

departed King Arthur," said a second Saxon. "Or mebbe 'e's been spyin' on us."

Swords were out in a flash, including Bedwyr's. He had been about to buckle his sword belt when the Saxons came upon him, so he held his scabbard in his left hand and his sword in his right. His belt with his long knife fell back to the ground, next to the short-handled axe he liked to tuck in his belt behind his back. Although he did have the two thin-bladed stilettos tucked away in his boots, a habit he'd adopted from Emrhys.

The Saxons had formed a circle around Bedwyr and were tightening it; their intentions clear. Bedwyr saw the tell from the first Saxon when he shifted his stance to an attack posture. But Bedwyr was faster.

He jumped inside the Saxon's sword thrust and rammed his own sword blade right up through the Saxon's jaw and into his brain. Before that first Saxon even knew that he was dead, Bedwyr was on the ground, rolling over his short-handled axe. He jumped back up on his feet and threw his axe in one fluid motion. It flew fast and true, splitting the skull of the second Saxon wide open.

Bedwyr had dropped his scabbard and retrieved one of the long knives from his boot. He stood poised and ready, facing the two remaining Saxons and brandishing naked steel in both hands.

The two Saxons blinked and looked at each other with fear and surprise. This young Briton had just effortlessly killed two of their fellow warriors in the blink of an eye. They had no wish to meet the same fate.

"Whattya want, boy?" one asked Bedwyr.

"Leave all four horses," he replied. "With all the packs. You can take your own weapons and water, but I'll have the rest."

The pair made as if to obey but halted once more when Bedwyr spoke again.

"Do this," he continued. "And I'll let you walk away with your lives—despite my hatred for your people!"

◆──────◆◆──────◆

The four companions from Ljós made much better time now with the four horses, although Emrhys walked as much as he rode. He was concerned that his large size would wear out his horse if he rode all the time, and his long stride did not slow the others down.

They worked their way west along the coastline at the channel for the next several days, entering an area just south of the channel with extensive moorlands. Emrhys and Vaelwyn seemed to be in a heated personal discussion. Their voices were low but insistent, and they kept glancing at their companions as though they wanted to ensure their talk was private. Bedwyr and Alantir quickly got bored, so the two mortals went for a walk down to the water.

There was still a mild chill in the air, common for early winter in Terra. They were sitting on the ground together, looking out at the water. Bedwyr was twisting and plaiting meadow grass into a sort of braid. Alantir was playing with the end of her own long braid.

"Let me see what you're crafting," she said.

"No, don't be so nosy!" he replied.

Alantir leaned over and snatched it out of his hands. Bedwyr laughed and lunged for her, and they rolled over in the meadow with Alantir managing to hold onto the plaited meadow grass. They stopped with Bedwyr astride Alantir, looking down at her while they both tried to catch their breaths. The laughing stopped, becoming serious as they held each other's gaze. Alantir put her hand up and gently touched Bedwyr's cheek and he leaned into it, kissing her then, gently at first and then hungrily. Alantir responded, her hand moving to the back of Bedwyr's head.

"I've wanted to do this again for so long," said Bedwyr.

"And I also wanted this again for a long time as well," Alantir replied.

They rolled over on their sides, and Bedwyr ran his hands over Alantir's back and down to her long legs and back up again. They kissed with a deep, passionate hunger and Bedwyr's hands returned to her lower back, then lower. They surrendered to their passion in the Wessex moorlands, lovers returning to their familiar embrace.

— ◆ —

The four companions had crossed most of the large expanse of moors that ran south of the channel without encountering any other travelers. Now, at the far western edge, they could see a group approaching on horseback. It looked like a dozen or so Saxons. Well-equipped and with the royal arms of Wessex emblazoned on their shields. Probably an official border patrol. Of course, that meant that Dumnonia was close behind them.

"We need a battle plan to deal with these Saxons," said Bedwyr. "And move past them into Dumnonia."

"Yes, I agree," replied Emrhys. "Here is what I suggest that we do." And he laid out a plan that they all agreed with.

They waited until the Saxon horsemen drew closer and then split into two groups as the Saxons watched. The Saxons divided into two separate groups of six riders each and gave pursuit in both directions.

Emrhys and Alantir rode north towards a small hill. Once on the far side of it, Alantir could clearly see the approaching Saxon horsemen. Emrhys positioned his horse around the bend, further along the straight path that passed the hill. He had a clear sight of where the Saxon riders would approach once they cleared the hill.

The Saxons came thundering towards them, their horse's heavy hooves tearing up the soft soil of the moorlands. Alantir had her bow ready with one arrow nocked and more arrows stuck in the ground in front of her, ready to use as soon as the first arrow was off. She sighted carefully and let the first arrow fly. It took the lead rider in the throat, toppling him from his horse immediately.

Steady now, she thought. *Just stay calm. Breathe deeply and focus …*

She had the second arrow off in a heartbeat, just as the Saxons were riding past her position. That second arrow caught one of the remaining Saxon horseman in the eye. He did not fall from his horse immediately, but the horse faltered and fell back from the pack. A minute later, his lifeless body hit the ground, his leg caught twisted in a stirrup. The remaining four Saxon horsemen thundered toward Emrhys.

As the horsemen approached Emrhys, he took the unusual step of dismounting. The Caomhnoir of the Breacadh and Lae stood eight feet tall, higher than the horses themselves. And he was brandishing naked steel in both hands. This was an unusual sight on the moorlands of Wessex for both the horsemen and their horses.

As the front two horses faltered at this sight, Emrhys surged forward and took out both of the Saxon riders quickly and cleanly. Emrhys gave the remaining two Saxons his wide and wicked grin as Alantir also rode up with her bow drawn and arrow nocked.

The Saxons turned and rode hard for the heart of Wessex.

Bedwyr and Vaelwyn had ridden south with the other six Saxons in pursuit. Vaelwyn had already outlined her variation on their plan, and the two turned their horses on an open plain in front of the oncoming Saxons.

The two groups clashed as the Saxons charged in, and Bedwyr took out one Saxon with his sword while Vaelwyn took out another with her rune staff. The remaining four Saxons thundered past before they could turn their horses.

"Now!" shouted Vaelwyn. "Turn and face them!"

Vaelwyn and Bedwyr turned their horses to face the remaining Saxons as they turned as well. Rather than raising their weapons, however, both Vaelwyn and Bedwyr raised their hands to work the magic of the elements they controlled.

"Concentrate now Bedwyr," Vaelwyn said. "But focus on the amulet as you seek your inner balance."

Now controlling his own innate magical powers as well as the power of his amulet, Bedwyr raised his arms and called on the power of air. He had not yet been fully trained to gain his inner balance when invoking his magical powers, and he was buffeted about wildly by the storm of chaos as he reached for his abilities. But Bedwyr held firm. Flickering cold flames of bright blue energy surrounded both his hands and slowly he raised them, a column of raging wind rising up between his palms. Bedwyr twisted the wind sideways and gestured toward the Saxons. Two of the riders were blasted right out of their saddles by the sudden, powerful gust of wind. Their bodies were raised up high and then slammed to the ground. There was no movement.

Terrified, the two remaining Saxons looked on, frozen, as Vaelwyn raised her arms where larger, flickering, cold flames of multicolored energy crackled ominously. As a Prime

Adeptus of the silver elves, Vaelwyn controlled the power of all the elements. Her right hand gestured toward the ground in front of the horsemen, ripping a line of green fire on the ground. There was a loud rumbling and crunching sound, and a huge chasm opened along the line the green fire traced.

The Saxon riders and their horses desperately tried to flee but the earth opened faster than they could move. Quickly, they were all swallowed by the ground; horses along with riders. Then, the chasm closed.

It was quiet again in the moorlands.

CHAPTER EIGHTEEN

Dumnonia

Four Weeks Before Winter Solstice

The group of companions continued to ride hard after their encounter with the Saxons, leaving the moorlands behind them as they rode further into Dumnonia. Another week had passed since they had stepped through the silver-limned doorway in the White Henge.

"Who was this King Arthur?" asked Alantir. "You speak of him as though he were a great and renowned king throughout your human lands."

"He ruled the southern regions of the lands of the Britons," said Bedwyr with one hand on the hilt of his sword. "But he was also renowned and respected in our regions north of the sea."

"It's noteworthy that his reputation remains so strong, even after his passing," Emrhys rumbled.

"Aye, he was a great warlord as well as a wise king," added Bedwyr. "Even the Saxons respected his military prowess as their conquest of our eastern lands became more difficult throughout his reign. He was well-known for his use of heavy cavalry, which was unique, whether Briton or Saxon."

"Unique?" asked Alantir, her dark brows raised.

"Well, I suppose he uses—used untraditional methods," Bedwyr mused. Roman, Cataphractarii, you know, all covered up? I'd say his style was more of a shocker than anything else, people didn't know what they were looking at. Maybe?"

"The element of shock and surprise," Emrhys quipped, nodding sagely.

"Where was King Arthur in Dumnonia?" asked Alantir.

"His court was located in Tintagel," answered Bedwyr. "Far to the west."

"We will not travel that far down the coast," said Emrhys. "I think we need to go to the port of Ilfracombe and seek passage from there to Dyfed."

"It will be a shame to find myself here in Dumnonia but not have the opportunity to visit the former seat of King Arthur," replied Bedwyr. "However, our task comes first. We must do what is best to support it."

"We are all agreed, then. We will travel directly to the port of Ilfracombe and seek passage."

They did not have far to travel. Whereas Tintagel was much further south and west along the rugged coastline, Ilfracombe was a short distance beyond the edge of the moorlands.

The talk of Arthur prompted one of Vaelwyn's memories of Arthur's half-sister, Morgan le Fay. This memory was from many years ago, as humans measured time, but it seemed recent to Vaelwyn.

Traveling through the western end of Dumnonia, Vaelwyn was passing time in a forested area near the southern coast when she heard a female voice in a vale nearby and went to investigate. As she reached the edge of the clearing, the voice became clearer.

It belonged to a woman, lamenting, "Why is my brother, Arthur, given such power to lead armies and rule men?" it exclaimed. "While I am left without any power or influence?"

The clearing was empty. Vaelwyn looked carefully, even venturing into the foliage in several places, but the voice seemed to remain in the center.

"Grant me powers of my own," continued the voice in the clearing. "I will pledge my loyalty to anyone or anything that grants me the power I so desperately crave!"

With that, Vaelwyn stepped into the clearing and addressed the speaker, "Be careful what you request out loud, foolish human," she said. "You will invite the cold touch of Shadow into your life without knowledge or struggle."

The woman was now visible to Vaelwyn as an attractive middle-aged woman. She was well-dressed, with raven dark hair and a fiery spark in her eyes that hinted at an inner tempest.

"Who are you to be instructing me?" replied the woman in the vale. "I am Morgan le Fay and my brother is Arthur, king of these lands."

"I am Vaelwyn," Vaelwyn replied. "And I am a simple servant of Light. Although they are both now constrained, Light and Shadow each still have some influence here in your realm, and I oppose the influence of Shadow wherever I find it."

Morgan le Fay stalked away to the far side of the glade.

"Look around us now," Vaelwyn continued in her frosty

voice. "Look at the bright sunlight in the leaves of the trees, smell the rich soil of the earth beneath our feet, feel the breeze touch our faces as it rustles the leaves, and feel the warmth of the sun on our faces. If you open yourself to the beauty of life and the elements all around you, you will embrace Light. And Shadow will have no hold on you."

"And you call me a fool!" hissed Morgan le Fay. "What power comes to me from simply enjoying life around me? I need power! I need to become as strong as Arthur but in my own way. And I care not where that power comes from!"

Vaelwyn was saddened as she recalled that encounter. She knew the residual magic in that part of Terra was strong, and she had conjured a special charm for Morgan. As a result, even though Shadow could make a claim on her, Light would always be there, too. If it worked as Vaelwyn hoped, then Morgan might become an ambivalent creature, sometimes serving Shadow but then redeeming herself with service to Light. Better than being lost to Shadow entirely.

Vaelwyn's recollection was interrupted by Emrhys' booming voice:

"We approach the harbor town of Ilfracombe."

Having sold their horses at the edge of town, and now unhorsed, they were made more aware of their group's unusual appearance as they walked through town. Emrhys' giant stature was unusual enough, and Vaelwyn and Alantir's cloaks and large hoods added to their unique overall appearance. They received less attention in the harbor area, where seamen traveled widely and had more experience with unusual-looking groups of people.

Bedwyr made some inquiries as they moved through the harbor front and was directed to the captain of a sturdy little merchant vessel. The captain, who was currently picking his teeth with a variety of toothpicks, was readying to cross the channel to the port of Tenby in Dyfed.

"Ho, captain," Bedwyr hailed. "We are seeking passage to Tenby. Have you room for us on your ship?"

Eyeing Bedwyr somewhat lackadaisically, the captain put away his dental sticks, albeit slowly, slotting each one back into a well-worn cylindrical tube, and appraised Bedwyr. He then raised his eyebrow, inviting Bedwyr to speak. Then, just as Bedwyr was about to, he shook his head and slotted a final pick home.

Bedwyr cleared his throat and simply waited.

When the captain smiled, it was shockingly revealed he only had three front teeth.

Captain Mabon acknowledged that he had room for the travelers but negotiated sharply over the amount of the fare for their passage.

Everyone boarded the vessel, with Alantir looking especially unsteady. She looked warily around as the ship's shifting deck swayed back and forth.

"I have never been aboard a large boat on open water before," she said simply.

CHAPTER NINETEEN

Dyfed

Three Weeks Before Winter Solstice

———◆||||||◆━━━━▶———

The sturdy little boat, *Gray Gull*, navigated into the channel with gray, cloudy skies. Alantir was fascinated. There was nothing like this at home. Woodland elves had little reason to travel via boat. And she did not like it. She'd felt queasy from the moment she first stepped onto the deck, and it got even worse when they'd made it to open water.

Alantir was not given a fair chance to get her sea legs, as the gray skies turned very dark ahead and the winds picked up dramatically in anticipation of an oncoming storm.

The waves grew larger, and the boat's movements became increasingly dramatic. Violent rocking from side to side, accompanied by sudden, dramatic rises and falls with high volumes of rain drenching them, in between peals of lightning and the rumbling of thunder.

She hated every minute. Cold, tired, sick, and frightened; this was an experience she'd be only too glad to leave to the humans.

"That gale has blown us well off our course," Captain Mabon said to Vaelwyn and Emrhys. "But we will make up some time and get back to our last good position. From there, we should make port not too long after our original plan. Just a few days lost."

Even Bedwyr was glad to see solid ground again as they sailed into the harbor of Tenby in the Kingdom of Dyfed. He was concerned about Alantir. She was pale and drawn, her step unsteady as disembarked.

"She needs a quiet woodland vale to sit and relax for a while," Bedwyr said to Emrhys. "She cannot just keep going, and I don't see her recovering quickly in a noisy, smelly pub."

"I doubt you'll find any quiet woodland vales nearby," answered Emrhys. "But a walk in the fresh air outside of town will work wonders. Walking on solid ground and seeing green growing things will probably help quite a bit."

"While you two take a walk," he continued, "Vaelwyn and I will get us some horses."

Emrhys had been correct. Alantir did improve with their long walk, and there were horses ready when they returned.

"We need to ride north to Cardigan," said Bedwyr. 'That is where the king of Dyfed is located right now. Llywarch ap Hyfaidd was a friend of my father, and I expect that we will find ourselves welcomed by him. Also, Cardigan is a good position from which to continue up the coastline to Gwynedd," he concluded.

"Perhaps you will find news of your own kingdom of Powys while we are in Cardigan," said Emrhys.

It was a long ride to Cardigan, and they were glad to arrive by nightfall two days later. Bedwyr was still concerned about Alantir. The long horseback ride had taken its toll on her after her seasickness. He explained who he was at the gates of Cardigan, and a runner was sent ahead to the king. Their group was directed to a local tavern where they could relax and refresh themselves after their journey. The tavern had ow ceilings and dark wood, and the smoke from the hearth filled the one large room, along with the pleasant smell of burning wood. The companions settled themselves at a table in the far corner and Bedwyr joined Emrhys at the bar. It was better for the women to stay in the shadows, with their large hoods concealing their elfin ears.

"Oi," the barkeep grunted at them. "Wha' is it you'll be 'aving now?"

He looked up and down at Emrhys's giant frame stooping under the rafters.

"This here's a calm and peaceable 'stablishment, ya hear," he said, "We don't go in for no funny business here—if ya know wha' I mean."

"Nothing fancy for us, friend," Bedwyr said, while Emrhys glowered at the poor barkeep. "Just some hot food to warm our belie and some cold drink to slake our thirst."

"Aye," he said. "I'll have the wench bring it over to ya."

"And we will also need rooms for the night," Bedwyr added.

The companions were glad to have the refreshments when they were brought to them. Just as they were finishing, a messenger from the king arrived.

"Bedwyr ap Cynfor, the king sends his warm greetings,"

the messenger said. "He asks that you meet with him, alone, at breakfast tomorrow morning."

"Aye," said Bedwyr. "Thank the king kindly for his welcome and I will gladly join him for breakfast in the morning."

As the messenger left, Alantir started to speak.

"Bedwyr," she said, "I know that he knows who you are already. Does he know that we ..."

"Shh ..." Vaelwyn broke in. "Let's not have any further discussions in this public place. Wait until we get to our rooms."

Soon afterwards, their meals finished, the travelers were taken to their rooms. They actually had only one large room with four beds and a round table with chairs. Although the room was roughly finished, it was adequate. Bedwyr was sure that Emrhys was not going to fit in any of those beds, but he could simply put the bedding on the floor.

"I think that we must plan to be on our way right after you finish your breakfast with the king tomorrow," Vaelwyn said in her calm voice. "We were able to remain cloaked and hooded to hide our ears tonight since we are tired travelers arriving late in the night. And in a similar way," she continued. "If we are packed and mounted when your breakfast is concluded, nobody will challenge the fact that we are cloaked and hooded as we depart on our travel further to the north."

"Yes, I see the wisdom in that," replied Alantir. "I would not have thought so carefully about how to keep our ears hidden from the humans."

"Bedwyr, you must see what you can learn about the best route to Northern Gwynedd," said Vaelwyn. "And whether we are likely to encounter any hostile forces along the way." Then she turned to Alantir, speaking in a low voice, "Alantir, you must rest and regain your strength. Please eat at least a light supper and then get some sleep. Tomorrow you will feel better."

It was a cold and gray morning as Bedwyr went to have breakfast with King Llywarch ap Hyfaidd, but at least it was not raining or snowing. His presence, alone, had been requested by the king. Although Bedwyr realized it must have to do with his father, worry gnawed at him, nonetheless.

Bedwyr remembered the king as a large, loud and boisterous man – forthright in his words and his deeds. Fair and loyal in his dealings with fellow Britons. The king was in good spirits as he welcomed Bedwyr and bade him sit and breakfast with him. There were fresh-baked oat cakes with honey, dark, soft wedges of rye bread, a humungous wheel of cheese and freshly churned butter. Bedwyr drank a tankard of gruit ale thirstily.

"I want to say again how sorry I was to learn of your father's death," said the king. "Along with your two older brothers."

"Thank you for your kind words, Your Majesty," replied Bedwyr. "It was a shocking series of events, followed by an unwelcome homecoming; the treachery of King Eluad ap Glast, now the self-styled King of Powys." He looked up at the king.

"Aye, lad," said Dyfed's king. "He is a treacherous cur, and that for certain, but this makes him even more dangerous. His war bands range far and wide from Powys and Dogfeiling. You must be careful in your travels when you leave here."

"I will be, my thanks to you, Your Majesty," said Bedwyr. "Have you, perchance, heard any news of my brother, Dylan? He was off to Gwynedd when last I saw him."

"Only that he was safely ensconced with your ally in Gwynedd," the king replied. "King Merfyn Frych has recognized your brother's claim to the throne of Powys with the deaths of your uncle and his sons, along with the loss of your father and your older brothers. And both Dylan and King Merfyn Frych are eager to promote armed conflict between Gwynedd and Powys. What do you think of that? After all, you must realize that this makes you the new crown prince and heir to the throne of Powys after your brother?"

Bedwyr blinked his eyes a few times and shifted in his seat.

"Aye," he said slowly. "I reckon that be true enough, me as the new crown prince. But I don't feel any different because of it. I am still burning for revenge!"

"I fully support ousting the traitor and pretender Eluad ap Glast from the throne of Powys by all force of arms available to us, my lord," Bedwyr continued, not without some bitterness as he thought of his family's fate in the fields. "Would you join with Gwynedd in such a conflict?"

Unseen by the mortals, Magwei's avatar worked his dark magic from the safety of the shadows. As he conjured, he spoke poisonous thoughts to plant in the mind of the king. He wanted to weaken any opponents of his quisling amongst the Britons, Eluad ap Glast.

Caution now, caution now, he intoned, *you are just a weak little king, easily overwhelmed by greater powers all around you ...*

"Here in Dyfed, we are not anxious to engage in any new battles," the king answered hesitantly. "The Vikings increasingly besiege us from the sea to the west, and the Mercian Saxons from the land to the east. People used to talk of the great King Arthur as the hope of the Britons, but however great he may have been, there is nobody who can offer much help in our struggles now." There was a protracted sigh as the king bowed his head in thought. When he continued, he avoided looking Bedwyr in the eye as he spoke, and his hands twitched and his feet shuffled nervously "For this reason, we do not welcome the idea of taking on fellow Britons to the north in Powys."

This is very unlike the king. He does not seem himself all of a sudden, Bedwyr thought. *And why is my amulet now warm and faintly glowing?*

Magwei's avatar continued with his conjuring and his poisonous thoughts, trying to have the king reach out to another of Magwei's dark subjects, this one amongst the Saxons,

You are so overwhelmed little king, that you need help from other ... stronger kings ...

"In fact, we have held discussions over reaching out to the Wessex king regarding an alliance. That may be the most useful alliance to us as we battle Vikings and Mercians," the king said as his hands shook more violently and he clawed at the side of his head.

Hearing these words spoken by the king, and watching his hands convulse, Bedwyr came fully alert. His amulet flared brightly as he heard words from the elemental King Aeryn in his ear.

"See your enemy's hand in this," he heard, "... and smite him!"

With that a luminous white haze blew through the room on a strong breeze—and outlined by that haze, Bedwyr could see a shadowy figure lurking behind the king. Bedwyr recognized that avatar immediately.

"You dare!" he thundered as he drew bright steel. "Begone from this king!"

Strong blue light streamed from the amulet around his neck as Bedwyr charged toward the gölge yürüteç brandishing his sword. The entire room was bathed in bright blue light now. Too bright for any shadows. And Magwei's avatar fled—unable to stand before Bedwyr's steel.

Llywarch ap Hyfaidd sat with his head in his hands, rubbing his temples. He shook his head as though to clear it.

"What ..." he mumbled, "What happened? It felt like a dream ... but here I sit in my own seat ..."

"The devil take them all!" he suddenly thundered as he regained himself. "Was I attacked somehow right here in my own hall?"

"Aye, good king," Bedwyr said. "You were indeed. There are forces of darkness now loose in our lands. And they do not battle as men do. They sneak and they hide, They strike treacherously from the shadows. These are dark times for all men now."

"As though we didn't have enough to contend with already!" the king yelled. "Well, damn them all. I will tell you this, Bedwyr, as clear and direct as I can be."

"We maintain good relations with Gwynedd, and we do recognize your family's legitimate claim to the throne of Powys. We recognize your brother as the Powys King in exile," the king concluded. "And we will ask you to send our hearty good wishes to Dylan and to King Merfyn Frych when you see them. And tell them that Dyfed will join with Gwynedd if we can devise good prospects for successfully ousting Eluad ap Glast for all time."

"Thank you," Bedwyr said. "Your courage and your loyalty to your fellow Britons are an example for all. You are a stalwart ally indeed!"

"You have my best wishes for a safe and successful journey north, my friend," the king concluded.

His companions were waiting by their horses when Bedwyr left his breakfast with the king. Alantir seemed well-recovered after a good night's rest.

"You can share any news with us on our journey north,"

boomed Emrhys. "Let's mount up now and get on our way to the north of Gwynedd."

CHAPTER TWENTY

Gwynedd

One Week Before Winter Solstice

Bedwyr was leading his companions north along the coast-line towards Gwynedd. As they left Cardigan in Dyfed, they had entered the small country of Ceredigion, which lies between Dyfed and Gwynedd. Since this was a small province with Powys to its east, they proceeded carefully, with a watchful eye out for war bands from Powys. Another two weeks had passed since their boat had docked in Dyfed.

Like much of the land of the Britons, the area through which they were traveling had a rugged beauty. Lush green patches were scattered between the rocky coastline and the harsh, obdurate hills that lay inland. They had to set a hard pace as the winter solstice was rapidly approaching, and they needed to be well into the north of Gwynedd within a few more days. Seeking a good location to make camp on one night, they spotted a small group of warriors with a fire already blazing. After some deliberation with Emrhys, Bedwyr thought they were from Gwynedd, but he and his companions approached carefully.

They hailed the small group before they got too close, and it turned out that they were, in fact, from Gwynedd. Once introduced, the four companions were invited to join the warriors around their fire. One of the men, Garth, knew Bedwyr's brother Dylan, which warmed relations between the two groups of strangers. Garth was a grizzled veteran, a captain of the rangers that patrolled the border regions. Thin and wiry, but well-muscled, Garth's weather-beaten face reflected a lifetime spent outdoors.

"Why are you here near your border with such a small number of warriors?" asked Bedwyr.

"We stayed here near the coastline while the rest of our group went to explore the southeast corner," was the answer. "That area has had many reports of incursion from Powys."

"Our king, Merfyn Frych, is determined to defend every single mile of our border," another man named Berwyn added. "And treat interlopers from the renegade king of Powys as harshly as they deserve."

"Aye, especially as he has now recognized your brother as the legitimate King of Powys in exile. Dylan, the true King of Powys, often rides with our border patrols to harry the false king's men," said Garth, "He gathers more fighting men from Powys to join under his banner with every day that passes. Eluad ap Glast is widely scorned and hated for the traitor and interloper that he is."

The two groups shared the food between them and also shared some amiable banter.

"Why do the women in your group keep those large hoods up?" asked Berwyn.

"They find the winter of Gwynedd extremely cold compared to their warmer climes in the far south," answered Bedwyr vaguely.

Before the conversation could continue any farther, they were interrupted by the sound of horses approaching rapidly from the east. Everyone around the campfire immediately scrambled to stand with their weapons ready.

Presently, a group of eight warriors wearing the arms of Gwynedd came riding into the camp at a rapid pace. They pulled up hard when they saw the populated campfire.

"A large group of Powys warriors tails us!" they shouted. "Make yourselves ready to defend our position!"

"How many are there?" Berwyn shouted.

"Twenty," came the reply. "Or more."

"We are outnumbered, then," Garth said. "And we should deploy defensively."

People moved quickly. They placed six Gwynedd warriors close on the eastern side of their fire where they would be clearly visible to the approaching Powys warriors. Then two separate groups of the remaining warriors hid behind them, flanking them, but invisible to the approaching war band. Bedwyr and Emrhys were in one such group of four warriors, and Alantir and Vaelwyn in another.

The Powys warriors rode right into the camp with no sense of caution and apparently every right to be there.

"Hail!" Garth, the Gwynedd leader called out. "What are you curs from the renegade king of Powys doing in our fair territory of Gwynedd?"

The leader of the Powys warriors looked the speaker right in the eye as he spat on the ground, "We go where we wish," he said simply. "Either defend your territory or tuck your tail and run."

Twenty seasoned warriors from Powys lined up in front

of the six Gwynedd warriors near the fire but the horses were now still, which removed the advantage of charging that horsemen usually enjoyed. Garth stepped forward and looked at the Powys men thoughtfully before suddenly lunging forward; he rolled on the ground and cut the hamstrings on the leader's horse.

His five men followed suit.

In the first moments of the battle, almost half of the Powys warriors were immediately unhorsed, and the remaining horses were spooked by the blood and chaos in their midst. The two groups of Gwynedd forces, hidden in darkness, now attacked the Powys warriors on both flanks, taking full advantage of the chaos and confusion. Many of the Powys warriors were dispatched immediately.

Two riders with uninjured horses broke away and rode hard back to the east, no doubt intending to bear news of this to their king.

As the initial fog of battle cleared, the two sides were more evenly matched. Ten of the Gwynedd warriors survived, along with Bedwyr and Emrhys. Those twelve faced thirteen from Powys, who had lost more of their men. But those thirteen could now see the giant warrior who aligned himself with Gwynedd.

Emrhys looked even more frightening in the flickering firelight. His towering figure held his sword and his battle-axe upraised. To everyone's surprise, one of the Powys warriors now held a crossbow ready. It was pointed right at Emrhys.

Suddenly, an arrow whistled through the darkness. Only the fletching was visible as the shaft buried itself deeply in the man's flesh. He clutched at the arrow buried in his throat for a few frenzied moments before falling lifeless to the ground.

Alantir followed her shot with two more in rapid succession. Arrows sprouted from the eye sockets of two more Powys men, and they also fell lifelessly to the ground.

Now, there were just ten Powys facing twelve Gwynedd, which included the terrifying giant as well as the fearsome archer hidden in the dark.

Garth spoke clearly, "I will offer you the same that you offered us," he scoffed. "Defend yourselves or tuck tail and run ... back to your renegade king."

"You will slaughter us if we run," said Powys.

"You have my word that you can leave unhindered and unmolested," he responded. "A far better treatment than you would have offered us."

<hr/>

The two groups from Gwynedd and Ljós were mounted and ready to move out shortly after dawn. There were only two days left until winter solstice now.

"Thank you again for your assistance," said Garth. "We would have been hard pressed to prevail against those curs without you."

"We were pleased to help strike a blow against that renegade king," said Bedwyr. "He who has taken my kingdom and my blood by treachery—and whose betrayal has earned my wrath. Please, if you can, make sure Dylan learns that I helped to strike this blow."

"Aye, Bedwyr," Garth replied. "We will make sure that your brother hears the entire tale, along with our own Gwynedd king, Merfyn Frych. I am sure that King Dylan and his growing band of loyal warriors will be greatly heartened to learn that their crown prince is alive and well and preparing to join the coming battle. Perhaps allying with

267

King Llywarch ap Hyfaidd of Dyfed as your brother has done with Merfyn Frych. In the meantime, fare well!"

"Farewell yourselves!" shouted Bedwyr as the two groups rode off in different directions.

CHAPTER TWENTY-ONE

Winter Solstice on Yr Wyddfa

Travel was bleak and exhausting in the winter season in northern Gwynedd. The light snow made for a pretty landscape but created treacherous footing. The companions made slow progress through the rugged terrain. When the terrain got particularly difficult, they sheltered their horses as best they could and proceeded on foot. Before entering the foothills, they had made arrangements with the villagers at their last stop. These folks had agreed to come into the foothills and retrieve the horses a few days after the travelers departed their village.

"We know that we can't just go straight to the summit of Yr Wyddfa," said Bedwyr. "There something else we must do first—as we have talked about."

"We still have a long trek ahead of us," Vaelwyn replied,

"but yes, we must work through our interim destination before we go to the summit. As we have talked about in our travels, we have go to the western shore of Llyn Llydaw, looking across to the eastern side," she continued in her strong, low voice. "And we must be in exactly the right position before sunset on the eve before the winter solstice."

"So we just do what we discussed when we reach Llyn Llydaw before sunset?" asked Alantir."

"Yes, when we look across the lake at that time from that location, we will all see the special vison that we talked about," said Vaelwyn. "And once our conjuring has enabled our access, we will retrieve a special key that we will need to complete our mission."

The group continued across the rugged terrain, strong winds blowing the light snow all around them.

"Llyn Llydaw is just ahead," said Vaelwyn. "We need to get in place on the western shore."

The group of travelers lined up on the lake's shore and looked around. Across from Llyn Llydaw rose the heights of Yr Wyddfa, along with the other peaks in the group: Y Liwedd, Crib Goch, and Garnedd Ugain. The calm water of Llyn Llydaw stretched out before them as the sun started to settle into the western horizon behind them.

As the last rays of the setting sun touched the far side of the lake and the gloaming was upon them, Vaelwyn raised her rune staff high in the air.

"Ceiliúradh a dhéanamh, Solas! A thógáil, staighre!" *Celebrate Light! Build a Stairway!* She called out as she pointed the tip of her rune staff to the far shore, then pulled it backward as though she were drawing a line across the lake.

Bedwyr felt goosebumps on his arms and the hair rising on the back of his neck as a series of silver lines spanned the body of water in front of them.

As the light from the setting sun faded on the eve of the winter solstice, a silver outline emerged. A light-limned walkway across the lake took solid form and in the middle of the lake now stood a small tower, with stairs ascending on one side and descending from the other.

"We must enter the tower quickly and retrieve the key," said Vaelwyn. "My conjuring the element of water has brought this tower up, but we will need Bedwyr's use of air magic to keep it aloft while we complete our task. Since this is all new to him, I am not sure how long Bedwyr will be able to sustain it."

"Thanks for the vote of confidence!" Bedwyr said. He grimaced as he concentrated on channeling his new abilities with air magic to keep the luminous tower and stairs lifted out of the water.

"Are you sure that we can walk on that?" asked Bedwyr. "I ... I don't want to let anyone down."

"Only one way to find out," said Alantir as she stepped onto the walkway. "Come on, let's go." She smiled at him as she stood solidly on the silver walkway.

Vaelwyn took the lead, and their group followed her the rest of the way across the walkway and up the silver stairs to the tower. Once inside, they were surprised by what they saw; the tower looked like a cavernous hall—but it was missing any walls or other structural features.

"Alantir," Vaelwyn said crisply, "you know what must be done."

Alantir concentrated and raised her hands in the air. As she swept her hands forward stone walls appeared along the sides of the hall.

"Nice!" Bedwyr said.

Alantir then pointed both hands at the far end of the hall and conjured a large stone hearth.

"And now," Vaelwyn said, "let's add some heat!"

And she put her hands together and conjured a small fireball which she sped toward the new hearth. A crackling fire now blazed in the new hearth.

Vaelwyn strode briskly to that hearth, where, on the mantle, a glass case slowly formed out of thin air. Inside it, a large silver key was suspended on a silver chain. With the case fully formed, Vaelwyn carefully grasped it, opened the front, and removed the silver key. She settled the key around her neck on its chain.

As soon as the key settled around her neck, they all felt a slight trembling under their feet.

"I, Uh, I ..." Bedwyr stammered, "... I think that my hold is weakening!"

"Me too!" shouted Alantir.

The stone walls of the tower glowed silver as the stone started to fade away. Vaelwyn led them through a doorway behind the hearth that led to the descending stairs from the tower.

As they left, Bedwyr could see that the silver light of the walkway behind them was starting to dissipate, and the tower itself was starting to fade.

"Aargh ..." he grunted.

"Run!" shouted Vaelwyn as she led them across the last stretch of the silver-lit walkway to the far side of Llyn Llydaw.

As they stood on the eastern shore catching their breath, they could see the last bits of the silver walkway fading from view. A minute more, and there was no sign that it had ever existed.

"That was a close thing," laughed Emrhys. "What would have happened to us if we hadn't made it out?"

"Nothing good," said Alantir. "That seems clear!"

"Now that we have this key, we must make our way over to the base of Yr Wyddfa," Vaelwyn answered. "And then climb to the summit to be in place by dawn on winter solstice."

With that, the group of travelers moved ahead toward the base of Yr Wyddfa.

━━━━━━ •◆• ━━━━━━

As they started on their way, Bedwyr felt some small rocks siding into him from further up the slope. *Must be windier than I thought up there,* he thought.

Emrhys led his companions forward. As they approached the sharper slope leading up from the base, he stopped suddenly. "Alert!" he thundered before he was engaged in a full hand-to-hand struggle.

Although it was now dark, it appeared that his attacker was about as large as Emrhys himself.

"Trolls!" yelled Vaelwyn. "Prepare yourselves!"

Vaelwyn illuminated her rune staff enough for them to see what was happening. A large, green-skinned creature was battling Emrhys. The troll had a bald head, pointy ears, and very thick, heavy-looking limbs. Emrhys was taller, but the troll was wider.

As they watched, the troll raised a huge stone club in the air and brought it whistling down toward Emrhys' head. Emrhys blocked the blow with *Dawnslayer*, but the force of the impact was clear to see. Emrhys himself delivered a strong blow to the troll with his black axe mace, but it barely seemed to register on its thick, slimy skin.

"I can't get through to help him," said Bedwyr." And I think I see a second troll behind that first one."

Before Vaelwyn could answer, they felt something whistle through the air between them. As Bedwyr watched the struggle between Emrhys and the troll, he saw the green monster suddenly sprout an arrow's fletching from its right eye. It staggered backward and Emrhys gripped his black battle axe in a two-handed grip and struck off the troll's head with one powerful blow.

Bedwyr looked behind him and saw Alantir just lowering her bow after having taken out the troll's eye with a single well-timed shot.

"Bedwyr was right. There is another troll right behind the first," Alantir said as she nocked another arrow. "But I do not have a clear shot at this second one."

"There is not a lot of time here," Bedwyr shouted. "Ah, I wish I could get up there to help! I hate feeling helpless!"

"We will not all survive if your second arrow misses," Vaelwyn stated.

"I know, I know," Alantir spat out. "But you know what happens to my aim when I am not calm. And you are not helping! I am trying …"

"I've got this one," Vaelwyn said as she raised her right hand in a fist with her heavy gold ring pointed toward the second troll and a searing bolt of bright red light shot out, drilling a hole through the second troll's head. As its lifeless corpse fell to the ground, the companions moved quickly up the slope, climbing toward the summit as steadily as they could.

"Our presence here is clearly no secret," Emrhys observed, "I wonder what else the forces of Shadow may have in store for us?"

They approached the summit of Yr Wyddfa just as dawn was illuminating the horizon to the east. Vaelwyn seemed to know just where to position herself in between a number of rock outcrops and large boulders. As the first rays of dawn's sunlight touched the rock face in front of her, Vaelwyn's face showed deep concentration. A diagram became illuminated on the summit's face, not visible a few moments ago; an ornately detailed circle with a pattern of interlocking leaves and tree branches. At the circle's heart was a slot to insert the key she'd obtained from the tower, now worn around her neck. There was also an ancient elven script illuminated. The translation was:

Beware the key holder,
'Ware the path chosen,
Upward Light will call thee,
Downward Shadow claims thee.

Vaelwyn removed the key from around her neck and moved it to the slot within the center of the circle on the rock face. As she looked at the key and the ancient elven script, she turned the key downside up.

It seemed unnatural to have it turned around like that, but she was now certain this was the hidden message in the script illuminated before her, "*Upward Light will call thee* ... "

She inserted the key as she had positioned it.

For a moment, nothing happened. Then, the outline of a doorway illuminated on the rock face, and it opened inward.

"Ha! You fools!" they heard a nasty-sounding voice cackle behind them.

They turned and saw a tall, slender being that looked somewhat like one of the Álfur but with lank, greasy hair. He was slightly stooped, with bent shoulders and red-rimmed squinty eyes. He wore a long, dark cloak, and he carried a twisted black rune staff. There was a faint but unpleasant smell to him, and he almost crackled with unseen power.

Bedwyr felt the hair on the back of his neck rising, and there was a deep, threatening rumble coming from Emrhys that sounded like a growl.

"My name is Magwei," the dark elf said. "I am one of the gölge yürüteç of my people, and you are all fools. You were lucky to escape from my avatar in the forest of Skógur. Here on this mountain in Terra, though, I am fully incarnate with all of my powers."

"Vaelwyn," boomed Emrhys. "You must not tarry here. You alone can complete the first step. We will deal with this servant of Shadow."

"I would never have been able to open that door myself," he gloated. "But now that you have opened it for me, I can sabotage the Elemental Seal of the North forever."

"You have no magic, Emrhys!" Vaelwyn countered. "How will you stand against a Shadow Walker of the Dark Fae with no magic of your own to call upon?"

"We stand with him," Alantir stated firmly. "And our magic is now awakened within us."

"And we have our amulets," growled Bedwyr. "With the increased power that comes from our Elemental friends."

"You must enter now!" shouted Emrhys. "Leave this dark creature to us."

As Vaelwyn reluctantly entered the doorway, Magwei cackled, "Yes, yes," his grating voice said. "I will be along to take care of you quickly enough. After I dispose of your friends here." He gestured with his left hand, and a dirty gray shield appeared, shimmering in his grasp. "Good luck," he said simply, with an evil lopsided smirk on his face.

Emrhys lunged forward, but *Dawnslayer* was stopped cold by the dark elf's gray shield. It did not look very substantial, but it certainly stopped *Dawnslayer*. Enraged, Emrhys pulled out his black battle axe. This, too, was stopped cold by the dark elf's shield.

"What's the matter, you big oaf?" Magwei taunted, "All those muscles not helping?"

Alantir and Bedwyr looked at each other. They could see in each other's eyes that they shared the same idea. They stepped forward, one on each side of their friend Emrhys.

A blue glow shimmered around Bedwyr and grew stronger and brighter with passing seconds. And a similar green glow now shimmered around Alantir.

The wind swirled around Bedwyr. It steadily rose to a howling gale. He clenched his fists and glowered at Magwei.

"You and your evil friends were behind the slaughter of my family!" he yelled. "Conspiring with those stinking Saxons—spreading murder and mayhem through Briton lands!"

The earth rumbled. Beneath Alantir's feet the soil rippled like waves in a stormy sea.

"Yes," she said with a firm set to her jaw and fire in her eyes. "And you unleashed your soul-sucking shadows on my innocent elves in Beechwood!"

Bedwyr clenched both fists and pulled them up against his chest. His amulet shone brightly as he then pushed both fists straight out toward Magwei, cold blue flames dancing around his hands as a powerful blast of air pulled the darkling into the air and then crashed him back down into the ground.

As he slowly got up from the ground, Magwei chortled. "That's it?" he said. "You really think that just knocking me over is going to save your precious quest?"

Alantir had used the time Bedwyr had gained for her to balance herself in order to wield her magic more forcefully. As Magwei started to rise, she raised her arms over her head. Cold, green flames crackling around her hands. Then she thrust them down sharply. Her amulet burned bright green around her neck as a deep and jagged chasm opened in the ground below Magwei.

The dark elf had a look of astonishment on his face as the earth swallowed him.

Emrhys, Alantir, and Bedwyr, stepped through the doorway into the mountain after Vaelwyn and dropped their gear just inside the entry. They found themselves in a stone corridor, where the walls pulsed with softly glowing light. Farther ahead, a short passageway opened up into a chamber that had a variation of the quaternary sigil embedded in the floor. This version had only two of the elements inscribed into the floor of the chamber: earth and air. Vaelwyn was standing in the center of the room.

"The elements are supposed to be illuminated," she said, not looking up. "But as you can see, they are dim. This is the first of the reasons why the Elemental Seal of the North is failing."

"How do we illuminate them?" asked Bedwyr.

"You must stand over the element of air," Vaelwyn answered. "And Alantir must stand over the element of earth. I will stand in the center. I will use some of my life force, my Fjör, to illuminate the elements here."

Vaelwyn drew a deep breath and concentrated, seeking balance within herself before she conjured. That faint silver aura surrounded her, pulsing and shimmering.

"I'm not seeing any difference," Bedwyr said.

"Neither am I," said Alantir.

"Ughh," Vaelwyn said. "Okay, I will push much more of my Fjör into the pattern."

The silver glow around Vaelwyn got brighter. And brighter. There were sounds now too. Her arms were fully extended and her fingers were rigid like claws. Tremors racked her body.

"I hear a howling wind—but there is no wind!" Bedwyr yelled.

"And I hear a raging thunderstorm—but there is no rain!" Alantir yelled back.

The ground trembled under their feet, and the rocks around them were giving off heat from an inferno.

"Wait!" Emrhys shouted. "You can't keep pushing more and more of your Fjör into this. You could burn out your Talent—or even kill yourself!"

"I must try!" Vaelwyn shouted back. "I don't know what else to do—and failure is not an option!"

"Wait!" interjected Alantir. "Wait! Let's just think this through—together—I am sure we can find another solution. There must be one!"

"There is no way to illuminate the elements here without a tremendous amount of Fjör," responded Vaelwyn soberly.

"Ok, so let's quickly figure out a way to provide the Fjör we need," responded Alantir as she yanked at her cloak. "There are four of us here. What if we link together and whatever Fjör is needed can be drawn from all of us equally?"

"Yes!" said Bedwyr, standing beside Alantir. "Let's try that."

"Yes," boomed Emrhys. "Our mortal friend has an excellent suggestion here."

"But all of us will then be left severely weakened," protested Vaelwyn.

"Yes," replied Alantir. "But you will still be alive. We can all recover from temporarily losing some—even a lot—of our life force, but nobody can recover from the loss of all their Fjör."

"I don't know about this, " Vaelwyn said as she thought quickly. "All of us would be weakened by this, making us more vulnerable to the Dark Fae."

"Aye," Emrhys broke in, "and if you burn yourself out trying to light up this pattern all. by yourself—then you leave these two fledglings alone to face the dark magic of the gölge yürüteç!"

Vaelwyn thought quickly and concluded that this was a solution that could actually work. Three weakened mages were better than only two; both of them only recently empowered and still unsure of themselves. "Ok, I will agree," said Vaelwyn heavily, "but we will have to move very quickly now."

She inserted her rune staff into a slot in the center of the chamber designed for this purpose as Bedwyr stood over the symbol of air, and Alantir over the symbol of earth. Vaelwyn and Emrhys each stood at one of the other two unoccupied points. Slowly, all four joined hands.

As Vaelwyn began to speak, her rune staff started to glow, as did each of the four companions. The glow from everyone else seemed to pulse toward Alantir, and she began to glow bright green, pulsed brightly and then passing into the symbol of earth inscribed into the sigil beneath her feet. The ground trembled, and a scent of freshly turned soil filled the room.

Then, the glow from everyone else shifted toward Bedwyr, who began to glow bright blue. In turn, his light passed into the symbol of air as a strong breeze blew through the chamber.

Suddenly, words illuminated in the air above Vaelwyn's rune staff. The letters rotated slowly so that they were visible from any point in the room. Magic made the words appear in the native language of each reader:

Find the Saxon warrior next,
Spear and shield among the best,
Her fencing swords have brought her fame,
Golden hair, her face does frame.

"*Saxon warrior?*" said Bedwyr. "Must we do this?"

"Yes, Bedwyr," replied Vaelwyn. We must follow exactly. Did you notice the final words of the verse?"

"We must find an accomplished Saxon warrior, a woman. A shield-maiden, as the Norse would name her," said Emrhys, his face alight.

"Look!" said Alantir. "More words are appearing."

The suspended magic verse continued:

The task complete, you now must leave,
Complete your next by Imbolc eve,
Scafell Pike is where you must go,
Accomplish this; twill strike a blow.

"All right," said Vaelwyn. "Now we know more about the next step. We know who we must find and where we must go to complete another repair to the Elemental Seal of the North."

"And we know we must reach Scafell Pike by Imbolc Eve," said Emrhys.

"Where is that?" asked Alantir.

"North," answered Bedwyr. "Into the hills and lakes of Cumbria. A chaotic land claimed by Britons, Saxons, Picts, and Norsemen."

The companions gathered their gear and slowly started their exit from the chamber. They were all exhausted and not moving quickly. But they were moving. And the symbols of the two elements glowed bright and strong in their settings inscribed into the floor of the chamber behind them.

The illuminated doorway on the mountainside disappeared as it closed behind them, leaving them standing on the summit of Yr Wyddfa in the bright midday sun.

Their respite was brief as a malevolent voice welcomed their return.

"You can't really think that you could get rid of me that easily? "cackled the voice of the dark elf, Magwei. "You do not look your best, Vaelwyn," his voice grated. "This may be easier than I thought."

The tired companions turned to face Magwei and were chagrined to see that he had two trolls there with him and a second gölge yürüteç. They prepared to fight, thinking their tired eyes were playing tricks on them at a shift in the air. The temperature didn't so much drop as cease to exist, sound was replaced by a void. Everything started to look blurry. Their companions, the dark elves and the trolls, as well as the rock-strewn summit—it all looked blurry.

Then, everything seemed to dissolve into nothingness and a sizzling white haze surrounded them.

Bedwyr heard voices that sounded familiar, but he was still half asleep. He opened his eyes and saw the unmistakable blue skies of Ljós. He slowly sat up and rubbed his eyes. He was in a very comfortable bed, with a fire burning in the hearth across the room. He recognized the elvish design and architecture that was a part of Ljós.

Alantir was sitting next to him with a warm smile on her face. She gave him a huge hug and kissed him gently. "I woke up a short time before you," she said. "But I had to wait for you to wake up on your own."

"What happened?" asked Bedwyr, somewhat muddled, but slowly realizing how much he enjoyed kissing her. "How did we get here? How did we get away from those annoying Shadow Walkers?"

"I can explain that for you, Bedwyr," said Vaelwyn from behind him. "When Caedwyn conjured the doorway that sent us into Terra, he added an unusual feature. He tied our continued presence in Terra to a short interval after the completion of our task," she explained. "So, having completed our repair the magic quickly returned us to Ljós."

"Well, that was a helpful trick," answered Bedwyr. "Very grateful to Caedwyn for that one."

"We all need to rest here in Ljós for a while," Vaelwyn replied. "Then we will need to start preparing for whatever Caedwyn and the king have planned for us next."

Bedwyr reflected on everything that had occurred in such a short period. He had learned a great deal and met many new people. He had acquired new skills and abilities that he had never even dreamed of previously; and Dylan was alive and well. He had traveled between realms, helped battle the forces of the Shadow. He was with Alantir. Of everything that had happened, this seemed the most important.

"King Aneirin of the silver elves has gifts that he would like to present to each of you," said Vaelwyn. "As soon as you both feel recovered enough."

Alantir and Bedwyr smiled and reached out to hold each other's hands.

A short time later, Bedwyr glanced at his surroundings again. They had walked to some sort of small natural amphitheater in the middle of a woodland glade unlike any that he had ever seen before; high in the mountains with beautiful vistas beyond them.

"Alantir," he said. "Look at how they carved benches right into several tiers of the earth. That small rise gives them seating for several dozen of these Adepti, but it seems like a natural part of the terrain."

Alantir sighed. "Bedwyr, how can you look back there

when just behind where the king is standing are such beautiful woodlands. The hills and valleys below us seem to be on display just for the Adepti. Crisp, clear sunshine and bright, colorful foliage. And some lingering mist on the floors of the valleys. Truly a wondrous view on such a beautiful morning!"

King Aneirin had a broad smile on his face as he greeted Bedwyr and Alantir, "Ahem …ahem …"

Bedwyr and Alantir turned to give the king their full attention.

"First, my heartfelt thanks to both of you for your assistance with this first task to repair the Elemental Seals," the king said. "We are all deeply grateful."

"Second," he continued, "we will need your help to complete the next set of tasks as well. As we will discuss later."

"But now, Bedwyr of Powys, please step forward," the king said.

As the tall, broad-shouldered Bedwyr approached the king, he smiled at Alantir, his brown eyes sparkling with mirth and his long dark hair tucked behind his ears.

"I am pleased to present you with an elven sword of great distinction. This sword was forged of special alloys by the master smiths of the Álfur and is imbued with elven magic. It is perfectly balanced; it will never tarnish, and its blade will never lose its edge. The name of this sword is *a Sciúradh*, which means 'sunder' in our tongue, and I hope that you use it to rent asunder many of our foes that oppose Light."

Bedwyr bowed slightly in respect, "Thank you, Lord King," he said beaming, "This is a gift that I will always treasure—and will always enjoy using against our Shadow enemies!"

"Alantir of the woodland elves, or should I say Princess Alantir of Skógur, please step forward," Aneirin said.

Alantir now smiled at Bedwyr as she moved forward. She was wearing her long dark hair in a braid, with the gold circlet given to her by King Mandáron on her brow. Bedwyr admired her and the sinuous movement of her walk as she approached the king.

"For you, Alantir, I am pleased to present you with an elven bow that has been carefully crafted from rare woods by the expert bowyers of your people in Skógur. Its unique design, rare wood, and craftsmanship give this bow the power of a much longer and heavier longbow, despite its compact size and light weight. And they have also crafted a special case for this bow that will protect against impact as well as inclement weather."

Bedwyr and Alantir smiled at each other again and moved into a warm embrace.

"Ahem, uh … now I must also say a few words about the tasks we face next. You will continue to work with Vael-wyn and Emrhys, and you will also add new companions to your team."

Bedwyr and Alantir reluctantly broke their embrace and turned to King Aneirin.

"You have another major challenge ahead to complete the repair of the Elemental Seal of the North; and then, you will have other tasks ahead to repair the other Elemental Seals. For now, I catch only a glimpse of one more such journey in the North, but that is all I have been able to scry so far."

A movement outside the window caught Bedwyr's eye. It was a hawk soaring above the open field outside. His thoughts tumbled, *I am glad to help my new companions with another quest, but I also have responsibilities to my family in Terra. I must help Dylan to avenge ourselves on the Saxons – and to retake our kingdom from that wretched usurper from Dogfeiling, Eluad ap Glast!*

"Also, I think that you have both now learned the real source of your personal misfortunes," Aneirin continued soberly. "You now know that the Dark Fae are your real enemy. They are behind all of the personal loss and tragedy that you have both suffered. Your real true enemies, the ones who caused the deaths of your beloved family members, are not Saxons or shadows. These are mere pawns on the game table that we are living through. Save your hatred and your thirst for revenge for the Dark Fae!"

Bedwyr and Alantir looked at each other again. Their eyes showed a shared understanding of exactly who their real enemy was. And the hard set to their jaws showed their shared resolve to avenge their families. Whatever it takes.

"Now, for your next challenge, Vaelwyn will lead you where need dictates. I do scry that you will travel deep into the Saxon kingdoms of East Anglia and Northumbria to start. And I foresee that you will complete the final steps in this challenge in disputed Cumbria.

"You have accomplished much with this first challenge," concluded King Aneirin. "But you must now know that your work has just begun. *Balance must be restored.*"

EPILOGUE

One Week After Winter Solstice

Magwei moved slowly across the rock-strewn surface, heading towards the range of jagged peaks in front of him. High, thin clouds obscured the starlight and did little to illuminate his way. He passed the petrified remains of long lifeless trees scattered around a putrid pool of standing water. The familiar sound of bats screeching in the air above him was comforting, as was the sound of small, scaly creatures scrabbling through the rocks surrounding the path.

Magwei knew that he had rough treatment awaiting him at the hands of his fellow outrunners when he got back to the Dark Henge. It was not the first time he had been on the receiving end, and it probably would not be the last. He would survive it, but he certainly preferred to be giving the harsh treatment rather than receiving it.

He approached the large, ornately wrought gates of the main entrance to the city of the Dark Fae. These gates of Pûlnoc were cast from some long-forgotten alternative to iron that their ancestors had discovered long ago as they delved deeply into the dark earth beneath the mountains. It was here at the center of Myrkur, within this gigantic ring of jagged mountains, that the Dark Fae had built their city.

The inner perimeter of these jagged mountains was impressive. It would take a full day to traverse one side to the other at the widest point. The Dark Henge, of course, sat at the center of this outer ring of mountains.

Pûlnoc was built into the inner face of the mountain ring, carved from dark granite. Polished human skulls sat atop the entry stairs leading to almost every doorway. Here and there, one could see an occasional Álfur skull or the very rare and very large skull of a Breacadh an Lae. The city rose high above the valley floor, but not too high. Each building had a wide veranda in the front, and the floor of the valley had four separate arenas, one at each cardinal point of the compass, affording the verandas a clear view.

The four arenas were the locations where the blood sports competitions were staged, ravenously celebrated by the Dark Fae. It was here that the most physically robust human slaves were forced to engage in mortal combat. All of the Dark Fae watched this bloody sport from the comfort of their verandas. Once in a great while, they were able to watch a pair of Álfur engage in this mortal combat, but it was a very rare event and highly prized. Even the use of human slaves had become very rare for long ages after the Great Sundering. It was only recently that the flow had increased again. Since the Elemental Seals had started to fail, human slaves had slowly started to rise in number once more. One could even see a few of them; ragged, frightened looking, scurrying about the city, running errands for their Dark Fae masters.

The main gate to Pûlnoc was set on the western side of the

city, and Magwei's destination was south. He was heading for the Council of Éjfél. This was the home of the Varázsló, whose ranks included the gölge yürüteç, or Shadow Walkers, like himself, as well as the inquisitors—the elite masters of the Dark Fae who rarely left the city. Both the gölge yürüteç and the inquisitors commanded the evil magic of all four of their dark elements. Blood magic and bone magic required dark rituals involving torture and sacrifice of other living beings. Ice and magma magic required dark rituals that involved the torture and sacrifice of the Earth itself. The rest of the Dark Fae wielded the magic of just one of these dark elements, the one that corresponded to their location within the city. The Dark Fae living north, south, east, and west each controlled the magic of just the one element that was aligned with that cardinal point.

It had taken months for Magwei to recover from the torture—a consequence for his failure to stop Prime Adeptus Vaelwyn's successful first step to repair the Elemental Seal of the North. Teeth regrew slowly and he could still only eat soup—something that bothered him possibly more than the still-open sores on his back and chest. Everything leaked.

Still, he was now sitting as a council member for the first time since his return, listening to the interchange between his fellow gölge yürüteç and the inquisitors.

"We will have many more opportunities to interrupt their efforts," said a large inquisitor named Bufol. "The fools have not yet realized that although they must succeed with every single step to completely repair the Elemental Seals, we only have to succeed once, and the barriers between the worlds will remain broken forever."

"And they are also vulnerable to our hidden threat," said Nalwei, the southern Shadow Walker. "They have no idea we have an ally who sits on the inner councils of the Álfur.

* * *

GLOSSARY

PEOPLE	DESCRIPTION
Aelfgif	Daughter of East Anglia Chieftain – Saxon Shield Maiden
Aelle	King of East Anglia; Aelfgif's uncle
Aeryn	King of Air Elementals
Afan	Son of Powys King
Alantir	Woodland Elf from Terra
Alderon	King of Lán Léargas in Ljós Realm of Fjall
Aldorthyn	Prime Adeptus of Silver Elves; Warden of West
Aneirin	King of the Silver Elves
Arawn	Son of Powys King
Arthur	Briton King of Dumnonia and Armorica
Baldyrien	King of Teilatua in Ljós Realm of Fjall
Bedwyr	Son of Powys Chieftain – Briton warrior

PEOPLE	DESCRIPTION
Caedwyn	Senior Prime Adeptus of Silver Elves; Midgard Warden
Caradoc	Brother of Alantir
Cerwen	Sister of Alantir
Cuthbert	Brother of Aelfgif
Cynfor	Briton Chieftain of Powys, father of Bedwyr
Cynric	Saxon Chieftain of East Anglia; father of Aelfgif
Dalamyra	Queen of Tishina in Skógur Realm of Ljós
Danderion	Prince of Lán Léargas in Ljós Realm of Fjall
Delbaeth	King of the Breacadh an Lae ("Dawn Kin")
Dylan	Brother of Bedwyr
Eardwulf	King of Saxon Mercia
Edyth	Aelfgif's mother
Eluad ap Glast	Usurper King of Powys and Dogfeiling
Emrhys	Warrior-Prince and Caomhnoir of the Breacadh an Lae
Garth	Gwynedd ranger captain
Griffin	Brother of Bedwyr
Gwendlyn	Alantir's mother
Hengist	Saxon Master at Arms for Cynric
Kalderion	King of Tulipesä in Eydimörk Realm of Ljós

PEOPLE	DESCRIPTION
Löswellyn	Queen of Tulipesä Eydimörk Realm of Ljós
Llywarch ap Hyfaidd	Briton King of Dyfed
Lyndelle	Alantir friend from Teilatua
Madoc	Brother of Bedwyr
Magwei	Dark Elf; gölge yürüteç, Shadow Walker; One of "The Six"
Maltrin	Bedwyr friend from Teilatua; rider giant war hawk
Mandáron	King of Garmoniya in Skógur Realm of Ljós
Merfyn Frych	Briton King of Gwynedd
Meriel	Friend of Alantir
Myrwei	Dark Elf; gölge yürüteç, Shadow Walker; One of "The Six"
Nalwei	Dark Elf; gölge yürüteç, Shadow Walker; One of "The Six"
Neldorin	Prime Adeptus of Silver Elves; Warden of the South
Rhedwyn	Prime Adeptus of Silver Elves; former Warden of North
Rhynwei	Dark Elf; gölge yürüteç, Shadow Walker; One of "The Six"
Selyf ap Cynan	Briton King of Powys

PEOPLE	DESCRIPTION
Sylvane	Queen of Earth Elementals
Tallendal	Champion Archer from Garmoniya
Taorlyn	Prime Adeptus of the Silver Elves; Warden of the West
Tarandyl	Alantir's father
Toland	Envoy from Eardwulf of Mercia; Slain by Cuthbert
Uulwei	Dark Elf; gölge yürüteç, Shadow Walker; One of "The Six"
Vaelwyn	Prime Adeptus of the Silver Elves; Warden of the North
Velkwei	Dark Elf; gölge yürüteç, Shadow Walker; One of "The Six"

PLACES	DESCRIPTION
Abhaile	Island of the Breacadh an Lae in Ljós
Armorica	Briton Kingdom South of Dumnonia (in Brittany)
Beechwood	Home of the Woodland Elves of Terra
Cardigan	Town in Dyfed
Clun Forest	Location of the Woodland Elves of Terra
Dogfeiling	Briton Kingdom ruled by Eluad ap Glast
Dumnonia	Briton Kingdom ruled by Arthur
Dyfed	Briton Kingdom ruled by Llywarch ap Hyfaidd
Ekaitza	Kingdom in Sjávar Realm in Ljós
Eydimörk	Realm of the Red Elves in Ljós
Fjall	Realm of the Blue Elves in Ljós
Fjall Bay	Large Bay at Far Northwest Region of Ljós
Garmoniya	Kingdom in Skógur Realm in Ljós
Gate of Dendalyn	Valley of Respite; soul-weary Álfur pass to The Sojourn
Gwynedd	Briton Kingdom ruled by Merfyn Frych
Ilfracombe	Port Town in Dumnonia
Lán Léargas	Kingdom in Fjall Realm in Ljós
Ljós	Land of Light, Home of the Álfur & Prime Adepti
Llyn Llydaw	Lake in Northern Gwynedd

PLACES	DESCRIPTION
Mercia	Saxon Kingdom in Terra
Myrkur	Land of Shadow, Home of the Dark Elves & gölge yürüteç
Powys	Briton Kingdom ruled by Selyf ap Cynan
Pûlnoc	City of the Dark Elves in Myrkur
Rélegur	Kingdom in Vatnid Realm in Ljós
Sjávar	One of the Realms of the Grey Elves in Ljós
Skógur	Realm of the Green Elves in Ljós
Northern Gwynedd	Region of Mountains in Gwynedd
Teilatua	Kingdom in Fjall Realm in Ljós
Tenby	Port Town in Dyfed
Terra	Land of Mortals
Tintagel	Town in Dumnonia
Tishina	Kingdom in Sjávar Realm in Ljós
Tulipesä	Kingdom in Eydimörk Realm in Ljós
Vatnid	One of the Realms of the Grey Elves in Ljós
Vesë	Kingdom in Vatnid Realm of Ljós
Vilnis	Kingdom in Sjávar Realm of Ljós
Wessex	Saxon Kingdom in Terra
Yr Wyddfa	Tallest Mountain in Gwynedd

THINGS	DESCRIPTION
Álfur	The High Elves of Ljós
Breacadh an Lae	Giant Warriors of Ljós ("Dawn Kin")
Caomhnoir	Warrior-Prince of the Breacadh an Lae ("Guardian")
Daemons	Dark Elementals; allied with Dark Fae
Dark Henge	Stone Circle of the Dark Elves, Celebration of Shadow
Éjfél	Ruling Council of the Dark Elves
Elemental Seals	Magic Barrier That Seals Off Myrkur
Fjör	Life Force Used in Magic of the Álfur
Great Sundering	Event of Barrier to Myrkur with Elemental Seals
Imbolc	Mid-winter Festival
Inquisitors	Senior Members of Dark Elf Ruling Council
Gölge Yürüteç	Dark Elves, Shadow Walkers; "The Six"
Quaternary Knot	Interwoven Knot Pattern with Four Corners
Sidhe (Aos Sidhe)	"People of the Mounds" (ancient human term for Fae)

THINGS	DESCRIPTION
Triquetra	Interwove Knot Pattern with Three Corners
Vålnad	Masters of the Living Shadows
Prime Adepti	Silver Elf Wizards ("Wardens")
White Henge	Stone Circle of the Silver Elves, Celebration of Light

… If you enjoyed this book, here's a sneak peek at Book Two in the series.

SAXON KINGS AND DARK FAE

CHAPTER ONE

Shield Maiden of Anglia

Eight Weeks Before Festival of Imbolc

Aelfgif washed the dark sticky blood from her bright steel sword, then wiped it down with the greasy woolskin she kept for precisely this purpose. She held her sword out at arm's length and once again admired the beauty of the hammered whorls on her blade and the balance of the hilt and leather handle crisscrossed with wire. It had been a gift from her favorite uncle and was her most prized possession. +VLFBERHT+ engraved on the blade just below the hilt marked it as one of the finest blades in the realm. The few blades that bore that mark were prized by all swordsmen—made by a master swordsmith on the continent. These blades were not prized because they were pretty or bejeweled—but because of their unique combination of lightness, strength and perfect balance. The sword was deceptively simple looking, nothing ornate about it, a perfect tool for an accomplished swordsman. Or swordswoman.

"Why do these Britons keep sending their young men to steal our cattle!?" Aelfgif shouted. "I am so tired of killing untalented young fools, but they keep coming."

The Saxon shield maiden stood 5'6" tall with wide shoulders and a well-toned, athletic physique. She had piercing blue eyes and straight blond hair, blunt cut at shoulder length with short bangs. Her dark blue quilted tunic fit snugly over her ample chest and was belted tightly at the waist. Her sword belt hung low on her hips, and her dark brown leggings were tucked into well-worn knee-high boots. She wore a long knife, a seax, on the other side of her sword belt.

Aelfgif absent mindedly fingered the silver amulet that she had always worn around her neck since childhood. It showed a large tree contained within a circle, with some of the branches losing leaves, and had a small ruby in the center. It was heavy and well-worn from long years of constant handling. Her uncle Osgood had given it to her when she was young and told her that it had been in their family for many generations. Her other uncle, Aelle, was their king in East Anglia. Their family traced their ancestry back to the fabled royal family of Sweden, the Wuffingas. The East Anglia descendants of the Wuffingas had come and conquered these lands many years ago and drove away the native Britons. The Angles and Saxons had been so successful in their conquests that the Britons were now reduced to holding only the far western fringes of these lands.

Memories of her uncle and his harsh training regimen came unbidden to her then.

I have not thought about those years of early training with Uncle Osgood for a long time now, she mused.

----------- ◆ -----------

The large man's sword slammed into the young girl's helm. Then he planted his foot in the middle of her chest and sent her sprawling in the mud.

"Ha, there you go, Arse-gif!" Uncle yelled. "You're damn lucky girl, that my wooden practice sword is what just banged your head!"

Aelfgif said nothing to this, but sat up, dazed. Her uncle Osgood pulled no punches with her.

"Aye, if you're goin' to keep beggin' me ta sneak around and teach ya swordcraft behind your lord father's back, then ya'd better get much more serious about it. And fast."

Aelfgif spat blood in the mud and said, "You know damn well I'm already far better with a sword than my brother ever was at the same age!" she shouted. "Even with the miserly amount of time you spare for my training!"

Her thoughts returned to the present as she took the long walk back to her family's estate. Her small band of men would follow more slowly with the recaptured herd of cattle.

----------- ◆ -----------

Aelfgif took a deep breath of the cool morning air as she reached her family's manor house. The morning sun filtered through the leaves of the trees and created a carpet of dappled light on the forest path. Her younger siblings, Bryce and Devona, would just be waking up now. Of course her older siblings Cuthbert and Aedre would have been up for a while now, working with Mother and Father. She wandered into the practice yard to see if gruff old Hengist would be there. He had been the master at arms for her family since her father was a young man. He was still a robust man, even in his later years. He had lost a couple of teeth somewhere along the way which gave him a perpetually battered appearance; and he walked with a slight limp from an old wound. Hengist was under strict instructions from her father not to indulge Aelfgif's warrior pursuits, but the old man admired her grit and determination. And he knew that she was damn good with a sword, probably better than her brothers.

"Ah, bollocks girl!" he said. "You're never 'ere when your father comes lookin', child! 'Ave ya forgott'n? The king's comin' ta visit tonight, with 'is typical large gaggle of followers."

Aelfgif patted the crusty old warrior on his shoulder as she picked up a hefty battle axe and went through some fast moves.

"Don't get yourself all worked up, Hengist, I am here now. What did my father want with me?"

"To see your lady mother as soon as is decent," Hengist said. "Something about not dressin' like a dirty warrior tonight, but like the beautiful young lady we all know she is!" His lopsided grin widened as he saw Aelfgif's less-than-impressed expression, and he added, "And he is right ya know. Those dirty and smelly clothes. You're worse than Bryce!"

"All right Hengist," Aelfgif said. "If you are going to badger me like a cranky old bull, then I will go find my Lady mother straight away."

"But I'm starving and I'm going to raid the larder for some ham and cheese before I go," she said. Then she spent lots of time in the larder where she carved herself big hunks of ham and cheese. She strolled out with a self-satisfied smirk on her face.

Lady Edyth was an attractive woman and leading member of the Angle and Saxon royalty of East Anglia. She always made sure that everyone knew that the royals of East Anglia were descended from the Wuffingas, the legendary royal family of Sweden. She proudly displayed her house's version of the East Anglia coat of arms, with the three gold crowns of the Swedish royals included. She strongly detested her middle daughter's obsession with a warrior's skills and pursuits. To her, women of the Saxon royalty should develop their feminine skills, which she saw as beauty, poise and mastery of their domestic domain.

"I don't know why that child insists on these warrior trappings," she mumbled to herself as she tidied up her sitting room. "A beautiful young girl with a comely figure. But she never shows it! An eligible bachelor, how in heaven will she ever find one!? Of course, being told what to do by her father and actually doing it are two different things for Aelfgif."

"Hello Mother," Aelfgif interrupted. "I was told that you wanted to see me.

"Oh, have you re-done your sitting room?" she continued. "Again ..."

"You know perfectly well why I wanted to see you," Edyth replied. "I have your lovely clothes laid out on your bed. The king and his party will be here in just a few hours—and you must bathe yourself and dress accordingly!"

"Here we all are," Aelfgif said to Cuthbert. "All bright and shiny and lined up in a row for uncle Aelle. Are we real people or puppets?" She giggled at her own humor.

"You always have to make light of our formal traditions," Cuthbert observed. "What is it with you? You look beautiful in that dress and we can all relax and have fun tonight. Why do you have to make fun of it all?"

"Because this is not who I am, stupid!" she said as she poked her brother in the ribs. "We both know that. I come truly alive in the dirt and muck with a sword in my hand and enemies to slay—not simpering around in a pretty dress batting my eyes at the eligible bachelors."

'Besides," she added, "I am a princess and I should be able to do anything that I want—just like the other princesses." And she laughed again.

Despite everyone waiting to formally greet King Aelle, he wanted to have a private word with Cynric before the feast. So the two brothers huddled over in the far corner of the hall.

"What are you planning to do about the Danes this year?" Cynric asked his brother. "With winter upon us, we need to prepare for next season."

"Well, we used to worry a lot about our northeastern border with the Danes," Aelle replied. "That was always where the heaviest fighting took place between us. But in the past few years, we seem to have settled into a stable border situation there."

"So you are less concerned about the Danes now?" Cynric asked. " 'cause I'm not."

"Well, exactly." Aelle said. "Because now the border wars are moving to your western regions here. You, brother, in this western region, border on some hotly contested territories. Fortunately you have Wessex to your southwest and Kent to your southeast, both strong and dependable allies."

"Yes, but ..." Cynric scowled.

"Exactly," Aelle finished. "Eardwulf to your west is completely unreliable and untrustworthy and he worries me more and more."

"The Britons sneak in along the Severn river valley and steal our cattle in the southwest corner, and the Danes we have out here on our northwest boundaries are increasingly restless. They keep pushing down on that northwest corner and are starting to open a corridor for themselves wedged in between us and Mercia. We cannot allow that to continue any further," Cynric concluded.

"You are absolutely right, Cynric," Aelle said. "We cannot allow that to happen."

———— ✦ ————

Toland, the envoy of King Eardwulf of Mercia, was greeted with a noticeable lack of enthusiasm by Cynric's family. He was an arrogant fool who served an untrustworthy king. Average height and average build, with dark lanky hair and a bulbous nose, he carried himself like he was lighting up their lives with his presence.

"Welcome Toland," Edyth greeted him. "How is Mercia's leading ealdorman doing today?"

"Tired and hungry, my lady, tired and hungry," he replied. "I hope that your people have prepared a good feast for us. And some pleasant entertainment."

His eyes always seemed to shift as he spoke. Aelfgif felt a chill down her back when his shifty gaze landed on her – and lingered far too long.

"That ealdorman from Mercia always makes me uncomfortable," Aelfgif said to her brother. "It's like he is undressing me with his eyes. And worse, I don't like what I see in those eyes."

"Aye, sister," Cuthbert replied. "Just stay away from him. I hear very unpleasant rumors about him and his unnatural appetites with young women."

Aelfgif shivered slightly and then stared down Toland the next time that he put his gaze on her. Toland looked away first.

All of the women noticed Godric, envoy from Wessex, when he entered the hall. Tall and confident, he carried himself with the air of a confident warrior. And the women usually agreed that he was the most handsome man at any event that he attended.

"Lady Edyth," he greeted. "What a pleasure to see you again."

"Oh, Godric," Edyth purred. "The pleasure is all mine, I assure you."

"My king sends his greetings," Godric said. "And wants me to strongly reaffirm our alliance when I speak with your husband."

Godric looked around at his surroundings and liked what he saw. In more ways than one. Cynric's hall looked festive. Wall hangings, fires, and lamps had transformed the large space. Extra tables and benches provided space for many guests.

Bryce, Aelfgif's younger brother, also liked what he saw.

"This is incredible!" he said. "I don't think that I've ever seen so much food in our hall!"

"Yes, well," Aelfgif replied, "you'd best keep your hands off it until after father's welcoming toast, or mother will have your hide!"

"But look at it all!" Bryce said, practically drooling as he whined. "There's all that roast meat – beef and boar, as well as deer and hare …"

"You can't eat it all!" Aelfgif chuckled.

"I can sure try!" he said. "I don't care about the fish or the vegetables, though. But that fresh bread looks really good!"

"Before you know it, little brother," Aelfgif said, "you will be drinking the ale and mead with the other grown men. A fearsome warrior needs to have a fearsome thirst – as well as a big appetite!"

"Are you keeping Bryce on his best behavior?" asked Cuthbert, seated on the other side of Aelfgif. "Mother will get very upset if he puts his paws into the shared platters before everyone else. Tell him about the entertainment to distract him."

Aelfgif looked around her. The warmth and flickering flames created a welcoming hall, and the look and smell of all that food was almost intoxicating. No wonder her younger brother could barely contain himself.

"Bryce, you know what else we have to look forward to?" she said. "In addition to all this food?"

"There's more than just food?" he giggled.

"Yes, yes," Aelfgif replied. "There will be jugglers and a scop to tell us tales!"

"That sounds great!" he said. I love the stories the scops tell!"

"And there will be music and dancing too," she added.

"Yuck!" Bryce said. "I don't care about music—and I certainly don't care about a bunch of grownups dancing their silly dances out there."

Aelfgif laughed heartily.

"I like a little man that knows his own mind," she said as she ruffled his hair.

Cynric stood up just then and the noise in the hall subsided.

"I would like to welcome you all here," the large man boomed out. "And I am offering a toast."

"To my brother," he continued," our king—on his birthday!"

There were raucous cheers and banging on the tables.

"And may his next forty years be as happy as these first forty have been!" he shouted as he raised his tankard. "Please, drink deep and then dig in my friends. Enjoy this feast I offer to celebrate my brother.

And with that, the eating and drinking and entertainment commenced.

A short time later Aelfgif looked up sharply.

"May I ask you to dance?" Godric asked.

Aelfgif blinked her eyes once or twice.

"I am surprised, sir, by your request," she replied.

"Why is that?" Godric smiled. "If I might ask?"

"Well, it is a noisome and boisterous hall," she answered, "and there are only one or two couples dancing right now."

"I don't care if we are the only couple dancing," he said as he extended his arm to her and they joined the few other people dancing.

They looked like a perfect couple on the dance floor. Of course, this made some of the other women very jealous.

"She is playing him for a fool!" Wilda huffed. "If he only knew what she is really like!"

"Why would you say such a thing?" Odella asked. "I am a personal friend of his sister and he is a perfectly charming man. Any woman would be thrilled to have the attention of a man like that."

"Yes, well," Wilda looked around to make sure that nobody was listening and then leaned in to Odella with an air of shared secrets. "The 'man' part, that is the problem ..." she said with a smirk.

"Whatever could you mean by that?" Odella replied. "Why would being a man ever be a problem. Why ..." A look of surprise lit Odella's face then.

"Oh!" she said. "You can't mean ..."

"Oh yes, my friend," Wilda said with a grimace. "She does not like men—not in that way. She prefers women!"

"No!"

"Yes!" Wilda said. "She seduced my cousin—that's how I know it's the truth. My poor cousin, she was so confused and intimidated because Aelfgif is a princess after all. But yes—no interest in men for that one." she clucked.

They were interrupted by raised voices at the far end of the hall. Cuthbert and Toland were having a heated argument.

"What the hell are you saying?!" Cuthbert yelled at Toland. "Are you intentionally insulting my family and my country?"

"I don't know why you accuse me of making an insult," Toland sneered. "After all, I am simply stating the facts."

Cuthbert lunged toward Toland, but two of his friends held him back.

"As I said," Toland sniffed, indifferent to Cuthbert's rage. "You East Anglians are clearly not doing your job of protecting Saxon lands here in the center of all our kingdoms."

"Just look," he continued, "at the lands that the Danes have taken away from what used to be our own shared northern frontiers."

Cuthbert shook off his friends that were restraining him and stood there, fists clenched, glowering at Toland.

"Why," Toland continued in his supercilious fashion, "Just look at how little land they have taken from Mercia. Very little. On the other hand they have taken vast amounts of territory from you East Anglians. Either you are all incompetent at arms, or you are just too stupid to figure out how the Danes are fucking you over—in plain daylight—for all the world to see!"

"I challenge you to back your insulting words with your sword, sir!" Cuthbert yelled. "Either retract your insults to my family and my country—or draw steel and defend yourself!"

"I accept your challenge!" Toland shouted back.

"Now see here!" Cynric thundered. "I'll not have you interrupt the king's feast with your dispute. If it's a duel you both want, then we'll arrange for that tomorrow morning. But we will follow all the traditions. If it is to be done, then by Woden, we'll do it right. This will be a formal holmgang!"

The morning sky was gray with low clouds the next day, and heavy winds blew.

Toland still looked ashen with concern. Most Saxons had long abandoned the practices of their Scandinavian cousins, but not the Wuffingas of East Anglia. As soon as Cynric had announced that this duel would be fought as holmgang, Toland knew that he was at a disadvantage. For one thing, holmgangs ended with death. Or disablement at a minimum. This was not a "fight until one man yields" type of duel, which was what Toland was accustomed to.

This would be brutal hand-to-hand combat, fought on a stretched-out hide about ten feet square and a two-to-three-foot boundary around it. To step out of the boundary for any reason amounted to fleeing. And that would mean cowardice of the worst kind. A man could never carry himself as a man again after showing that sort of cowardice.

To make it worse for Toland, Cuthbert was a physically intimidating specimen of a man. Much younger than Toland, as well as taller, faster, fiercer, and much more heavily muscled. He chose the long-handled battle axe as his weapon of choice. Toland chose a longsword, the only weapon where he was at all competent. Although all combatants in holmgang were allowed three shields, Toland could probably be assured that burly young Cuthbert would smash all three of his shields to pieces in short order.

As the contestants were lined up within the boundaries to begin, sweat could be seen streaming down Toland's face and neck; even though it was a cold winter's day. As they began, it seemed that Cuthbert was stalking Toland with heavy footsteps, and the smaller man scurried around the small space that they had to use. Toland's next moves, though, indicated that he thought his several escapes from Cuthbert meant that he had some sort of advantage in speed over the big man. The crowd could see an evil grin start to spread across Toland's face. He pulled up, squared himself, and then launched a series of rapid steps toward Cuthbert with his sword held out in front of himself—almost like holding a short spear.

Cuthbert, though, had cleverly concealed his actual speed. Blindingly fast that battle axe spun down. Toland's arm was lopped off at the shoulder in one single blow. As Toland stood there in shock, and before he could even react to that first mighty blow, Cuthbert's long-handled axe swung back and struck off his head. The crowd was stunned by this violent and sudden ending, and there was complete silence for several moments. But scattered laughter and cheering soon broke out. The wretched envoy from Mercia had not been well loved.

"I can't say that I am surprised by the outcome," Hengist said. "Toland always was an arrogant ass—with a bigger mouth than a strong arm."

"Aye," Cynric replied, "nor am I. But there will be hell to pay now. You'll see."

———— ✦ ————

The day after the duel with its tragic outcome, Cynric and Aelle sat alone by the hearth.

"This could not have gone worse for us!" Aelle spat out. "Your son has put all of East Anglia in peril."

"And what was the boy to do?" Cynric replied. "Let that Mercian dog insult us on our own territory—in my own hall!"

"He could have just wounded him—maybe made him beg for his life in front of a crowd," he replied. "The we could have humiliated him and his damned Mercian king – but given them no basis for war."

"Aye, easy to say now brother," said Cynric, "as we sit in our chairs before the hearth. But the boy's blood was up. We both know a man can't think straight when his blood is up and he has cold steel in his hand."

"And that king of Mercia is a cold and arrogant bastard," he continued, "that would be coming for East Anglia soon—regardless of this event. And we both know it."

"Aye, aye," Aelle replied. "You are right, but we have been preparing to fight the Danes to the north. Now we have to shift a lot of those warriors here to face Mercia to the west. You will have a larger command here now, brother. And a lot more to be watchful for."

"It was already going to be a long, cold winter," he replied. "But we on the western front will be ready to face this traitorous Saxon king when he comes!"

───────── ✦ ─────────

In a dark room in the shadowy depths of Myrkur, the Shadow Walkers of the Dark Fae plotted and planned. All of these gölge yürüteç were there, "The Six" as they were sometimes called.

"I am telling all of you," Velkwei hissed, "this plan is perfect."

"You idiot," growled Nalwei, "you always think your plans are perfect."

Velkwei snarled and bared his canines.

"This time, I have to agree with him," Myrwei cut in.

"Yes, why don't we have Uulwei tell us everything again?" said Rhynwei. "After all, these are his vassals."

Magwei grumbled his agreement. Velkwei and Nalwei continued to glower at each other.

"It's actually very simple," Uulwei said. "I have the two kingdoms in the center under my control. With my help, they have each become the strongest kingdoms in their own areas. As long as the other kingdoms do not unite against them, they are unstoppable. And they have my dark magic to help them as well.

I will have them raid and conquer east and west, and then north and south. When this campaign is over we will control all of this northern realm of Terra. The Britons and Saxons will all be mine!"

"Ours!" Velkwei growled. "Not yours!"

The Six grumbled their approval and murmured contented words about the darkness they would soon spread across the north of Terra.

"What the hell!" exclaimed Eardwulf. The King of Mercia was caught off guard by the sudden appearance of the shadowy apparition in his chambers.

"You should be used to dealing with my avatar by now," Uulwei hissed. "Do you really startle that easily?"

"No, I am never going to be used to you popping up whenever and wherever you feel like," the king replied. "And I am tired of it!"

Uulwei's avatar clenched his fist and Eardwulf crumbed to his knees gasping for air.

"You will breathe again when I decide that you can!" Uulwei spat out. "Who do you think you are—you arrogant little human. You would be nothing without me!"

After another minute of watching the king scrabble around on the ground gasping for air, Uulwei's avatar opened his clenched fist and allowed Eardwulf to breathe again.

"Now listen closely you fool," he continued. "Thanks to me, you will have my other vassal, the Briton king Eluad ap Glast to guard your western flank. I want you to spread chaos an fear to the east—and conquer the other Saxon kings."

"But first," he growled, "you must kill Aelles's brother, Cynric, and all his folk and family. He guards their western flank too well. And when you kill them, make sure the Danes get the blame. We will have all of Terra aflame if we do this right."

Uulwei's avatar stood in a shadowy cloud of darkness, right in front of the erstwhile King of Powys.

I hate this creature, Eluad ap Glast thought to himself, *but I would be nothing without hm.* He shivered then, *and to cross him is ... painful.*

"I want you to crush the revival of the legitimate royal house of Powys. This Dylan must be dealt with—and quickly," Uulwei commanded.

"How am I going to do that?" Eluad replied.

"Just do what I tell you to do," the avatar replied. "I have a plan—and you will just execute that plan."

"Sow chaos and fear wide across the lands of the Britons," the avatar continued. "And with my other vassal, Eardwulf of Mercia, protecting your eastern flank, you will march west and conquer the kingdom of Dyfed."

"If you can help me do that," Eluad replied, "then we will hold all of the south and central lands of my people."

"Yes," the avatar hissed. "And then we will march north to Gwynedd and take it all!"

It was the hour of the wolf. Aelfgif walked through the forest in the total darkness found only in the deep of night. It was still hours before dawn would touch the horizon and she felt the rush of wings sweeping past her head in the dark. A moment later, with prey firmly grasped in its talons, the owl swiveled his head toward Aelfgif, two golden orbs gleaming. The owl blinked and swiveled his head back to its prey, its cruel beak swiftly tearing the hare apart. Aelfgif shivered. The owl's baleful gaze falling upon her was an ill omen. Not that she cared much about omens, but uncaring was not the same thing as being unaware. Aelfgif pulled her cloak tighter. There was a smell of approaching snow on the cold wind that blew from the northeast.

As Aelfgif got close to her home she saw a large number of men moving furtively in the surrounding trees. Shadowy figures moving through the darkness. She saw small flames flickering here and there, and she could smell smoke.

The forest was unusually quiet.

Instinctively, she hunkered down on the ground, where nobody could see her silhouette.

Aelfgif heard the jangling of gear, metal weapons scraping against each other, and the unique sound of men's leather harness when weapons are drawn. She could hear boots stepping on fallen branches and forest debris. And she could hear Saxon voices—with Mercian accents.

These men are dressed like Danes—but they are not, she thought to herself. *What manner of mischief are they about tonight?*

A bright light flared up in the night.

What was that! Aelfgif thought to herself. *By Woden's eye, there are torches all around our hall!*

"Awake in the hall!" a loud voice called out in Danish.

Rough men in fur cloaks stood in a group outside the door to the hall. There were rustling sounds from inside.

"We don't speak that language here!" a voice called out. "It sounds like pigs fucking!"

The leader of the group outside gestured to his men. Most of them fanned out in separate groups along the outside of the house with lit torches. A small group with bows stayed by the main door to the house with arrows nocked and ready.

"All right, you had your chance," the leader shouted back in Danish. "Prepare to get fucked by this pig then!"

In unison, the men with the torches threw them up onto the thatching on the roof of the house. The dry thatch caught fire quickly. Another group of men boarded up the other, smaller doors in the back of the hall. In a short time, the entire hall was engulfed in a raging inferno and thick smoke was everywhere. The sounds of people choking and coughing inside the hall could be heard all the way to where Aelfgif lay concealed in the woods.

I have to go help them somehow, she thought frantically, *but what can I do? All the warriors are away this week; my family is left alone and vulnerable. I can't just lay here and do nothing ...*

The main door to the hall flew open and several arrows immediately flew into the opening from the group outside. The sound of arrows thunking into wood came out of the open doorway. And then nothing.

Cynric then charged out of the door with arms and armor. He was flanked on either side by Hengist and Cuthbert,

"You cowardly scum!" he snarled at them. "You burn innocent women and children instead of challenging other warriors to fight! I spit on you! You are less than pigs..."

"I'll take your heads!" the old master at arms roared. "You are all sons of poxy whores!"

Cuthbert immediately took several arrows to his throat and chest and his steps faltered. Blood poured out of his mouth and he looked at his father with a sad and puzzled look. Then he fell lifeless to the ground.

Cynric roared with anger and pain at the death of his son. He rolled to the ground and sprung up in front of the first two bowmen. He took the head of the first one in a single vicious swing of his sword and took the bow hand of the second archer a moment later. Then the second group of archers let fly. Fletchings blossomed from his chest as he roared again and took several more steps toward the archers. Another flight of arrows finally put him down. And he was still roaring and cursing as his head fell into the trampled earth.

Two small battle axes came swirling out of the flame-flickered darkness toward the remaining archers. One axe split the skull of the larger archer, and the second axe was deflected before it struck home. The surviving archer put an arrow through Hengist's eye and deep into his brain. He dropped like a heavy sack and did not stir.

The fake Danes ignored the screams of the women and children as they boarded up the main door to the hall. They waited several hours until the hall was completely burned down, drinking and gambling as they waited.

Aelfgif had used up all her tears watching the death of her father and brother and being helpless to do anything. Someone had to survive to avenge her family! And then she had to watch the horrible burning death of the rest of her family. She felt hollowed out inside. Not sad, just empty. The only thing that filled that emptiness was a red-hot rage and an overwhelming drive for revenge.

I have to escape, she thought, *I am the only one left to avenge my family. And the only one that knows that this was done by Mercians—not Danes!*

She ran into the night, away from the glowing embers of her family home. When she thought she had run far enough she curled into a ball and cried herself to sleep.

Foul breath reeking of sour ale awakened her, with an ugly face looming above her in the still-dark sky. She could feel hands tightly holding her ankles and her shoulders.

"Hold 'er tight now lads," she heard. "I'm goin' to show 'er wot a real man feels like when I ram it home."

She tried to struggle free, but she was firmly in the grasp of her attackers. She felt hands rip open her tunic and tear her undergarments apart, the cold air on her naked breasts. Then she felt rough hands groping her, She could also feel her amulet, strangely warm, between her breasts.

Her attacker's hands moved down to his waist, freeing his manhood. Her medallion suddenly felt scorching hot.

"Oh, I love it when they's strugglin' like this," he cackled, "I think I'm harder than ever a'fore!"

But just before he penetrated Aelfgif, there was a blinding flash of red light from her amulet, accompanied by searing heat directed outwards.

"My eyes! My eyes!" she heard from three different voices in front of her. She no longer felt the hands grasping her ankles amidst the surprised cries of pain from her erstwhile attackers. The further ones fell lifeless to the ground; their eyes melted completely away by the blast of red light from the amulet.

Recovering rapidly, she swung her feet up and kicked the remaining attacker in the face. She quickly retrieved her long-knife from her belt that they had thrown to the side and slashed his throat open. And spat on his dead body.

"Who fucked who now!" she screamed.

She had no idea what had just happened with her amulet, but there would be plenty of time to figure that out later. Once again, she ran headlong into the night.

Thank you for reading the first book in this series:

Book 1: *Ancient Kingdoms of Ljós,*
(Takes Place in Gwynedd, Wessex and Ljós)

I hope that you also enjoy reading the other books in this series as they become available:

Book 2: *Saxon Kings and Dark Fae*
(Takes Place in East Anglia, Northumbria, and Ljós)

Book 3: *The Sidhe Return to Caledonia*
(Takes Place in The Scottish Highlands and Ljós)

Book 4: *Dark Magic in the Atlas Mountains*
(Takes Place in Algeria, Morocco, and Ljós)

Book 5: *Rising Strife Amongst the Álfur*
(Takes Place in Iceland, North America, and Ljós)

Book 6: *Always Darkest Before the Dawn*
(Takes Place in Mexico, South America, and Myrkur)

Book 7: *Dark Fae Ascendant*
(Takes Place in Japan, Mongolia, and Ljós)

Book 8: Caomhnoir *of the Breacadh an Lae*
(Takes Place in China, Angkor Watt, and Ljós)

Book 9: *Balance Must Be Restored*
(Takes Place in India, Nepal, Ljós and Myrkur)

* * *

ABOUT THE AUTHOR

 David Harris is an outdoors enthusiast and former Eagle scout. He has spent a lifetime hiking, camping, and skiing in the Adirondack mountains. He has never read a fantasy novel or an action thriller that he did not enjoy. David is a long-time member of Mensa, an Ivy League graduate and a former boxer. He enjoys living in the mountains of upstate New York.

www.davidharrisbooks.com